BAD SEED

First published in 2019
by Eyewear Publishing Ltd
Suite 333, 19-21 Crawford Street
London, WIH IPJ
United Kingdom

Graphic design by Edwin Smet
Author photograph by Angel Navarro
Cover photograph by Shutterstock
Printed in England by TJ International Ltd, Padstow, Cornwall

The editor has generally followed American spelling and punctuation at the author's request.

Set in Bembo 12,5 / 17 pt
ISBN 978-1-912477-76-0

WWW.EYEWEARPUBLISHING.COM

RICHARD LIEBERMAN

BAD SEED

EYEWEAR PUBLISHING

Richard Lieberman
is the author of two critically-
acclaimed, award-winning, best-
selling books. His work has been
praised by the *Washington Post*,
Book World, *Library Journal*,
Publishers Weekly, *Forbes* and
Booklist, and awarded a Society
of Midland Authors Adult
Nonfiction Honourable Mention.
He has also written numerous
articles in national magazines.
Lieberman lives in Sarasota,
Florida and Door County,
Wisconsin. He was previously a
partner in the Chicago and
Los Angeles offices of the
international law firm,
McGuireWoods.

Science, my lad, is made up of mistakes, but they are mistakes which are useful to make because, little by little, they lead to the truth.

Jules Verne
1864

TABLE OF CONTENTS

AURORA

I knew what my so-called peers said about me, and it didn't bother me one fucking bit. What they didn't understand was that in order for me to do what I did, I'd had to be strong – every hour, every day. My competitors, the press, government regulators – they all wanted me to fail. Despite them, I fought to get to a place where I could do good for everyone. I'd never let my enemies bring me down, not as long as I had a breath in my body.

Backstage, I listened to the man who was introducing me. He was the CEO of the world's largest company, and also my neighbor in Silicon Valley.

"This year's TED Prize is awarded to the recipient not because she is America's youngest billionaire and a cutting-edge inventor. Yes, yes, those things are all true but that is not why we are honoring her. When the twenty-first century concludes, she will be considered, I am confident, one of the greatest individuals of our time based on her watershed achievement: single-handedly conceiving, founding, and leading a major American corporation that provides a product that significantly enhances the health of everyone."

He paused, letting his words resonate. The audience was quiet, respectful. He continued, addressing my life's work.

"Using bioengineering, she has transformed one of the most harmful staples of the American diet into a nutritious food that extends life and improves health. While many believe that Silicon Valley and its leaders are money-obsessed purvey-ors of entertainment and toys, this individual, this Silicon Val-ley giant, has proved that our American place of innovation can produce something that advances the physical well-being of millions across the socioeconomic spectrum. I am proud to present the Ted Prize to Aurora Blanc."

The monetary award (a million dollars) meant nothing to me. I spent more remodeling my house this year. But the prize itself placed me in the same league as the most admired people on the planet.

I walked out on the stage. Spread in front of me, in an ocean of burgundy velvet seats, were the eminent, the wealthy, and the powerful. I recognized many of them, and I knew they could not believe that a twenty-eight-year old woman was standing here, above them. I greeted them in my most self-as-sured voice, and began my story. Of course, I didn't tell the whole story, only what they needed to know.

PART I
STANFORD

CHAPTER 1

The day my mom helped me move into the dorm at Stanford, it immediately struck me that the room was not much better than the places where we'd lived. Linoleum floors, bare white walls, and two stripped-down beds. While we were unpacking my new Walmart wardrobe of billowy tops and mom jeans, my roommate and her mother walked into the room and introduced themselves. Phyllis, the roommate, was a supercharged version of the type of girl who had ignored me my whole life — slim, groomed, shiny reddish hair, and oh so confident. She looked like her mother. I favored my dad with my big frame and rolls of flesh. We were of Norwegian descent, and I had his dishwater-colored hair, a bland, featureless face, and a lumberjack's torso.

Mother and daughter were friendly, if intent on the minutiae of Phyllis's possessions. I watched out the corner of my eye as they hung up a dozen color-coordinated scarves in her closet.

"Do you want to join us for dinner after we finish unpacking?" Phyllis's mother asked.

I looked at Mom, knowing that paying for a meal with these people would blow her budget for the month.

"Unfortunately, I have some work I have to do this afternoon," said Mom. "Next time."

"It's amazing that you live so near here," said Phyllis, who had apparently read the materials the school sent her about me.

"Yes, Menlo Park," said Mom. "We are so blessed to live in such a special place."

"Blessed," said Phyllis's mother, clearly wondering whether Mom was a born-again Christian. I knew that the elite did not characterize things as "blessed".

Phyllis said, "Where is the nicest place for us to eat in the area?"

Phyllis's mother brightened up. "Yes, yes. What is the best restaurant? We need to celebrate Phyllis's first day at the best university in the world."

Mom didn't miss a beat. "Oh, there are so many. Just walk along Main Street in Palo Alto and you can't go wrong."

Mom knew nothing about restaurants, except for McDonald's and Jack-in-the-Box. She thought she could bluff it, but Phyllis had probably already figured who she was. It's okay, I told myself. I didn't care what anybody thought of us, especially a rich East Coast bitch.

CHAPTER 2

The Stanford biotech lab did not fit my vision of what it would look like. I thought it would be ultra-high-tech, with flashing digital lights, mysterious vapors, and walls made of some gleaming substance. It was a drab space, with harsh florescent lights, standard kitchen refrigerators, plasterboard walls, and Formica-top tables. The real-deal lab equipment was all there, however: DNA gel boxes, thermal cycler machines, shaking incubators, micro-centrifuges, UV-visible spectrophotometers, computers, microscopes.

It was the middle of my first semester. I was studying for a Bachelor of Science degree in the Bioengineering Department. I liked the work. The standards were rigorous, the professors were Nobel-Prize-winning, and there was no B.S. You either made the grade or you didn't. There was none of the silly subjectivity of the liberal arts courses that my roommate Phyllis was taking.

Biotechnology is defined as a science where biological processes, cells, or organisms are exploited to develop new technologies. The word "exploit" excited me — it still does — for what other scientific discipline has exploitation as the centerpiece of its work? I felt this was where I belonged, especially in this lab.

At the end of one day's session, as I was cleaning up, Professor Fraser from my Protein Engineering course came in.

"I'd thought I'd pop in and see how you're doing."

"Doing fine," I mumbled, wondering why he was there. I had forced my way into his advanced course.

"Do you have a minute?"

"Yes?"

"Don't be worried." He had a kind expression on his narrow, long-nosed, middle-aged face. "We've noticed that you're very quiet in class and distance yourself from the other students. I want you to know that you're doing fine. Better than fine — the faculty is impressed with you."

I didn't know what to say and nodded my head stupidly.

"It's too early for you to know what you will do you when you graduate, but have you thought about going on for an advanced degree and perhaps into academia?"

"I haven't really thought about it."

He frowned. "You've never given it any thought?"

Actually, I had thought about it. I wanted to make something new — to change things in nature. My education would give me the ability to genetically modify plants or animals. Of course, I was aware of the controversy about what the big companies had done to make crops resistant to herbicide sprays, pests, and diseases, but that didn't bother me. On the contrary, the power to change living things excited me. I knew that if I became a research scientist, I would probably remain a social outcast, but so what? I'd been ignored my whole life and it was unlikely that I would ever be looked at as anything other than the overweight geeky introvert I was.

He looked down at me, a slender man in baggy khaki pants and button-down pale-green shirt. One of the buttons was unfastened.

"I have thought about doing my own research on GMOs, maybe even trying to come up with something new," I said. "But I wouldn't know how to get the funding to do that, so, well, I really don't know."

Despite this amorphous response, he lit up. "You know, only thirty-five years ago any serious work in the computer field required big industrial-size mainframes, teams of people, millions of dollars. That changed with the personal computer. The PC democratized computing, it permitted people to cheaply create software and apps, and make advances in every field. They could do it at home or in garages or in little offices. They no longer needed a big company or massive funding. Of course, you know all that, but the point I'm making is that it's going to happen with biotech research."

"How could that happen?"

"The resources that a company like Monsanto has will no longer be necessary because the new processes and equipment will be readily available to small businesses and even individuals. They'll be far faster and more efficient. The way we do genetic engineering now is crude, slow, laborious and expensive. The public and the press believe we can easily do all kinds of miraculous things now, like how scientists changed a gene in a mouse to produce a new mouse. But that single genetic modification required a team of top researchers, a fully equipped laboratory, and over two years of work, and they still didn't know what they were doing. That's going to change: soon we scientists are going to get much better control over our science without needing millions of dollars, and your capacity to research and create will be limited only by your ability. And you have a lot of ability. That's what I wanted to tell you."

CHAPTER 3

To my surprise, Phyllis stayed on as my roommate second semester. I thought she'd clear out as soon as she had a chance.
Of course, she wasn't around much but when she was, she was
pleasant enough.

One afternoon, as I sat on my bed surrounded by a pile
of textbooks, eyeing her as she slipped her impressively toned
body into her Lululemon workout clothes, she looked across
the room at me. "You know, Aurora, you have a pretty face. If
you took some time to work on yourself, you might even get
a date sometime."

I wasn't offended because she was right. Like my Dad, I had
no will power – I ate horrible food, never exercised, had no
social life, and never went on a date. Of course, she overlooked
that I didn't have the time for taking care of myself nor the
money to buy the kind of clothes that you needed to look like
a Stanford student. I accepted how I was. I had bad genes because of my Dad and bad jeans because I had no money. There
were other ways to be happy, I told myself, and maybe that
would happen once I got my degree and a career.

Taking my silence for agreement with her assessment,
Phyllis looked at me and said, "I'm going to the recreation center. You're coming!"

I trudged obediently across the campus behind her, wearing
my rumpled once-white, now grey, high school gym clothes.
The Stanford campus looked a lot like the pictures I had seen

of Ivy League campuses – stately oak trees, green lawns, and august brick and stone buildings. Stanford may have been on the West Coast but it was culturally like my imagined Ivy League school – traditional, preppy, reserved.

The workout room at the Arrillaga Center was a vast space with red and grey exercise machines as far as the eye could see. In less than an hour, Phyllis taught me how to use ten of them. "You don't need to make notes on how to do this," she said sternly. "You will remember what I'm telling you." She was like a drill sergeant.

The process was exhilarating. I actually got my blood flowing as Phyllis scrutinized and corrected my every movement as I worked my way through the machines.

"Come here three times a week!" she ordered. "And it will also do your fat ass good if you walk around campus more often and don't eat those disgusting desserts on the meal plan."

Because this was the kindest communication I had had with any student since I'd arrived at Stanford, I dutifully nodded.

As we walked back across a quad, Phyllis took my elbow. "I started to work out in high school to help my depression. I was taking meds from my shrink but I think the exercise helped me more. I don't take the pills anymore and I'm afraid if I stop doing this every day, it will come back. It was so bad in high school, I could barely get out of bed."

I was astonished – this was the opposite of who I thought she was. "I had no idea," I whispered.

"No one here does. And don't you dare say anything to anyone about this. I don't know why I told you. Probably because you're so fucked up, I thought it might help you to know.

Actually you can fix yourself a lot easier than me because there is nothing fundamentally wrong with you as far as I can tell."

I couldn't think of what to say.

"You're welcome. Just get yourself together. OK."

"Thanks, Mom."

She rolled her eyes, smiled a tight little smile, and let go of my elbow.

CHAPTER 4

It was late afternoon in Professor Fraser's lab. I was his assistant and I appreciated that he had taken me under his wing.

It was clear from the beginning that Professor Fraser was a nice person. He spent a lot of his valuable time trying to impart his knowledge to me. It boosted my shaky self-esteem that this distinguished professor thought I might amount to something.

He was doing work on pest-resistant peaches, getting a stipend from some big company, which was probably why he could afford to pay me to do grunt work.

As was his custom, he began holding forth, presumably to educate me, even though he was providing information I already knew. "The work we're doing here – genetically engineering a peach – is nothing new. Farmers have always improved crops by taking the best seeds from the most desirable crops and planting them the following year. They crossbred different varieties to change them. Did you know, the original tomato was hard as a rock and the size of a marble, not something you'd want on your salad?"

I did know this, but nodded and continued working.

When he started up again, I interrupted him. "I really don't think what we are doing here is the same as just taking the best seeds like farmers do when they cross-breed. We are literally ripping a gene from one organism and transplanting it into another organism. I don't think a farmer from one hundred years ago would have seen this as the same."

"Aurora, we are inserting genes containing a desirable trait into another organism. That's essentially what farmers have always done — improving the crop."

"They were not doing anything like what we are trying to do — transferring genes across dramatically different species. I mean, this is what I want to do with my career, Professor, but I can't accept that it's the same old, same old. This is new, we're trying to push the envelope."

He smiled, clearly enjoying this. This was his idea of fun and I was only indulging him. But, generally, I found this whole discussion boring. We didn't need to justify what we were doing. The negative stories in the press about GMOs and big companies were noise to me.

"Say what you will, Aurora" he went on, "the yield of crops and animals has improved exponentially in a very short time. The average American farmer produces enough to feed over twenty times the number of people he did in the first part of the twentieth century. Americans used to spend over thirty percent of their income on food; now it's about half of that. That extra disposable income has changed peoples' lives and fueled this country's economic growth. And we are going to do the same thing for the rest of the world."

"I'm not so sure about the rest of the world. Most countries in Africa, Europe and Asia are afraid to use GMO crops." Of course, Professor Fraser knew this. It was as if we were hitting tennis balls back-and-forth to each other, and each player knew exactly where the next shot was coming from.

He countered, "The more we can engineer crops and livestock to combat hunger, provide nutrition and enhance overall quality of life, the more likely it is that everyone is going to adopt what science is providing. It's inevitable."

I nodded, and he thought I was conceding the point, but I was bored with the discussion and wanted to end it. Nevertheless, he looked delighted. For someone so brilliant, he was quite simple.

I did follow the nationwide debate on genetically modified organisms because I didn't want to have a science career where the rug would be pulled out from under me by new restrictive laws. But so far, the government agencies were sticking to the line that GMO products were completely safe and that there was no need to label them in the grocery stores. From my vantage point, this seemed like a big leap of faith; we didn't really know what was safe or not. Government had been holding back on regulating our genetic engineering because of the heavy pressure from big companies on the politicians not to mess with their businesses. Monsanto, in particular, had a monopoly on corn and soybeans because their seeds were genetically engineered to thrive when the crops were saturated with glyphosate, an herbicide that killed weeds that threaten crops. Since Monsanto made not only the genetically modified corn and soybean seeds but also the herbicide, Roundup, they essentially owned everything including the politicians who gave the company free rein to do whatever. All this gave me comfort that if I worked in this field, there would be plenty of freedom to experiment.

CHAPTER 5

My sophomore year was an improvement over my first year. For one thing, I lost twenty pounds and put some actual muscle on my flabby self by working out. As a reward, I guess, for diligently following her orders to go to the gym, Phyllis began inviting me to hang out with her friends. This consisted of sitting around drinking overpriced flavored coffee drinks at Peet's. These girls were out of my league: not only were they pretty, groomed, and expensively dressed, but, much as I hated to admit it, they were articulate and intelligent. In contrast, I was a slob, sporting my cheap Walmart wardrobe, lovingly selected and paid for by Mom. And try as I might, I couldn't adequately engage in their conversations. My topic range was limited to bioengineering and the *Star Wars* films, and I certainly was not going to hold forth on that. It's not that these girls were just too cool for me; it's that I was genetically uncool. They treated me nicely enough but we all knew that I was not one of them. After a few get-togethers, I declined Phyllis' invitations. She seemed surprised that I didn't want to come, but I wasn't one of them. I could handle any physics problem thrown at me in a Stanford classroom, but I had no ability to talk or look like those girls. Soon Phyllis' interest in me cooled, and we barely spoke. In mid-semester, she found a new roommate and moved out. It didn't bother me; it was nice having my own space for the first time in my life.

It did worry me that a socially inept person like me was

likely to end up as an educated lackey in some research lab. That would be an improvement over Dad's career, but that wasn't why I went to Stanford, and it wasn't what I wanted for myself.

My mom continued to be my best friend. She did my laundry, brought me snacks, and told me how great I was doing. She seemed oblivious to the fact I was a social outcast. Or maybe she knew but didn't care because she was an outsider herself. She took comfort in her religion. I never talked to her about my self-doubts, nor did I share my ambitions with her. She was proud because I had moved to the other side of the tracks, at least for school. And, I had to admit, her blind confidence in me helped keep me focused on getting through school.

At this point, I should have been more confident of my looks. I was slim and strong now. At my height (5'10") and with my newly lean face – I had cheekbones – I looked better when I stood in front of the mirror. But my colorless hair and mousy hairdo, my lack of makeup, and horrible clothing took away whatever I had achieved at the gym. Maybe someday if I made some money, I could take advantage of the hairdressers, clothiers and the makeup people available in this wealthy enclave. But the minimum wage stipend I received from Professor Fraser for lab work barely helped me meet expenses even with my scholarship. I was a poor girl and poor girls don't look good – I understood that.

CHAPTER 6

By the end of sophomore year, I did have something of a social life. I became part of a clique of bioengineering students. On Wednesday nights, we hung out at a dive bar called Antonio's Nut House on California Street in downtown Palo Alto. It was a loud, dark, sprawling place with pool tables and bar food. We liked the place for its nineteen-seventies arcade machines, perfect for geeks like us. While waiting my turn for the next pinball game, I stood at the bar trying to get the bartender's attention. I wanted a Diet Coke (a drink within my budget and without calories). The girl next to me, someone I had never seen before, and who was also vying for the bartender's attention, nodded in my direction. "Go ahead," she said. "I'm still trying to decide what I want. I like the Dogfish Head IPA, but it's got so much alcohol that it will put me on my ass."

"Isn't that the point of coming to this place?" I said, noticing that she was beautifully groomed and expensively dressed. She was a sharp-featured, dark-haired woman in her mid-twenties who knew how to make the most of her appearance. She was not pretty in any traditional way, but the overall effect was of a very attractive person.

"I have to go to San Francisco tonight for a meeting, and I better remain semi-lucid," she said.

"Sounds like you really want to impress him." Looking at the bartender, I said, "I'll try a Dogfish Head IPA." I tried not to think about the five dollars I could not afford to spend on the beer.

She ordered a drink with a Scottish name. "It's a business meeting. What's your name?"

"Aurora Blanc."

"That's a wonderful name. I'm Jane Abbott. Plain Jane."

"Ha. You are anything but that."

"When I was growing up that's what my friends called me."

"You must've grown up in a pretty nice place if they thought you were plain."

"I lived right near here. Belle Haven."

That left me speechless.

She continued, "Actually, it's not in a very nice area. In fact, it's pretty low-rent and kind of dangerous if you are in the wrong place at the wrong time."

"I know. I grew up there. I still live there."

Now she was the surprised one. "Really! I thought you were a rich Stanford kid."

"I am a Stanford kid who goes to this bar now and then."

"I'll bet you're the only Belle Haven person who ever went to Stanford. The kids I knew who went away to school went to reform school."

"Lucky for me, I guess." What a stupid comment, I thought. Half my beer was gone and I was already feeling light headed.

I expected her to walk away, but she settled in next to me, and looked at me from head to toe. "So, you're really brilliant and you got a scholarship so that Stanford could look good because they took someone from the local working- class community."

I tried to change the subject. "What do you do?"

"I'm a consultant."

"What kind?"

"Oh, I do work for Silicon Valley people and companies. Different things. So many opportunities here. And so much money to be made by resourceful people."

By her dress and appearance, it appeared that she was very much part of the elite Silicon Valley tech world. She was what I wanted to be – confident, successful, and young. The alcohol and her interest in me loosened my tongue. "I intend to start my own business after I graduate – in science with something new that I come up with. I want to have a Silicon Valley start-up."

"This place is where the money is, so stay right here. There are the VCs, you know, venture capitalists, and the angel investors. If you're doing this on your own, look for an angel. A lot of them like to help young people and are not doing it for the big return; they're happy if they just get their money back and have some fun advising the startup. The VCs get their money from pension funds and big institution investors so they make you much more accountable. You're an attractive young person with a Stanford education. Your best play is to find an angel. If you get off to a good start, then the money will flow in from other investors. In the beginning, just be cautious in using the money. Don't blow it on champagne and cocaine. If your business gets off to a good start and shows promise, even if it's never profitable, you can get moderately rich. That doesn't happen a lot, but it does happen; there are plenty of people around here who never had a profitable business but everyone thinks they're hot shit."

"Have you done this yourself?"

"No, I don't have that kind of talent. I'm good at providing services and support. But I've worked with a lot of people in tech. I have a good understanding of how it is. I can tell you that for founders, you know, kids like you who start businesses here, they work 24/7 with their employees in tiny rooms, immersed and obsessed, never taking a day off, riding an emotional roll coaster. Even if I had the talent to do it, that's not for me."

"I do think it is for me."

"Well I admire that. Let's keep in touch."

We exchanged contact information and she left for her meeting in San Francisco.

CHAPTER 7

"You're doing what?" I was having difficulty grasping what my mother was saying.

"Denver. It's not like I'm moving to Europe or something." She was sitting on my dorm room bed, blissfully smiling, oblivious to the fact that I was in shock.

"How did you meet him?"

"I just told you, Aurora. At work."

"At the motel where you clean rooms?"

"He was staying there. You'll like him. He's a good guy."

"You don't even know him."

"I do. He's been here working on a construction job for three months. He's a Christian, a good man.

"And you never said a thing to me."

"I didn't want to distract you, honey."

"I'm pretty distracted now. You can't leave me."

"I'm not leaving you. You're nineteen and you'll graduate in a few years and have your own life. This is a chance for me to have a life too."

"A life without me."

"You're overreacting. You should be happy for me"

"How can I be happy that you are running away with a stranger you met in a motel?"

From a rational point of view, I couldn't blame her; it was her life after all. When I met him, this new love of her life, he was nice enough – a friendly blue collar working guy – but I was devastated.

After she moved away with him, Mom and I talked on the phone and texted but we couldn't afford to travel to see each other. After she was gone for a few months, I began to harbor a coldness towards her. Even though I knew better, I could not get over the feeling that she had deserted me.

CHAPTER 8

My work with Professor Fraser was slow going. To develop a pest-resistant strain of peaches, we were laboriously inserting genes from various species into a peach seed, trying to make it resistant to the weeds and pests that usually kill it. This transfer and insertion of genes was the essence of our genetic engineering. The result, if we were successful, would be a genetically modified organism; that is, a new, improved peach. The problem with the whole process was that it was like the game "Where in the world is Waldo." I was searching for a gene from any organism in the world, hoping against long odds that it would provide the right immunities for my peach. Once I located a gene that I liked, in order to isolate it from the rest of the organism's DNA, I needed to clone it and then mass produce thousands of copies. Only then could I inject it, using an old-fashioned micro-glass needle, into the microscopic pronucleus of my peach. If I got it right, the injected "exogenous" gene would become part of the peach's genome (the peach's DNA which contains all the information that makes up the peach).

This process was tedious, imprecise, extraordinarily expensive and almost impossible to get right. Most of the time the injected genes ended up in the wrong place in my peach. Sometimes I couldn't make copies of the genes or, even worse, the whole thing would careen out of control resulting in too many copies. The big companies that developed GMO crops might go through millions of these gene injections to come up with something useful, taking anywhere from six to fifteen years for a new crop seed to be ready for the marketplace. Some scientists spend years changing a single gene. I understood all too well that the work I was doing in this lab was likely to be a waste of time. And I knew perfectly well that the pipe dream of starting my own Silicon Valley company was not a realistic goal.

I was sitting alone in the lab as the vivid California royal blue sky displayed itself through a little window. I was using an injection micropipette connected to a stainless steel apparatus suspended above my peach, making no discernible progress, when Professor Fraser came up behind me. He was aware of my pessimistic state of mind. He had become such a genial presence in my life that I opened up to him when he asked me what I was doing. "I've been thinking about... what I mean to say is, I can't really see, you know, how I could actually start a career as an independent researcher."

He frowned, clearly angry. "There are plenty of things you can do. Don't be so negative. Use that intelligence of yours to think creatively. Most people are trapped by their circumstances because they think they are. I know you're a scholarship student. You don't have money, but you've got capital, Aurora. It's what you're learning here. Think about how to spend it lavishly. Don't hoard it like most people. You can do whatever you want with it."

"I don't know. I..."

He interrupted. "I don't want to hear it. I wouldn't have you in this lab if I thought it was a waste of my time. Don't make me regret choosing you."

CHAPTER 9

Professor Fraser's home was all beige and brown: somber walls, couches, and carpet. Even his wife, who insisted that I call her Ellen, blended in. Their house was on a tree-lined street in Menlo Park near the university; they had lived there for thirty years and they said that if they sold it today, they could easily retire on the proceeds. I looked around the living room for pictures of their children and grandchildren but saw none.

I knew that some of the professors in the Bioengineering Department made big money consulting with the large corporations. This clearly was not the case for Professor Fraser. From what I could see, everything about the couple was modest; he had devoted his life to teaching and she was his traditional support mate. I knew that I should respect him but I didn't. He was a classic underachiever – exactly what I did not want to be.

Ellen worked intensely in the kitchen while the Professor and I chatted. I understood that it was an honor for a Stanford student to be invited to her professor's home.

When we sat down to eat, Ellen brought out the most beautiful food I'd ever seen: asparagus – forest green and plump (so unlike the scrawny vegetables served in student dining); a whole fish, golden and glowing on the platter; minute potatoes covered with grill marks; red, yellow, and orange carrots; and corn on the cob. It was way too much food for three people, but I wanted to taste it all to find out if it could be as good as it looked. I was so taken by this spread that I forgot to compliment Ellen.

"You've done it again, dear," said Professor Fraser.

"Yes, yes, it's so beautiful," I lamely added.

"Well, it's my passion and joy, but thank you for appreciating it."

We were eating what was the most exquisite food I'd ever consumed in my life. Professor Fraser said, "Ellen's a master chef. If she wanted to, she could have a restaurant that rivaled anything in Napa Valley."

"Ha. Not true. It's a hobby."

"She buys the ingredients every day at the local markets. All organic, sustainable, fresh and perfect."

"It's easy to do that in this community. Everything I need is here. You're giving me too much credit."

"What is the fish?" I asked.

"Barramundi." Casting a corrective look at her husband, she said, "It's not local at all. It's a sea bass from Australia. And it is not my recipe; it's from the French Laundry. I did modify it."

Responding to my obvious ignorance of what she was saying, Professor Fraser explained, "It's not a laundry but restaurant in Napa Valley — one of the best restaurants in the country. I'm guessing that this fish is high in omega-3 fatty acids."

"Absolutely," Ellen said. "High in omega-3, the good fat with the healthy cholesterol, and low on omega-6, the bad fat that hurts you."

"And when you say you modified the recipe from the French Laundry, I know you came up with something brand new." Turning to me, adapting his stentorian voice, he began a lecture (he couldn't help it): "Everything she uses is nutritious.

This corn, for example, probably represents the tiniest fraction of the corn produced in this country. It's organic, of course; no GMO seeds generated it. Some local farmer nurtured it like a child. The media talks about how corn is bad for you but this corn is nutritious and healthy. The big industrial farmers raise corn for ethanol and animal feed, and there is a good reason why they use it for fuel; it's full of carbohydrates and has almost no nutrition. You can't even eat it."

"Animals eat it, but we can't?" I asked.

"You'd chuck it up if you did. Excuse me, this is an inappropriate topic for a lovely meal."

Ellen smiled. She obviously appreciated (or gracefully tolerated) that her man loved to hold forth, urging him on. "How can the corn be used for both car fuel and animal feed?"

"They shouldn't use it for feed. Cattle fed on this genetically modified corn have at least twice the amount of saturated fat, and it has almost none of the good omega-3 fatty acids. It's loaded with omega-6 that clogs and inflames the arteries and causes heart disease. A hamburger is basically fat disguised as meat. And steaks are almost just as bad."

"My Dad died at forty-three. He ate meat," I blurted out, even though meat had nothing to with his death.

"Someone told me you lost your dad at a young age but I didn't know the circumstances. That must have been very difficult for you. But it wasn't his fault; it's almost impossible to avoid unhealthy eating, particularly if you are not rich. Ninety-nine percent of the cattle in this country are GMO corn-fed. The economics behind it are the reason. You can raise an enormous steer in fourteen months by putting it in a feedlot and feeding it this Frankenstein corn and cheap grain. But if you raised all American cattle the old-fashioned way, in grass pastures, it would be too expensive – twice as much, would take too long to raise, and you wouldn't have nearly enough to feed the U.S. market. It's a tragedy. The grass-fed cows not only have plenty of omega-3 and very little of the harmful omega-6, but they also have CLA fatty acid that provides cancer protection and reduces body fat. Grass-fed cattle is good for you – our ancestors lived on grass-fed animals and didn't drop dead of heart attacks like we do."

Ellen, who had been silent during this discourse, said, "You two are experts on biotechnology. Why can't you fix the cows so they don't kill people?"

I shrugged and looked at Professor Fraser.

"If we had any idea how to approach that kind of experimentation, even if we succeeded, no one would eat a genetically engineered cow," he said. "The government wouldn't approve it and consumers would be afraid to eat it."

Ellen shook her head. "What about changing the corn feed? It's already genetically engineered, so why not try to make it so it doesn't ruin the cow?"

Clearly irritated, he said, "Because dear, the whole point is to provide feed to fatten the cattle as quickly as possible so they can be sold cheaply and the corporations can make big profits. If the corn doesn't accomplish that, there is no market. If you want healthy meat, you could just feed the cows grass, which is fine for rich people, but doesn't work for everybody else."

I didn't say anything. I just listened.

CHAPTER 10

We began a real friendship, Jane and I. At first, it was a one-way relationship: she talked and I listened as we sat on our bar stools in the dark, clamorous surroundings of Antonio's. She told me about her family: working class people, her dad was a truck driver and her mom stayed home. Like me, she was an only child and the first to go to college, a local community college as she didn't have the money for a university. When she graduated, jobs were scarce. She started a one-person consulting firm, doing marketing and PR. She had few friends because she left the people she grew up with behind, and didn't make friends in college because she was a commuter. She was a loner like me.

Jane asked about me, my daily doings, but when I told her about my classes in the lab, she listened without comment, bored. After a while she began inquiring about my Menlo Park childhood – my friends, my high school, where I lived, my father and mother. I evaded her questions but she was persistent. I thought hard about how to explain it to her. Slowly, I began to confide, starting with when I moved the black garbage bag stuffed with bedding and clothes by getting on my hands and knees and pushing it up the thirteen urine-scented steps to the second-floor landing, then dragging it down the walkway into a motel room smelling of cigarettes. I was big for an eleven-year-old, but carrying our family's possessions up these stairs, trip after trip, was too much for a child.

"It would be nice if your father could be here to help us move into this shithole," my mom muttered.

As we unpacked, my dad pulled up in his pickup and parked next to Mom's rusty Corolla. He lumbered up the stairs, smiling as if it were a normal day and he was arriving home from his security guard job. He carried stuffed pillowcases we had left by our car. When he reached the top, he was breathing hard. He smelled of liquor. I didn't really mind that sweet aroma because, in an odd way, it seemed to reflect his sweetness, his gentleness.

Mom glared at him. "You ought to be able to afford the rent in this place," she said. "It's public housing."

Dad grinned. It was hard to tell whether he was drunk, because he always acted pretty much the same.

A paperback book stuck out of his coat pocket. He was always reading, even when Mom was yelling at him. He often read his books to me. One was about a man in Russia who killed an old lady for some jewels and then worried that he would get caught, even though the police had no clues that he had done it. It was a long book, but I liked it. On the other hand, I preferred watching a science program like *Nova*, if the TV was available and Mom was not watching one of her religious shows.

Our new home had a bed, a fold-out couch and a tiny kitchen. As soon as we came in the door, Mom turned on the TV to her favorite evangelical station. Christ did this, Christ said that, the preacher said, over and over. It occurred to me that I would be in the same room with her all the time now, except when I was at school.

"At least, I don't see any roaches," she said, glaring at Dad. "They'll probably come out tonight when you're at work." She turned to me. "Put your stuff in that drawer next to the bed and if it doesn't fit, pile it nicely on the floor."

At first glance, I thought the carpet had an unusual brown-and-black pattern, but upon closer inspection I saw that the pattern was nothing but crusty stains. I crammed all my T-shirts, shorts, jeans, and sandals into the two small night-stand drawers. I didn't care if my clothes got wrinkled, because they were worn and frayed, anyway. The other kids at school had fresher, newer clothes, but new clothes wouldn't help me – I was a blob. I got perfect scores on every test and knew every answer when the teachers called on me, but that didn't help me with the other kids. I didn't blame them for ignoring me.

Mom hustled around the room, putting things away, while Dad searched for a chair that could contain his girth. Rather than flopping down on the bed, the only piece of furniture large enough to accommodate him, he stood, hovering over us, an enormous mass of a man, smiling sheepishly. "Hey," he said, to get our attention, and put his hand in his pocket, took out a wad of money and placed it on the bed.

Mom stopped what she was doing, picked up the money, and began counting it. "Where did you get this?"

"We live in a rich place," he said. "There's all kinds of money here."

She frowned. "If you had given this to me a few days ago, we could've paid our rent."

"We can't afford to live here in Menlo Park. We have to move to some other part of the country where we can get by."

"We don't live in Menlo Park," she said. "We live in Belle Haven."

"Belle Haven is part of Menlo Park," he said, to make his often-repeated point that we were trying to live beyond our means.

Mom had a grim look on her face when she was laying down the law. "Belle Haven is good for *her*," she said, nodding her head in my direction. "Smart, successful people live a few miles away. We're staying here, despite the drug dealers and gangs."

He shrugged his shoulders and watched us unpack.

My mom insisted on keeping me in the same school, even though it was in a different district than our motel. Because the school bus did not come to our new neighborhood, she had to pick me up every day, which meant I had to sit in a window-less school room until she finished her waitress shift. One afternoon, three girls from my class were also there. I could hear them on the other side of the room, talking about how they missed the bus because of their student government meeting, grumbling about the wasted time. I wanted to join in their conversation, to connect with them, but I did my homework, instead.

"Why are you here so late?" Melinda, the student government president, asked me.

Happy to be noticed, I blurted out an explanation of how we had moved to a different school district, which required my mom to pick me up after her work.

"That's horrible," said Melinda. "It's bad enough to do it

just this one afternoon — it's like jail. But you have to do it every day."

"I know. It's bad. I try to use the time to do my homework."

"Still."

Despite the long school day, all three of the girls looked fresh, in their cute jeans and T-shirts. I wished I had worn something nicer than baggy sweatpants and Mom's old blouse.

"I think I heard that you moved to a different neighborhood," Melinda said. "Did you get a bigger place?"

"We're still in Belle Haven, but it's outside the school district. But, yeah, we moved to a nicer home."

"Since you have to stay after school anyway, you should run for student government. You're such a smart girl. Everybody knows that. You'd be good at it."

My heart began to beat faster. I felt a surge of joy. "Well, thanks, maybe I will."

"I think the elections for the next officers are soon, like in February?" Melinda turned to one of the other girls, Beth, for confirmation.

"March 20," Beth said. "But you got to be honest if you're in student government. No lying politicians like in real life."

"She knows that," said Melinda, casting an irritated glance at her friend.

"No, she doesn't. She just lied to us."

The other two girls looked at Beth, waiting for explanation.

"Tell them how you just lied," she said to me.

I was at a loss. I shrugged my shoulders.

"She moved because her family was evicted. They're home-less now," Beth said.

The other girls shifted uncomfortably in their chairs.

"Well, maybe she couldn't help that," said Melinda.

The third girl snickered. "It's hard to believe she's home-less, since she is obviously getting plenty to eat. I'm worried she's going to break that chair she's in."

Melinda looked down at the floor.

I straightened up, forced myself to smile, and turned to-wards Melinda. "I would like to be in student government."

One of the girls' mothers came through the door. "Let's go, girls. Hurry."

The three quickly put their stuff into backpacks, and moved through the door. Melinda paused, turned her head to-wards me. "Sorry, Alice."

"Aurora. It's Aurora, not Alice," I said to Melinda's back.

In the car, Mom looked at me suspiciously. "Your eyes are all red. What happened at school?"

I wanted to tell her, but I couldn't face her reaction. "Noth-ing," I mumbled.

"Don't lie to me. They were picking on you again."

"It was my fault."

"You're better than them, Aurora."

I started crying again.

"Stop that right now. Enough!"

I managed to calm myself, but the tears continued.

"I'm ashamed of you." She hit the brakes, yanked the car over to the edge of the road, and slapped me. "You have no idea how much I sacrifice for you," she yelled, leaning so close that she filled my entire field of vision. "I work two crappy jobs to try to get us out of public housing, haul you back and forth to school every damn day, stay with your loser Dad because you like him for some reason I can't fathom."

She pulled the car back on the road. In her softest, kindest mom voice, she said, "I do it because I believe in you, Aurora. And I am telling you what you need to do: ignore all the crap around you, concentrate on school, play your stupid video games, if you must. But be strong. If you do that, it will get better. I promise you."

I knew she meant what she said – that she wanted to help me, but I didn't believe anyone could help me. People like me are who we are – we can't change no matter what we do.

We scraped by, living hand-to-mouth, moving from one cramped, crummy place in Belle Haven to another. Belle Haven consisted mostly of small rundown nineteen-fifties cottages gone to seed, with beaten up cars out front. We could not even afford to rent one of those cheap houses. We stayed in low-rent apartment complexes or, when things got extra-tight, in the public-housing motel. Our neighbors were a mix of lower-income whites, Latinos, Asians and African-Americans – a true melting pot, except each group was afraid of the others. While Belle Haven looked safe, gangs, drugs, and guns were a regular part of community life. Most people considered Belle Haven a slum, but Mom believed it was a good place for me, because it was next door to one of the richest areas in the world – Silicon Valley. It didn't feel that way to me. When I rode my old bike into Menlo Park, just a few minutes away, I felt like I was trespassing.

Dad was morbidly obese. Whenever I saw him, which was less and less as Mom's criticism of him became more and more, he was eating something or drinking liquor. He also smoked, which was supposed to keep a person's weight down, but, in his case, didn't.

When I was twelve, the security guard who was relieving Dad on his shift in an empty warehouse found him slumped over in his chair. He wasn't sleeping. The doctor at the hospital told us that Dad had probably been sick for a long time; his liver was badly damaged.

Mom was stunned by his death. I suppose she did love him despite her constant complaints about him. She walked around in a daze for months. For me, it didn't seem like he had gone away forever; I imagined he was still working the night shift and still doing whatever he did during the day. I kept waiting for him to come home, thinking about the books and ideas we would talk about when he got there.

Mom worked at various housekeeping and waitressing jobs, and I endured adolescence – no girlfriends, not to mention boyfriends. Mom continued to be my best (and only) friend. I was a nobody, except to my teachers, who appreciated my academic abilities. They suggested to Mom that we apply to a local private high school for economically disadvantaged gifted kids, and I got in with a full scholarship. I graduated as valedictorian of my class. But being academically gifted did not improve my social life. I took little pride in my academic achievements, because I believed my perfect scores on every test happened only because I had a freakish photographic memory. But the teachers and counselors thought I was special and helped me fill out the daunting college scholarship application forms. That fall, I packed my duffel bag and moved a few miles to the other side of the 101 to attend Stanford University.

CHAPTER 11

Waves of magnificent sound washed over me. The musical instruments were so powerful that it was difficult to understand the words of the singer, even though I knew them all from the record. "When you try your best but you don't succeed... When you feel so tired, but you can't sleep. Stuck in reverse. And the tears come streaming down your face."

"My favorite," I shouted to Jane, who was standing next to me, in the third row of the HP Pavilion in San Jose. All fifteen thousand people were standing, worshiping the performers on stage.

"I know, it means something to me, too."

The singer's voice was almost feminine, soaring above the instruments. "But if you never try, you'll never know just what you're worth."

I bent my mouth to Jane's ear. "I believe that, I think."

Jane took my hand. "Of course you do. I do too. That's why we're so close."

The spotlight intensified on the singer. "Lights will guide you home and ignite your bones. And I will try to fix you."

I turned to look at her. "I know you are trying to fix me."

After the concert, as we crossed the parking lot, I examined Jane from head to toe. High black charcoal boots (Chanel, she said), tight dark Seven jeans, floating cream blouse over a black tank top. Exquisite Jane and lusterless Aurora. I did not understand why she liked me, why she took me to this concert that must have cost her five hundred dollars, why me?

The other concertgoers walking by us were quiet, on this warm April night in an early spring that had been like summer, with some days close to ninety degrees.

Jane shook her head. "Me trying to fix you? No, you're fixing you. I'm just here for you to talk to."

"I don't know what you see in me," I said, not understanding why I kept saying things to drive her away. She was the best — actually the only — close friend I'd ever had, and yet I kept arguing with her about how unworthy I was of her friendship.

"I see myself in you," she said.

"Me in you? You are everything I'm not."

"Someday you're going to laugh when you think about this conversation, if you even remember this conversation."

"You know I'm trying. I'm just not getting anywhere and I don't think I ever will. I'm just a lab rat. I'm not being negative about myself; that's just who I am."

"You're wrong about that, Sweetie, completely wrong. You can make yourself into whoever you want to be."

"I want to be you but I can't."

"I'll help you. But you need to promise me that you will help yourself, too."

"Just like the song."

She fumbled for the keys in her purse, leaned over, and kissed my cheek. "Yes, just like the song but without the tears."

CHAPTER 12

Jane and I stood in line at the UPS office with our Christmas packages. I was sending out only one gift – to Mom in Denver. But Jane had an armful. It was a long line, with just one agent working, but suddenly, much to my relief, another agent opened a second window. I was already late for work at the lab. As I moved toward the second window, two people, behind us in line, their arms full of boxes and bags, pushed in front of me. I sighed.

"What the fuck!" barked Jane. "Are you going to let those assholes do that to us?"

"Well, I don't…"

"What do you mean you don't? Don't what! Grow a pair, Aurora."

I gaped at her.

"Don't just stand there like a dumb fuck. Do something. Otherwise, I'm not going to waste my time with a wimp like you."

I walked over to the two ladies, who were both wearing dark yoga gear and were already immersed in their transaction with the agent. "Excuse me," I said, "but we were in front of you."

One of them eyed me from head to toe. "Young lady, you were ahead of us in the other line, not this line. We'll be done shortly, so be patient. The holiday season is stressful for all of us." She turned back to the agent.

I looked at Jane, who was scowling at me.

I tried a different tack. Edging toward the agent, I said, "We were here five minutes before they even walked in the store."

The agent shrugged. "You'll have to work that out between yourselves."

I was standing in front of them now. I thrust my little package across the shelf, shoving aside their packages, and put my phone with Mom's address directly in front of the agent's face.

"My Mom lives in Denver," I informed the agent, as if this was necessary information. She hesitated and I moved the phone even closer to her face.

"You need to do mine right now," I said, in the coldest tone I had ever used in my life.

The agent accepted my package and began typing Mom's address on her screen. I glanced behind me. It seemed that everyone in the store was watching, frozen in place. I motioned to my friend.

"Jane, please come here so we can complete our transaction."

Jane walked around the two yoga ladies and squeezed my arm.

When we walked out, I made eye contact with the two women. "Have a nice holiday," I said.

"How do you feel?" Jane asked when we were outside.

I was so relieved, so euphoric that I began to laugh.

Jane looked at me as if I had lost my mind. "What?"

"Best day of my life," I said.

CHAPTER 13

Entering the lab to start my late afternoon work session, there was a gawky, long-haired man, clearly a student, at my workstation. He was so absorbed in the work (which was my work) that he didn't notice me.

"Excuse me. You are sitting at my desk."

He jumped and stared up at me. "No, it's not," he said, defensively. "Professor Fraser hired me to do lab work here for the semester."

"Oh," I mumbled, backing away. Unsure what to do, I walked out of the lab into the hallway. Wow, he fired me without even telling me. And for good reason, as I had made no discernible progress on the peach project. He decided to try somebody more competent. I couldn't blame him. But now what? That familiar cloud of depression descended on me. I shouldn't be surprised. The whole set up had been too good to be true and I had to face it: I didn't deserve the kind of support he had given me.

"Aurora!" Professor Fraser shouted. He was suddenly behind me. "Where are you going?"

I stopped, and waited for him to tell me how I failed.

"Where are you going?" He looked perplexed.

"There is someone at my workstation doing my job."

He looked as if he were trying to solve a complex bioengineering problem.

"There is a student working in there on the peach project," I said.

"Oh. That's Harry. Yes, yes, I hired him to do that work."

"Well, goodbye, Professor and thank you." I turned and began towards the door.

"Aren't you working today?"

"What work? Harry is doing my work."

"That's what I'm trying to tell you but you keep walking away. I've got a new project for you."

"I thought you fired me."

"Why in the world would you think that, Aurora? You are the best student in the Department. Come with me." He began walking toward his office. "By the way, I want you to get to know Harry Sumner. He's very talented and a nice boy. It wouldn't hurt if you had a social life."

I stared at him.

"I'm not blind to everything around me, despite what you may think, Aurora. You work too much. You need to get out, date, have friends."

In his sparse office, he sat behind a desk topped with several large computer screens. There was no paper anywhere. Professor Fraser had the personality of an old-school guy, but when it came to his work, he was up-to-date.

"You remember our conversation at my house about corn and cattle?" he said.

It took me a minute. "You mean how industrial corn feed for cows causes cholesterol and unhealthy omega levels in people?"

"Right, right. The meat that is killing the U.S human population. I want to try genetically modifying cattle feed so that the beef is healthy."

"You said that if people want to eat healthy, they can buy grass-fed cattle meat."

"It's too expensive – most people can't afford it, and production is limited. No, I'm interested in mass-produced cows, and whether we can change the genetic composition of their corn feed to make healthy meat."

I took a breath and patiently explained, as if to a child, "Professor Fraser, we do not have the resources – money, people, or time for something like this. It took Monsanto years to genetically engineer corn to be weed-resistant. I shouldn't have to tell you because you know this better than me – it would take millions of dollars for a project like you're talking about."

"No big company would undertake this, Aurora. The big cattle producers have an extremely profitable business model now and the general public is not asking for healthier meat. Some of the educated elite buy grass-fed steak but everyone else is happy with the cheap meat even though it makes them sick and kills them."

"We can't do it, Professor Fraser."

"I think we might. You and I can do it, and I hope to get it done before you graduate next year."

"Yes, sir," I mumbled. I wasn't going to refuse a job, no matter how ridiculous it was.

"We'll start tomorrow. You'll work in that corner section of the lab which has some privacy. Don't talk to anyone about this project. As far as the University knows, it doesn't exist. I'll pay you myself. Now go introduce yourself to Harry."

Following his instructions, I said hi to Harry, who, I suspected, also following Professor Fraser's orders, asked me if I wanted to hang out later.

CHAPTER 14

Nineteen-years-old and I finally had a boyfriend. Granted, he wasn't much – physically and socially awkward, too nice, and not sexy. In his little off-campus studio apartment, we lay on his couch and I let him kiss me and feel me up. But there were no sparks. My lack of passion didn't seem to discourage him, which further dampened any enthusiasm I tried to muster.

"I have to go to the bathroom," I said, disengaging myself from him.

"You always have to go to the bathroom when we're on this couch. I think there's a diuretic in the fabric that makes you pee."

When I came back, attempting to divert his attention, I asked, "How's your work coming?"

He optimistically put his fingers under my jean waistband and said, "You know how it's coming – it's not coming at all. If I work on this for the next few years, until I graduate, there will be nothing to show and then they can bring in another student who can waste her time, too." He massaged the skin on my stomach. "Even with a big research team working on this, it would take years. I think Stanford got some research money that it's using to just to give stipends to students like us." He shut his eyes, trying to push his hand further down as I shifted away from him. He was tickling me, not the effect he was trying to achieve. "What is that secret project you're working on in the corner?"

"I can't talk about it."

I pushed his hand away. He moved to the other side of the couch. "I can't believe you won't tell me. I don't know why you're even seeing me." He stood up and began pacing around the room. "You won't go to bed with me and you won't even tell me what you're doing in the damn lab."

"Come on, Harry. Please. Fraser swore me to secrecy."

"Ok. I'll take the vow of secrecy too. What is it, Aurora?"

I decided that if I couldn't do it with him, I could at least give him this. "If I tell you, I'll have to kill you."

"You are killing me."

"We're genetically engineering corn so that when cows consume it, their meat will have the proper omega 3 to 6 ratio, a lot of CLA and low-fat content. The meat will be healthy to eat."

"You need to leave now."

"What?"

"You have no respect for me. This whole relationship or friendship or whatever it is, is a total waste."

"Harry, I am telling you the truth. That's what we're doing. Honestly."

"If that's true, my project may be a waste of time, but yours is absolutely fucking nuts."

"No, it's not. We're going to do it."

"Sitting in our little college lab working a few hours a day! Not in your lifetime and not in this century. Fraser is giving you money to help you, just as he is doing with me. But at least he's not making me drink Kool-Aid."

"We're using a new way of editing genes," I said calmly.

"It's like a tool. It sends out this microscopic scout who travels to the exact location in the DNA of the corn that we want. Once the scout arrives, he uses a laser to cut into the gene in the right place. Then he removes or changes the DNA or if we want him to, he places new DNA from another organism into the corn DNA."

"What does he do then – have a party?"

"He sews it up."

He waited to see if I would laugh.

"It's revolutionary, Harry. In a week, I can do what a team of researchers would spend years working on. It took me about an hour to figure out how to use it. Right now, I'm working on putting flax seed genes into corn seeds because they have the health qualities we want."

"Where did this come from?"

"Researchers at Berkeley. They just invented it. Fraser is friends with someone there and he replicated what they were doing. Hardly anyone knows about it yet. It costs almost nothing. Someone is going to use it to cure cancer someday. But what we are doing now is just as good, and no one is looking over our shoulders telling us what we can't do."

"I don't believe this. It's science fiction."

I took a breath and explained it all to him – how a number of years ago, scientists discovered a weird clump of DNA sequences. These scientists stumbled upon the ability of this odd cluster of DNA called CRISPR to protect certain bacteria by identifying invading viruses that would ordinarily kill the bacteria. Once the CRISPR DNA spots the virus, it uses a special enzyme that functions like a scalpel to chop up the virus. Then it inserts the sliced-up virus genes into the bacteria's DNA to protect it from future attacks by the same virus. It's similar to an immunization process. This was all very interesting to scientists, but the big thing was the realization that if in nature, these cells could act as a delivery system to take any genes to exactly where they should go and then cut and paste them in precisely the right place, then scientists could use the identical process to do the same thing, to do whatever they wanted with any DNA. They found that by using this, they could easily alter, eliminate, and replace genes in any plant or animal – like using a word processor on a document. And since DNA and its subset genes determine everything about all organisms, this new process – actually a tool – could allow scientists to do essentially anything with them.

"I mean, this just happened, Harry, it's new. You can use it to take biological parts of anything you want and insert it into any other plant or animal you want to change. And you can do it almost instantly. They call it the CRISPR-Cas9. I can do in a month what it takes a corporate or university research team ten years to do, assuming they could do it at all."

Harry looked puzzled. Everything I told him was true, except that I was working on the corn seed in collaboration with Professor Fraser. The Professor had already determined what we should do. I was just his lab assistant.

CHAPTER 15

Jane insisted I accompany her to San Francisco to shop for clothes, even though I had only a couple of hundred dollars. Looking at the price tags as we walked through Barney's, I saw nothing I could come close to affording.

"Hey, Lana. Doing some shopping damage today?" said a suave, elegantly dressed man, walking up beside us. He flashed a confident smile at Jane and acknowledged me with a nod.

"You're confusing me with someone else," said Jane, continuing to move through the racks.

He laughed. "I understand. Have fun shopping." He eyed me and, in mock whisper to Jane, said, "Your friend is attractive but she needs a redo. This is the right store to do that – my favorite. See you later."

"Who is that?" I asked.

"I don't know. It doesn't matter. Let's try to find something you can afford."

Jane led me through the store at lightning speed. Within fifteen minutes, she had me in the dressing room, stuffed into a pair of tight Dolce & Gabbana designer jeans ($375, but on sale for $130) and a Milly silk, cotton V neck three-quarter length sleeve black blouse ($240, but marked down to $80). In the mirror, a stranger stared back at me – tall, slim, and confident. If clothes truly make the man (or woman), then these clothes were absolutely worth the $210 that I needed for my basic expenses. I calculated that I could make it up by skipping meals.

"You're better off wearing these two pieces of clothing as your uniform than the twenty pieces of horrible stuff you wear now," Jane said. "Steve Jobs wore the same black turtleneck and jeans every day, and he was the coolest guy around."

On the train back to Menlo Park, I said, "You never tell me anything about your job, Jane. What exactly do you do as a consultant?"

"I advise in a number of areas."

"Like what?"

"You know me. I'm a Renaissance kind of person. I know a lot about many things. People, clients, appreciate what I provide."

"So, like what companies do you work for?"

"I do this for people who are with all the name companies in the Valley."

We pulled into the station, gathered our packages and moved from the train onto the quaint, 1950 era wooden platform and to the tree-lined street. I felt lucky to have Jane as my friend.

CHAPTER 16

Harry and I stopped seeing each other as boyfriend and girl-friend but we continued to cross paths at the lab. I would have continued to date him, but my lack of any physical attraction to him was more that he could handle, and he stopped asking me out.

When I came into the lab one afternoon, he was clearing his things out of his work space.

"What are you doing?" I asked.

"I'm changing majors. This is not really me. It's boring and depressing."

I was surprised because I had always believed he was one of us. "What are you going to do?"

"Become an Econ major. If I go to school during the summer and double-down on courses, I can catch up and graduate on time, maybe a little bit late. I want to go into business when I graduate."

"I'll miss you." Now that he was leaving, it hit me that he was my friend.

He must have perceived my regret. He walked over to my work area and said, "What's happening with the secret project?"

"We're not working on it anymore."

"Sorry. I thought it was ridiculous when you told me about it. Did you accomplish anything?"

"We used the tool I told you about, you know, the CRIS-

PR. We took genes from flax and worked on inserting into the regular commercial corn seed's DNA."

He scowled at me. "Yeah, I remember what you told me. So, you weren't able to do it. It was too far-fetched."

"No, we did it."

"Did what?"

"We genetically engineered the corn seed just like we intended."

"You're saying you succeeded?"

"Yeah, we succeeded."

He shook his head. "I don't believe it. You won't know if it works until you raise cattle with the corn. So now what?"

"Nothing. Fraser just wanted to do it to see if it could be done. But in the end, he was worried that we'd done far-out genetic engineering. It's way more than just transferring a gene; we pretty much invented an entirely new corn seed, and we did it with this CRISPR tool that hardly anybody knows about. The whole thing is so out-there that he won't show it to anybody."

"Where does that leave you?"

"Nowhere. Nowhere at all."

CHAPTER 17

During Thanksgiving break of my senior year, I went out to visit Mom in Denver. She seemed happy and secure with her new husband in a nice little condominium downtown near the ballpark. She even looked different: thin, greying hair even though she was still in her forties. Her edginess was gone. She now moved more slowly and carefully as if she was afraid to injure herself. I had to give her credit: she actually turned her life around from ghetto mom to happy housewife. And she no longer had the TV blaring with evangelical preachers.

"Aren't you excited to be graduating?" We were sitting on her small balcony, looking out at the fresh grey three-storey condos bordering the baseball stadium. "Your life is really beginning, Aurora."

It didn't feel that way to me. To the contrary, I felt a kind of dread floating over me. I had no plans, no ideas, and anxiety about leaving the routine of my college life.

"I don't know, Mom."

"Don't know what?"

"I don't know what to do."

"What do you want to do?"

"I know what I don't want. I don't want to be a nobody anymore."

"Aurora, I don't understand you. Look at you: you're a different person than you were a few years ago: beautiful with that body and face and that nice jean outfit that you wear. You were a big plain girl and now, well, you've changed yourself, Aurora. You're graduating from the best school with the best grades. And you're not afraid of your own shadow anymore. You're assertive when you want something. School changed you. You have the world at your feet – believe your mom."

"No, Mom. I'm a poor girl with a science degree and no skills and no social contacts. I'm qualified to get a job working for some big company or university as a lab assistant. It will be the same as school."

The old anger flashed across her face. "I don't want to hear it. Listen to me, Aurora, don't disappoint me, understand. Don't let me down."

I nodded. But I didn't feel any different.

CHAPTER 18

Jane was even more unsympathetic to my malaise than Mom had been. Perched on our stools at our favorite bar, Jane, dressed to kill as always, said, "You are a loser only if you think and act like you are. You just need to start doing something to get out of your rut."

"Working in that lab everyday makes me feel like a drone."

"Work with me."

"As a consultant? Doing what?"

"I'm an escort."

"What?"

"I'm an escort. That's what you could do until you finish school and get another job."

"You're not helping me by joking."

"Listen to me. I get three thousand to spend the night with rich men. I can make about ten on a good week. That's what I do."

"You're not kidding?"

"No, Aurora, I'm not kidding."

"You, like, accompany them to events, provide companionship?"

"No, Aurora, they fuck me."

I just looked at her, trying to reconcile the Jane I knew with this other Jane. I couldn't grasp it.

"You should do it for a while. When you're dirt poor, you're vulnerable and weak. I know because that was me.

Money makes you strong. Whoever said money can't buy happiness was never destitute like us. You can't even think about being happy when you have nothing. Once you have it, you have choices."

I was speechless.

"Think about. I'll help you. I'll tell you what to do. You'll feel better about yourself."

I managed a nod.

"I got to go, sweetie. Stop looking so shocked. I'm the same person you've known all this time. What I'm telling you about is just a job. It's a good one, actually much better than the soul-killing work that you're doing in that lab. You can trust me. I would never do anything to hurt you."

CHAPTER 19

As I walked from Union Square to the Four Seasons Hotel, I took the deep meditative breaths I'd learned from yoga classes at the Stanford gym. I would do this once – for the money, to please Jane (if I backed out now, she would chastise me and I couldn't face that) and to show her that I had balls. Trying to move inconspicuously across the hotel lobby, I was aware of mocha and teal-colored walls and furniture. Following Jane's directions, I dialed the cell number she provided and responded to the male "Hello" by saying, "It's Vicky. I'm in the lobby. I'm wearing jeans and a black blouse."

Within a few minutes, a short, thin Asian man in an expensive, dark suit and a pale blue narrow tie, emerged from the elevator. He spotted me across the lobby.

"Vicky," he mouthed.

I followed him into the elevator. Jane did not tell me how to handle the elevator ride part, so I stood mute staring at the floor. He didn't speak, either.

He led me to his room, a suite, more elegant than any apartment I had ever seen. Then he walked over to the window and looked down at a large construction site – a block-wide hole in the ground. "An interesting view, is it not?" He spoke with an accent. I was trembling but his reassuring behavior calmed me a bit, although my heart was racing so much I worried he could hear it across the room. I can do this, I told myself. I just needed to meticulously follow Jane's instructions like a good student.

"An interesting view, but I have a view for you that I know you will like much more," I said, improvising a bit off Jane's script. I walked toward the bedroom and he dutifully followed, as Jane said he would.

"Let's take care of the business part first," I said.

"Yes, yes," he reached into his pocket and handed me a wad of bills. I avoided looking at his face, trying to stop my hands from shaking as I counted the money in accordance with Jane's instructions.

"Thank you. Let me put this away in my purse while you get to take off the tie and anything else you want to take off."

As he turned around to undress, I finished totaling the bills – nine hundred dollars, more money than I'd held at one time. Even with Jane's commission, there was plenty left for me. Despite my fear, I felt euphoric.

When I looked up, I saw him from the back, carefully placing his clothes on the chair. I had never seen a naked man before. He looked like the slim Asian girls I saw every day in the University gym locker room. Even when he turned around, except for the little male part of him, he looked like a girl with short hair and a little chest. He stood there as if waiting for orders. Now I understood why Jane gave me instructions and a script. With my photographic memory, the print was right before my eyes and I just followed it.

Forty-five minutes later, I caught a glimpse of myself in the hotel hallway mirror, flushed and glowing. I almost didn't recognize myself. I looked strong, competent, and alive. Jane was right.

★

"I'm going to spend my final semester studying and looking for a job," I said to Professor Fraser. He looked stricken that I was leaving his lab.

"You got perfect grades the whole time while you were doing your lab work with me. And I can help you with getting a job. You should also consider graduate school which I can advise you on." I couldn't believe he was pleading with me to stay on.

"I just need a little time for myself," I replied.

In truth, my new job was taking more time than I thought it would, between going into San Francisco and doing out of town trips to LA, Seattle, and Phoenix. The "tours," as Jane called them, to other cities were particularly lucrative, generating around ten thousand dollars for a three-day visit. I could do the new job, miss class and do well on my tests, but the lab work was too much to fit in, and paid next to nothing, of course. My new job was much better: I could finish my class work, change into my new designer clothes – Vera Wang, Milly, Rag and Bone, Vince – and head to work.

When I met up with my clients in their hotel rooms, I was in charge; I just did exactly as Jane instructed. It didn't matter how rich or brilliant or powerful or attractive or ugly or stupid they were, I was the boss. If they had their own ideas on how the session would go, I would disabuse them of any notion that they had any say in the proceedings. But they ended up happy because they wanted to be relieved of any responsibly or decision making. They appreciated what they were getting – a nineteen-year-old, tall, toned, educated, articulate, a skillful young woman providing forty-five minutes of dirty sex. They were lucky to get me and they knew it.

This job was also teaching me something new, something valuable: if I just took a script and followed it, like an actor, I could be so much more than the timid, mousy me. And maybe I could start writing my own script for the rest of my life.

CHAPTER 20

"Have you given any thought as to what you are going to do with our work on corn seed?" I asked Professor Fraser.

"I'm not going to do anything with it. It was an exercise to see whether we could do it. I wanted you to see what was possible and to know if you could work at a corporate or university lab leading a difficult project." He smiled at me.

"You could profit from what we did, assuming it works. Why not do something with it?"

"Theoretically, it works. But there is still a big question on the whole thing. It's a question that I could not in good conscience permit to exist unanswered."

"What question? If it works, it works."

"You know what I'm talking about, Aurora. With this seed, we spliced, edited, altered, and restructured corn DNA in a way that was impossible two years ago. What we accomplished could result in the outcome we intended or something completely different. We think we know what genes we turned off and on in the corn seed but we may have programmed something else with unintended consequences. It is impossible to know whether it's safe or not. And once that corn seed is out there and reproduces, it will be all over the place, and no longer within our control."

"Monsanto is making GMO seeds all the time with no oversight and those seeds have taken over agriculture in this country — they are just about the only seeds that farmers use now. No one is getting sick."

"You don't know that, Aurora. We don't know anything about the long-term effects of what we've done. The natural function of what scientists discovered in CRISPR is a defense of foreign genes entering cells; that is, to protect organisms from viruses. But we're using CRISPR in a completely different, opposite way — as a device to force the entry of the alien genes into organisms that have never known them before. Maybe it's not harmful to put genes from flax into corn as we've done but we just don't know. I'm concerned that by forcing genes into other genes, as we are doing here, we're creating immense stress in the organism. This process of cutting DNA, putting something new in it and then effectively stitching up again — we did a substantial amount of that to reprogram our corn seed, as you know — there could've been a massive disruption in the corn DNA, which resulted in producing substances in the corn that were not there before. It may be a harmless change, but maybe it produced toxins. We've got to leave it to the scientific community to deal with the enormous ramifications of what we can do with this CRISPR-Cas9 tool. I think there will be some world changing advances that come from this. It will probably cure cancer. But there could be some profoundly negative things as well. This little experiment is too much for us to play with, Aurora. Far too much."

"You are the most responsible and careful person to do it."

"If I pushed this forward, I would lose control over it. Listen to me, Aurora, let me give you some fatherly advice. Do the right thing — always. You probably think it's easy, like always picking up your trash from the ground. But it's a hard thing to do. You'll see — you will have choices where doing the right thing will hurt you — in your job or personal life. You might suffer by doing the right thing. You may lose the opportunity to make a lot of money by doing the right thing. You might lose your social position. I know you're thinking that what I'm talking about will never affect you, but it will. And if you remember this, it will help you in your life more than anything we ever did in the lab."

CHAPTER 21

I heard that Professor Fraser was on administrative leave for the rest of the semester. I stopped by his office several times, but the door was locked. He didn't respond to my emails. Finally, I went over to his house. I was worried that he would ask me how I could afford the used BMW convertible I'd purchased on a three-year loan with earnings from my evening job.

Ellen answered the door. I remembered her as sparrow-like, but now she looked gaunt. I was taken aback when she embraced me. "I'm so glad you came, Aurora. He loves you and wanted to help you when you finished here at Stanford."

I followed her out to the screened porch in the back of the house. He was in a wheelchair facing the yard, his head tilted downward. "Hello, Professor Fraser," I murmured as I stood in front of him. His face was impassive when he looked up at me. He shifted his gaze to the yard.

"A stroke. I found him in the kitchen on the floor last month. We thought there would be improvement. Actually I thought he would bounce back, but..."

He looked up at us again, like a dog trying to comprehend what was going on.

"The doctors. What do they say?"

"They say there's significant brain damage, but there's always hope. I don't know what I'm going to do."

"He'll get better. He is such a force. This is impossible."

I smelled shit.

"I'll have to take him in to clean him up," she said, apologetically. "You know, he was in the middle of doing so much work, trying to accomplish so much. Aurora, could you do us a great favor: take his current work files and organize them so they are ready when he can work again?"

"Yes, yes of course. Anything."

"Wait until I finish with him, and then I'll download his work, and get you the passwords you'll need. He respects you so much, Aurora. I wouldn't trust anyone else to do this but you."

CHAPTER 22

It was all there: a step-by-step road map of how Professor Fraser altered the genetic composition of corn. Following the instructions, I knew I could do it again in a few months with about $50,000 worth of used lab equipment and components. I checked online and determined that I would have no problem purchasing the Cas9 enzyme that uses the messenger RNA molecule to do the genetic engineering. The RNA molecule was the "photocopy" of the genetic information from the linseed (or from wherever we'd taken the info) that we wanted to transplant into another organism, in this case the corn seed. This mechanism, the Cas9 enzyme with the message RNA molecule, hunted down the particular DNA (the stuff that actually held the genes) in the corn seed to insert the new genetic sequences into it. Using this still secret CRISPR-Cas9 tool, I could do myself what a university or corporate lab would spend ten years and millions of dollars trying to accomplish.

When Professor Fraser was better and able to communicate with me, I intended to convince him to let me help him bring this project into the light of day. It was all there; it just needed his prestige and connections to get it over the finish line.

I moved through senior year without energy, showing up for my classes, escorting three or four nights a week, waiting for someone to tell me what to do. I felt more isolated than ever, Professor Fraser's condition did not change, and Jane was my business manager now, not my mentor; she set up my dates and collected her percentage. My former boyfriend, Harry, had disappeared into the business school.

I bought a plane ticket for Mom and her man to come in for my graduation day. She was euphoric over my so-called success – I was graduating from Stanford at twenty – and was not bothered by the fact that I had no job nor plans.

"You're like a lot of other kids. You just need to take a breather," she gushed. Of course, she didn't know that my "breather" involved fucking three or four men a week and sleepwalking through most of my waking hours.

Six months after graduation, still on my "breather," I saw Harry crossing University Avenue in downtown Palo Alto. He didn't notice me and I almost kept going, but the need for personal contact compelled me to shout out to him. He stopped, looking vainly for someone he knew.

"It's me, Aurora!" I yelled from across the street.

He hesitated as he stared at me, then crossed the street. We faced each other, standing in vivid sunshine. He looked good – no longer awkward, his frame filled out.

"Aurora?"

"Who do you think it is?"

"You look so different," he stammered. "I mean you look great, so, so – polished." He paused, searching for more apt words to describe me.

"You're graduating next month?" he asked.

"Yes."

Collecting himself, he shook his head. "It's so sad about Professor Fraser. I know how close you were to him."

"His wife says he could get better. What are you going do

when you graduate?"

"You'll laugh."

"Trust me. I'd never laugh about someone's job."

"I'm going to be a VC."

"A what?"

"Come on. You've lived in Silicon Valley your whole life. VC, a venture capitalist, someone who invests money to start new companies, you know, with high-tech or biotech products."

He was right; I did know that. Some of my clients worked for venture capital and private equity firms but when they talked about it, while I pretended that I was interested, I really didn't care.

"So, you have a job, Harry?"

"Not yet. Most of the firms want MBAs so I'm still looking. I might try to do it on my own."

"On your own? How does that work?"

"I'm looking for someone with an idea for a new business or technology that I could partner with. There are lot of people out here with new ideas, new things. I would like to be, you know, an entrepreneur – raise money, advise – for someone who is trying to launch something I could get excited about. How about you, Aurora? What are you doing?"

I paused for a minute, sizing him up. I had been intimate with dozens of successful men and with most of them, I could sense what made them winners. Standing on this hot sidewalk, I believed Harry had changed; he now seemed to possess the same thing some of those men had – intelligence, confidence, presence.

"I'm doing independent research," I said.

"On what?"

"Remember the work I started with Fraser on corn seeds?"

"You don't mean the corn seed that makes meat healthy?"

"Yeah. I've been working on it. It's ready to go."

PART II
HEALTHY HEART

CHAPTER 1

Transferring out of the Bioengineering Department turned out to be the right thing for Harry. By the time he made the decision, he knew he hated science. His dad, a chemist with DuPont had pushed him into bioengineering even though Harry's interests were in the arts. When he finally worked up the courage to transfer, he chose economics because it represented a compromise he could live with – practical enough to satisfy his dad but providing the liberal arts education that meant something to him.

The only meaningful thing about his two years in bioengineering was Aurora. Even before her miraculous transformation (he barely recognized her when he ran into her in downtown Palo Alto), he was in love with her, carrying a torch almost from the day he met her.

On the eve of graduation, Harry rightly felt he'd come a long way since his freshman year. The students in the Humanities Department, where his new major was based, were far better-rounded than the science students, and in that new environment he blossomed, losing his awkwardness, gaining confidence and social ease. He had a group of good friends, male and female, who liked and respected him. Stanford had been good for him; he had grown up and was ready to do something with his life. While his parents were prepared to pay for an MBA, he wasn't ready for more school, and besides, most universities wanted their students to have some real-life work experience before entering a business graduate program. It was fate, he decided, that he was residing smack in the middle of the biggest innovation factory in the history of humankind with its doors wide-open for young entrepreneurs. Harry was certain that he could play the game as well as anyone else. With his Stanford degree, his assured manner and nice looks, he was a member of America's educated elite. And now he wanted to realize his potential.

He thought a great deal about what he wanted from life. It wasn't only wealth; he was surrounded by money and that alone was not what he wanted. What he wanted was the adventure of pursuing the big achievement, the rich experience, not the riches alone. He just needed the right horse to ride to success and he planned to start looking for that horse right after graduation. And although it was unlikely that the horse would be a filly, he decided that it wouldn't hurt to follow up with Aurora on her far-out science project. After all, she was the most brilliant student in the Bioengineering Department, and, in his eyes, Stanford's most beautiful student. Well, perhaps not *the* most beautiful, but she had somehow put herself in contention. She seemed to have become a different person in the two years since he had last seen her. There could be no downside in talking to her further about her work. Maybe there was a chance, however slight, for a romantic relationship with her. In the past couple of years, he'd had a few hookups but none had turned into a relationship, even though a couple of the girls seemed interested in taking things further. At least he knew now that Aurora's lack of romantic interest in him was not because he was physically unappealing; he had done fine with girls. Perhaps Aurora had some personal problems back when they were dating and the new Aurora had overcome those difficulties, whatever they were.

Several months after graduation, Harry moved to an efficiency apartment in the reasonably priced, now semi-gentrified Belle Haven area. A few years ago that part of town had been dicey, particularly at night, but now it was relatively safe and provided Harry an opportunity to stay in the Silicon Valley area on his parent's modest allowance while he tried to get something going. But finding a business opportunity, an innovator with an original and commercially viable invention or business plan, was proving more difficult than he thought. He talked to a number of young people, all men, with ideas like a pornographic comic book app, a tiny microphone embedded in the user's nostril, a self-cleaning carpet (they demonstrated how it worked but it didn't), a marijuana store website that provided the best and most varied selection available, chargeable to the customer's credit card (interesting but unfortunately still illegal in all fifty states). One bad prospect led to another. After several months, Harry felt he was looking for a needle in a haystack, except that there was no needle. Even more discouraging was that some people didn't even bother to return his follow-up inquiries, including Aurora. She had given him her contact information that afternoon on the sidewalk in Palo Alto, but then did not respond to his texts, emails, or calls.

By late summer, his parents were pressuring him to either get a paying job or apply for graduate school. Their patience was running out and he knew they would soon cut off his allowance. He started looking at MBA programs.

Early one morning, unable to sleep, he decided to review his prospect list to see if he had overlooked any possible business prospect. Once again, he came across Aurora's contact information, which included her Palo Alto address. He put on his running gear, entered her address in his maps app, and set out on his route. Forty-five minutes later, he stood, sweating, in front of an upscale condo building on a side street off University Avenue, close to where he'd seen her last spring. Her name was on the lobby tenant screen; he studied it for a long minute, then pushed the buzzer.

"Who is it?" a small female voice in the small speaker said.

"It's Harry."

"Who?"

"Harry. Harry Sumner."

"What do you want?"

"I was in the neighborhood. I wanted to say hello."

"It's not a good time."

"When is a good time? I've been trying to contact you. Is everything okay?"

She did not respond. He thought she had disconnected but then she said something he could not hear.

"I'm sorry, Aurora, what did you say?"

In a tiny voice, she said, "My Mom died."

"Oh, I'm so sorry."

"I didn't even know she was sick."

"When?"

She murmured something he could not understand.

"Aurora, can I please come in? Please."

There was a pause. "Apartment 311."

He took the elevator to the third floor. She opened her door before he knocked, and immediately turned back into the apartment. He followed, passing through the kitchen, strewn with Diet Coke cans and Lean Cuisine boxes, over to a grungy brown couch in the living room, where she settled into a nest of pillows, magazines, and more empty boxes.

She was pale, with stringy, greasy hair sticking out at odd angles. She was dressed in food-stained black sweats.

"Aurora, I am so sorry," he repeated, looking for somewhere to sit. He settled on an armchair on the other side of the room.

She began to talk, almost breathlessly. "I didn't even know that she was sick. He — her husband — called me and said she died. He said she didn't want to worry me. I hadn't seen her for almost a year. She was here for graduation. She seemed fine then, but after she died I remembered she hadn't looked truly healthy. I hardly ever talked to her since she moved away; I was mad at her because she went away with this guy — her husband. He said she had cancer. I don't even know if she got the right treatment for it or any treatment. I could have helped her. I'm supposed to be a scientist but I didn't do anything, nothing at all to help her." She took a breath, and stared at the floor.

He understood she was grieving. But he saw no trace of the girl that he had encountered on the street only a few months before.

"When did she pass away?"

"In May — May 13."

"What have you been doing all these months since it happened?"

She shrugged. "Nothing."

"Are you working?"

"No."

"Have your friends been helping you?"

"I don't have any friends."

"Oh. What are you doing for money?"

"I have some saved."

Unable to think what to say, he repeated, "I'm so sorry, Aurora." Unable to resist saying it, he asked, "So what do you do all day, Aurora?"

Surprisingly, she didn't seem offended. "Nothing. Just kinda staying here. I can't seem to get motivated to do anything. I'm in a funk, actually – I can't do anything right now. Sorry I didn't call you back."

"I wanted to talk to you about your idea – your work on the corn seed. Can we do that sometime?"

"Yeah, I guess, if you want."

"Good, I'll come by tomorrow and we'll have lunch – a business lunch, ok? On me. Wear something appropriate for a business lunch, all right."

She took a long look at him for the first time since he'd entered her place and let out a little laugh. "Yes, sir."

"Tomorrow at noon."

The following day, she came to lunch as promised, but was unfocused and unkempt. They sat in in the garden of an upscale cafe, surrounded by attractive young business people engaged in intense conversations. He probed about the status of her work on the corn seed while she picked at her salad. She confirmed unenthusiastically that it would work.

"What would you need to actually create the seed?" Harry asked.

She looked puzzled. "What do you mean?"

"What resources do you need to actually create it?"

"Why are you asking this?"

"Because I want to do it?"

She looked at him, clearly surprised.

"Aurora, I want you to create the GMO corn seed, test it and then market it. I want to make a business of it with you. That is, if the thing really works."

"You're serious?"

"Will it work?"

Irritated, she said, "Yes, I just told you that."

"Then I want to do it. Do you?"

"Well yes. But how?"

"There is money here. You know that. People are investing in all kinds of things – some of them sketchy. There are angel investors who give seed money to get a promising idea going. What do we need to start?"

"Well, let me think. We'd have to have basic lab equipment. And, of course, the DNA itself. It wouldn't be expensive – all we are really doing is picking out the specific CRISPR molecules we need, which we can probably order from a commercial lab, and then injecting them into cells." Becoming animated, she explained, "That's the beauty of this – the hard, time-consuming work we used to do is done by the RNA that takes the injected DNA to the right place in the cell and inserts it there. It's fucking magic, Harry."

"So, it's a stripped-down lab setup. How much could this

lab equipment and DNA cost – like $300,000?"

"Oh no. Much less."

Harry asked, "How much less?"

"Maybe $50,000. Could be even less than that."

"And if you had these tools, you could do this."

"Anyone trained as a molecular biologist could do it if they had my process. You could do it."

"I want you to do it. Will you?"

"Yes, if you want me to."

After she left, Harry wondered why he had been so decisive, almost bullying her into committing to the project. Over the past few months, he had rejected any number of ideas that were as far-fetched as this one. Was it pity for her current state or maybe even unrequited love that compelled him to do something unwise? He could always pull out if he wanted; she was so grief-ridden, she probably wouldn't care if he changed his mind tomorrow. But as he assessed and reassessed her idea, he knew he wanted to do it. And for some reason he trusted her.

When Harry told his parents that he had identified a business opportunity that he planned to pursue, they were not happy. His father told him he needed to support himself; that he would not subsidize him anymore. His parents were practitioners of tough love and Harry respected that, but the reality was he could no longer afford his rent and had little money to eat. His parents assumed he would come home until he figured out what he wanted to do, but going back to St. Louis was out of the question. He needed to be here to raise money and help Aurora establish her lab.

He did not want to spook Aurora by telling her about his

financial situation but he desperately needed a place to live. He asked his friends if he could temporarily crash, but everyone had an excuse – "My girlfriend just moved in;" "Every bed is taken;" "I'm moving next month;" "I need absolute quiet because I'm studying for the law boards." Finally, with no other alternative, he called Aurora and told her that his lease had expired and asked if he could use her couch for a few weeks. She murmured her consent. She still sounded like a zombie. When he showed up several days later with his stuff, she seemed surprised to see him, and she and her place looked no different than when he had seen her the week before. While he cleaned up, she sat on the couch, staring at him. It hit him that she was suffering from clinical depression.

"I want to tell you exactly what we are going to do to get this going, Aurora," Harry said, filling a fourth large garage bag.

"Ok," she said.

"My first job is to go out and get some funding so you can set up a lab and do the genetic engineering to make this seed. Your job is to write a short business plan, ten minutes long at most, to deliver to investors. It should succinctly explain exactly what the seed will do. Don't put in any of the science. Just say that you've worked out how to do it, what equipment, space, number of assistants you need to make it, and how it will dramatically improve human health and longevity. I'll write up the part about the money we need and the money we will make. Can you do that, Aurora?"

She seemed to emerge from her fog. "Of course, I can do that, Harry."

"Good. Then let's get to work."

"Now?"

"Right now. And when we finish, I want you to prepare a detailed, I mean, really intricate, step-by-step protocol as to how you are going to genetically engineer this thing."

"I don't have to write it down. I know how to do it."

"Yes, but I don't."

CHAPTER 2

And so they began. Harry contacted every VC and Angel that he'd ever heard of to try to get meetings. Aurora prepared draft after draft of the pitch for his review, and wrote and rewrote the scientific protocol for the genetic engineering of the corn seed. They worked all day and all evening. It was as if they were back in Professor Fraser's lab, working long hours, grabbing catnaps. Over the next few weeks, Aurora came out of her trance, and became more and more engaged in the process, pressing Harry for the details of his work.

Harry started to get meetings, leaving for extended periods during the day to meet with potential investors in restaurants and offices. He did not bring Aurora, although he understood that if he got a bite, she would have to join him for a presentation. She began to go out sometimes too, dressed like a fashion model, telling Harry that she was hanging out with her friend Jane. She would disappear for hours, sometimes returning late at night, sometimes the next day. He assumed she stayed at Jane's place. He didn't ask any questions; he was relieved that the Aurora he had met on the street several months before was back.

She behaved as if Harry's presence in her apartment was of no matter, as if he were a brother visiting from out of town. She was careful to maintain her privacy, always emerging from her bedroom fully dressed. But to Harry she was a walking, talking aphrodisiac. He was careful to give no clue that he

90

was turned on by her physical presence, aware that the stakes were too high for him to do anything to upset the delicate balance of their business partnership. Their work conversations were intense, but at the same time impersonal, and they never discussed their personal lives. In fact, neither one had much of a personal life. What Harry thought about, obsessed about, dreamed about, was convincing an investor to provide $300,000 to get them started. He rehearsed his elevator pitch. He fantasized about someone saying yes. As to Aurora's inner thoughts, he hadn't a clue. The science geek that he worked with and had dated two years before was still evident in their work discussions, but the new Aurora was inscrutable.

After several weeks, Harry found the courage to ask Aurora how she was getting money to pay rent, buy food and put gas in her BMW convertible. (He didn't have the nerve to ask how she got a BMW convertible in the first place.) She sloughed off the questions, muttering something about getting money from her mom's insurance policy. While that didn't sound quite believable (she had the apartment and car before her mother died), he let it go.

The first half-dozen investor meetings went nowhere. The investors either did not understand what Harry was pitching or objected to the whole idea of GMOs, reflecting the green attitude of the Silicon Valley crowd. Some said that a startup could not possibly compete with Monsanto-type companies — a concern that Harry shared.

The seventh meeting was different. Frank Conrad, a lean, steel-grey-haired industrialist from the East Coast, who had sold his holdings and retired to the Bay Area to pursue offbeat investments, asked probing questions and seemed genuinely interested. Harry knew that Conrad was a guy who could throw a half million dollars at an investment for fun and not lose a moment of sleep if he lost it – a genuine angel investor. He also knew that Conrad was a man who wanted to win. At the conclusion of their meeting, Conrad told Harry he wanted to meet the founder-scientist. Could they meet at Frank's house?

Aurora was unfazed when Harry told her about the meeting, but to his dismay, she refused to rehearse her pitch, insisting she had it under control. She drove the two of them through the residential streets of Mountain View, with its backdrop of the grassy slopes of the Santa Cruz Mountains, to an address with a long private driveway. At the end of the drive, at the gate, Aurora pressed a buzzer, identified Harry and herself. The house was made of grey stone, impressive but something short of a mansion. Harry was glad they were driving a Beamer.

"Very modest house. Probably only seven or eight million," whispered Harry, as Aurora tried to figure out where to park. There was a Mercedes and a Porsche in the circular drive.

"Park any place," a male voice shouted from the vestibule of the house.

Frank led them around the side of the house to a yard with old oak trees shading a swimming pool, and then into a nineteen-thirties-style cabana. Harry and Aurora sat across from Frank on a big sloppily cushioned couch.

Frank said to Aurora, "So why should I trust you with my hard-earned money?"

"Well, my father loved meat."

Conrad looked puzzled but she continued.

"I can't remember him eating anything else, Mr. Conrad. Hamburgers, pot roast, chili, and sometimes steaks when we could afford it. If my mother tried to feed him fruits or vegetables, he would leave them on his plate. He was a working man – a man of simple pleasures and meat was one of them. He died when I was twelve. Massive heart attack. If he had been sick before that, we certainly didn't know about it. He was burly, a little overweight, but that's how a man is. His death had a profound effect on me. I loved him and I missed him. He had no money, no life insurance policy; our little family (my mother and me) were left with little, but we got by.

"When I was seventeen, I was lucky to get a scholarship to college in my town. My scholarship was to Stanford."

Conrad leaned forward, elbows on knees, eyes on Aurora.

"I don't know when it first occurred to me that my dad's love of meat killed him. Sometime during my education as a biotech major, I began to understand that the cholesterol in animal fat clogs and inflames the arteries in the heart and eventually kills or damages the health of the people who consume it. As a young science student, I asked myself why does beef kill? After all, our ancestors, the hunter-gatherers, consumed plenty of meat, but they didn't have heart disease. I began to educate myself about Western society and heart disease. And what I learned was surprising to me – the meat is not the problem; the problem is the corn fed to cattle by the giant beef companies. You see, throughout history, cattle lived mainly on grass. The cows were healthy and so were we. Our ancestors thrived on grass-fed meat. But in the last thirty years or so, the beef industry learned that by feeding cattle a certain type of genetically modified corn, the cows fatten and grow very quickly, only fourteen months to market. And it's much cheaper to raise the cattle with this type of corn – only three dollars a bushel.

"Now, let me be completely honest, Mr. Conrad. There are some good things about big agriculture's corn-fed cows. It used to be that beef steak was only available to the rich; now it's within reach of most people. In fact, the modern agricultural system is so efficient that Americans use only about ten percent of their disposable income on food, including restaurants. Sixty years ago they spent almost twice as much. This extra disposable income has enhanced peoples' lives and helped the U.S. economy."

She paused, assessing whether Conrad was with her. She decided he was and went on.

"There is a price for this cheap tasty food: big agriculture's beef is comprised of marbleized fat that ruins human arteries. The problem is cholesterol; that fat-like substance that the liver produces. The body actually produces most of its own cholesterol, which is necessary to digest food. But Americans consume much more than they need from eating fat-saturated cows. They pay a huge price: coronary heart disease, heart failure, heart attacks and strokes.

"At Stanford, I studied genetic engineering. Yes, I know GMOs are controversial and many people are rightfully concerned about what some of the big companies are doing to our food products. But genetic engineering also has the capacity to do great good. Over the course of my college years, I thought a lot about whether it was possible to make meat safer. Could the corn seed be altered through genetic engineering to produce healthy beef in a way that the meat was affordable? I experimented by trying to change the DNA in corn that causes cattle meat to provide dangerous cholesterol. Eventually I made a breakthrough. Mr. Conrad, with this seed, we can raise cows that are as healthy for human consumption as grass-fed cows, and can do it as efficiently and inexpensively as the big beef companies. We can extend our customers' lives and quality of life, and we can significantly reduce U.S. health care costs."

She paused, gauging his reaction. He was still with her.

"So, sir, whether you invest in this or not doesn't matter to me. I'll continue to devote my life to it."

Conrad said, "I'm sure I know you from somewhere."

Flustered, she said, "Oh no, I don't think so. I wouldn't have forgotten if I had met you before."

He shook his head. "For better or for worse, I have a photographic memory for faces and I'm sure I know you. Just can't quite place you."

On the way home, Harry was glum. "Conrad was completely unmoved by your presentation. I don't get it. He was so encouraging when I met with him."

"It's my fault. What I said was over-the-top."

"No. Your pitch was amazing, perfect. I never knew that about your dad. Well, the hell with Conrad. We'll find someone else. No one said this would be easy. I just thought we had him."

As it turned out, they did have him. Later that day, Harry and Aurora received an email from Frank. "I'm in. Let's start with $300,000. My lawyers will put together the papers."

CHAPTER 3

Six months later Aurora's new laboratory in Palo Alto was up and running, staffed with four graduate students and all the equipment and materials she needed. Frank, their angel investor, regularly stopped over to the lab, each time asking Aurora for a detailed description of what was going on. Harry tried to be there whenever Frank showed up to make sure that Aurora said the right things, but she didn't need him; she was a master at providing detailed, complex information about the project while not quite telling the other person everything.

"We are using clustered, regularly interspaced short palindromic repeats, which we call CRISPRs and CRISPR-associated (Cas) proteins," she explained to Frank, surrounded by her four lab assistants. "This is our tool set for genome editing. We use this CRISPR-Cas 9 technology to target gene cleavage and gene editing in a variety of eukaryotic cells, and because the endonuclease cleavage specificity in the CRISPR-Cas 9 system is guided by RNA sequences, editing can be directed to just about any genomic locus by engineering the guide RNA sequence and directing it along with the endonuclease to the target cell."

"I have no idea what you just said," Frank smiled, clearly delighted to be in the midst of this.

"I think you do, Mr. Conrad." Aurora had spent enough time briefing him to know that he was highly intelligent.

"Frank, call me Frank. I'm your partner, not your father.

I have a question. Why are you inserting flax genes instead of something else into the corn DNA?"

"I've experimented with genes from many other crops, but flax works best. Linseed, as it is also called, has genes with the optimum healthy, low-fat enzyme balance and it does not cause the high fat that cows get from eating commercial corn feed." Turning to one of the lab assistants, Aurora said, "Gina, can you please show Mr. Conrad how you are using CRISPR to edit the genes. This will demonstrate how straightforward the process is."

The process was straightforward but not as clean as Aurora explained to Frank. Her fear, which she kept to herself, was that the incision into the corn's DNA was a brutal intrusion. While she was able to achieve her purpose, making the cut and then inserting the flax gene, she worried that the editing process was also inadvertently changing other parts of the corn genome. As the CRISPR enzyme cut the DNA, it appeared that the cells were frantically trying to put themselves back together again and doing so in a way that made the repaired DNA look subtly different in the end. So while she was certain that she had succeeded in properly inserting the flax gene into the corn DNA, there was something about the overall corn genome that felt different, as if she had repaired a broken chair leg but wasn't quite sure it was as solid as before. She did not plan on sharing her worry with her two partners, because she could find no solid evidence that anything was wrong with her GMO. It would be one thing if she was playing around with a human embryo, but, after all, this was just a corn seed. Monsanto and other big companies had been messing around with seeds for years with no adverse effect on anyone. It just needed to be tested on the cows.

Harry wanted to use part of the $300,000 funding as salaries for the two of them. He also wanted to use the money to get his own apartment, but Aurora insisted on using all the funds for the business. Harry and Aurora continued their roommate existence but spent little time in the apartment. She worked long hours in the lab and came home either to crash or change into her part-time-job clothing. She tried to avoid having Harry see her in her provocative attire because when he did, he seemed uncomfortable. Aurora knew she was looking more attractive, not only during the evening, but all the time. Working constantly had revitalized her.

One evening, Jane scheduled Aurora with a client at the Palo Alto Four Seasons hotel. She told Aurora that she had seen this man before, about a year ago, so Jane didn't need to screen him again. Aurora had no recollection of who he was but that wasn't unusual. Despite her superb memory, she preferred not to remember the men she slept with. She was glad this was an early evening appointment, because then she could go back to the lab after she finished. She and her lab assistants were in the final stages of fine-tuning the corn seed.

When she heard the knock on the hotel room door, her mind was at the lab, running through the planned evening's work. Pulling the door open, it took a long minute for the full implication of what she saw to sink in. Even after she processed everything, she was speechless. He stood there, mute, then abruptly backed away and headed down the hallway to the elevator. Aurora followed, then heard the door slam shut behind her. Standing in the hallway, heart racing, frozen, she tried to focus on what to do. She needed instructions from Jane.

"Mr. Conrad," she shouted down the corridor toward his retreating form. "I just locked myself out."

He hesitated, then stopped.

She could see everything that she had worked for — the work, the funding, the promise of a future — coming to an end. All the repercussions of this disaster clouded her ability to think clearly. She breathed in and out, trying to stifle her panic. "Could you wait here by the door for a minute while I go down and get a key?" she said, trying to buy time. Even though his presence at her door had nothing to do with her ability to get a key from the front desk, he meekly walked back. As Aurora passed him on the way to the elevator, she murmured, "Thank you. Be right back."

Moving slowly down the hall, waiting for the elevator, then standing in line to ask the clerk for a new key, gave her what she needed — time to compose a scenario, a script. She could see it take shape in front of her, as if it were on a screen. She wrote it, deleted some lines, added some others.

Inside the elevator again, she examined herself in the mirror. She was shining with perspiration and flushed from anxiety. When she reached her floor, she held the door open with one hand while she patted her face with her dress sleeve, straightened her spine, and brushed back her hair. She exited and walked resolutely down the hallway toward Conrad.

"Now we can go in," she smiled, opening the door. He hesitated, then followed her inside.

"You recognized me when we first met at your house. That's why you acted so oddly," Aurora said.

He stood by the door as if he was going to leave. "I thought I knew you, but I couldn't place you," he mumbled.

"I can understand that." She smiled reassuringly at him, and he offered a weak smile in response. "We could not have met in a more different context. Sit down, please." She motioned for him to sit in one of the pair of oatmeal-colored armchairs. She settled in a chair, across the room, leaned back, and crossed her legs.

He did not move from his position by the door. In her husky escort voice, she said, "Mr. Conrad, I thought I was working for myself tonight, but when you showed up at the door, I got confused for a minute and thought I was still on the clock working for you. But actually I am working for myself for the next hour, then I've got to get back to the lab. I mean, I could extend it for an extra fee, but I've got another job I need to get back to." She continued to smile as she tucked her legs beneath her, pulling her skirt slightly up. "Before we forget, can you please put my fee on the table?"

He didn't move.

She crossed her legs Indian-style, smiling serenely.

He stared at her.

"I never wear underwear in this job," she said, noting where he was looking. "No reason to. Less to take off and no worries that I might lose them. Lingerie is expensive."

He shifted uncomfortably, glancing back at the door.

"No honestly, I don't. See." She wiggled her skirt up well above her waist as she continued to sit with her legs crossed.

"Frank, the fee. This is business for me."

He reached into his pocket, pulled out some folded bills, and placed them on the table next to the chair.

"It's business for me but pleasure for you. We both understand that, don't we? "She uncrossed her legs, sat up and leaned forward with her legs apart. "This is an extraordinary coincidence, don't you think?"

He put his hands in his pockets and seemed to relax.

Aurora leaned back in her chair, now fully exposed to him. "If there's anything you would like to kiss, its right here for you," she said, causally touching herself between her legs. "You just paid for it. It's alright. It's just you and me here, Frank. We're making the best of an awkward situation. It won't change anything. Tomorrow everything will be the same, like this never happened. But right now, I'm here for you. I'm ready."

Frank crossed the room to her.

CHAPTER 4

Aurora suggested a formal business meeting with Harry and Frank, something she had never done before. Frank scheduled it at his Palo Alto office. Harry thought it was strange that he didn't do it at his home where he usually met with them.

Aurora and Harry took the elevator to the seventh floor of the office building, and entered through the featureless door of FC Enterprises. The reception area contained graceful, deep mahogany, nineteenth-century Biedermeier chairs, desk and tables, purchased by Frank in Vienna. Aurora knew nothing about furniture but she knew these were museum pieces. Immediately, Frank stuck his head out of an inner office and motioned them in. This room had a long conference table in the same Vienna style, and the walls were covered with nineteenth-century portraits of Austrian society women in elaborate hairdos and billowing green and maroon silk dresses.

Frank was subdued as they settled in around the table. Aurora and Harry declined his offer of refreshment. Frank, addressing Harry, said "So, what's on your mind today?"

Harry turned toward Aurora, who said, "I thought it was a good time to give you a status report and talk about next steps."

Frank said, "Ok, but I'm comfortable that Harry has been keeping me up-to-date and I've got a good idea of your progress from my visits to the lab. I think you're on track."

Harry stared at Aurora, in the dark as to what she intended to say.

"Yes, yes, that's correct, you're up-to-date on status," said Aurora, sounding impatient. "I want to discuss moving things forward."

Frank gently said, "Right, I know the plan. We are going to raise a few test cows with our corn seed to see how long it takes them to reach maturity and then test the meat for fat content and enzyme balance. And then repeat the process until we are certain that our corn does what it is supposed to do. I understand we should be able to finish this in five or six years, maybe a little longer. I'm fine with the plan. Don't worry, I'm in for the long haul."

"We're ready to raise cattle for market right now," Aurora stated.

"What do you mean for market now?" asked Harry, not even trying to disguise that he'd had no prior notice of what Aurora was saying.

"Our initial cattle production should be enough to supply at least part of the California retail marketplace. We can produce the meat and sell it. We'll need an advertising and marketing campaign to explain the health benefits of the meat, and a sales and distribution organization."

They stared at her.

"Now?" said Frank.

"My corn seed will produce the same healthy fat enzyme balance in the cattle as grass-fed. I've taken all of the bad stuff out of the corn's DNA. It's ready. We can't wait for years with unnecessary testing. We can double-check everything by raising cattle for the market."

Frank shook his head. "We don't have the facilities to do this now – no farms, no cattle, I have no idea what all else we need."

"We are going to subcontract all the cattle operations. You know, feedlots – agricultural enterprises. We'll use their facilities and expertise to raise cows with our corn seed. We don't have to own anything and don't have to reinvent the wheel. You know how it's done with the big beef companies – the cattle spend the first year of their lives on rangeland grazing in healthy grass and wheat pastures; then they're moved to the fenced feedlots where they're fed a crappy, corn diet for about eight months until they're ready for slaughter. I've been working on this. Over the last couple weeks, I vetted a number of the big agricultural feed operators and picked some who will work for us as subs under our control. They have access to excellent calves raised on good grazing land. They'll take them to feedlots separated from the big commercial operations and raise them with our corn seed along with vitamin supplements, minerals, and roughage like alfalfa. I've negotiated all the fees and costs."

She removed two folders from her battered backpack, handing one to each man. "Please study these. Mr. Conrad, you may want to have your accountants check the projected costs against market data so you're comfortable that I negotiated a good deal. I believe they will confirm that we can bring these cows to market at the same price as the big producers. I think part of our marketing strategy will be to offer the beef at the same wholesale prices to the grocery stores as the big companies, even if our profit margins are tight. We want to show that healthy meat costs no more than the bad stuff. If you can sign off on this by next week, we can get going right away. Our operators can get year old calves right now and transfer them to the feedlots. I figure we can have our product in grocery stores in about a year."

Frank and Harry looked at her as if she had just turned stone into bread.

Taking their silence for acquiescence, she continued, "For marketing, we will need an ad firm without ties to the food industry. That's a little bit of a challenge because most of them do work for one food producer or another. Our marketing campaign will focus on slamming the ill health effects of corn-based foods. The established Madison Avenue firms won't want to offend their clients, but I've identified several boutique firms that specialize in tech. They want to make a name for themselves in a high-profile campaign like we are going to run. I'm interviewing them now and will have a recommendation for you this week."

Harry, ignorant of all of this, said, "How, how...?"

"How much will it cost to get this going?" she said. "Conservatively, it will cost us about $2300 per head to raise the cows to slaughter. As a practical matter, we can't start really big. I mean the large players like Tysons and Cargil can slaughter up to thirty thousand cows a day. But we can't come into this business too small. We need to go to market not just as some little startup. We've got to have credibility to get attention, publicity. We want to eventually have the option of whether to go public or not. So we must slaughter around twenty-thousand head during our first year of operation. That way we'll have enough product to make an impact on the California market. For the production, sales, distribution, and a modest ad/or campaign, we need about fifty million. And before we go to market, we've got to have office space, staff, and a living wage for Harry and me. That's about fifty-five million in capital."

Frank shifted in his chair.

"Nice job, Aurora!" Harry said resolutely.

"Thanks. Of course, I want your input, Mr. Conrad, but I think you'll fully agree with my plan."

Harry leaned forward, leveling his gaze at Frank.

"Well, I'll study this," said Frank. "It's quite a departure from where we were."

"No, no, it isn't," Aurora said. "This is exactly where we were headed. This is what I thought you wanted, Frank. We didn't go into business to waste our time with some theoretical project. We did this to be successful, help people and get rich."

Frank looked at Harry. "I'm rich already. I want to stay that way."

"Look at me Frank, all three of us are partners. I know you can raise this money, this is eminently doable. Harry and I relied on you when we committed to do this together. We are doing our part. Now it's time for you to do yours."

Frank shook his head as if trying to clear it.

"Well?" she said, clearly irked.

Frank stood as if to leave, studied his watch and sat down again. "Alright," he whispered. "We'll need to do some due diligence around your plan and the resources you've selected. I'll have my people work with Harry on that. But I'll start raising the money now. Aurora, you can proceed with what you are doing."

"I already am, Frank."

CHAPTER 5

Aurora and Jane sat in the back of their favorite dive, Antonio's Nut Bar. It was a good place to talk. They couldn't be heard above the pinball noise.

"You have to quit."

Aurora frowned.

"You have too much to lose, Aurora. You can't do it anymore. Look what happened with Conrad. Next time it could be someone else who knows who you are."

"It gives me a feeling of control. Everything else I do is so chaotic."

"No, Aurora."

"You're right. I don't even have time for it. I'm working 24/7 on the business."

"How are you going to handle Conrad now?"

"I don't know. He's been communicating only with Harry. He's raising all the money I asked for. He's gotten us more investors and there is going to be a board to advise us. But, Jane, I was scared when we met with him. When I was making my pitch, I expected him to walk out any minute. I thought everything we had worked for was going right down the tubes."

"I told you to go for it, didn't I?"

"Yes, but he wouldn't have done it unless he believed it was a good business plan."

"He wouldn't have done it if you didn't have him by the balls."

"What do I do now? Just pretend the whole thing never happened?'

"Let him decide what to do. Just act like nothing ever happened. He needs to own this. He's the one who bought you. And if he hadn't been so cheap with his funding, you wouldn't have been out there escorting to pay your rent. If he wants you, let him tell you. Don't discourage him and don't encourage him."

"It would be easier for me if nothing else happens between us."

"Don't be so sure of that. Never underestimate the power of the pussy."

"Jane, I want to do something for you. I just don't know what."

"I appreciate that. And you know I love you. You'll figure out how you can use me when the time is right."

Aurora soon realized her original plan overlooked the fact that she first needed a harvest of corn to feed the cattle. Consequently, there would be at least a six-month delay while she contracted with farmers to grow the corn. Still, things were moving at lightning speed. Harry rose to the challenge and proved to be the driven, passionate entrepreneur that Aurora believed he was. He rented office space in Palo Alto and hired several young people to staff the business side of the operation. He monitored farmers and beef operators to assure that everything was in place when the corn was ready. And with his seventy-five-thousand-dollar salary, he got his own apartment.

Frank was now immersed in raising funds and briefing investors on status. What had started as an inconsequential angel investment was now a major undertaking. After the meeting in his office with Aurora and Harry, he dealt only with Harry, avoiding Aurora.

The work continued to intensify for Aurora. She often arrived back at her apartment at one or two in the morning. One night, when she opened the apartment door after eighteen hours at work, she found a woman on her couch. She all but jumped out of her shoes.

"Calm down, it's just me," a familiar voice said.

Aurora hit the light switch. There was her mother holding her usual coffee cup. Aurora's legs trembled. She slumped against the wall.

"I know what you've been up to since the last time I saw you, Aurora. You've become a whore and a liar. What did this good education get you? The skill to cheat and steal. I know what you did. Stole the corn formula from that poor professor and whored your way into this job. I'm disgusted with you."

Aurora wanted to defend herself, but she knew her arguments would be unavailing. Her mother was right as always. Aurora murmured, "How can you be here?"

She shook her head no, and to Aurora's eyes, she seemed as always, in her old house dress with her hair pulled back. "You're not as smart as you think, Aurora. Now I'm going to tell you what to do. Tell your business partners that somebody else invented the corn seed formula and that the professor's wife should get a big share of this business. Give her three-quarters of your share. And tell your business partners that this corn seed is not ready to be sold. It needs to be tested real good for a long time to make sure it's safe and does what it's supposed to do. You understand me, Aurora?"

Aurora began to argue but stopped. She started to weep. It had been so long since she cried, she could not control it; it turned to sobbing. She gasped for breath, thinking that she was going to die. She looked at her mother for help, but her mother shook her head scornfully.

"I can't tell you how disappointed I am in you."

"Mom, I'll do better. I promise I will."

Her mother frowned. "I'm glad your father is not around to see this."

Aurora squeezed her eyes shut so she could block out that scornful face, but realized her reaction was childish. She willed herself to open them. Now the room was dark; she could no longer see her mother at all. She sat up straight to better search for her, then saw that she was in her bed.

She lay back on her pillows and tried to sleep. She asked herself, "what I am doing? Am I so driven to be successful that I will cut corners and disregard the scientific methodology that I believe in? So what if it takes five years to finish the testing? And if it doesn't work, that's the way it goes. That's what scientists do – we don't guarantee a profitable business plan. I'm not a businessperson; I'm a scientist. Do the right thing even when it is difficult – I believe in that. I may be a born loser – I probably am, but I'm not a bad person. I'm good. My Mom knew that – that's why she was here tonight."

★

Harry and Aurora were drinking the thirty-five-dollar a pound Jamaican coffee brewed by a lab assistant. Aurora had spent the day refining the corn seed and Harry had dropped in to see what was going on.

"Why are you doing this? I thought you were totally finished developing the seed."

"Yes, yes, just checking and double-checking. You know me."

"Ha, I should know you after all the time we spent together but honestly sometimes I'm not sure I really do. Frank keeps asking me about you – your background, what you're really like, how well I know you. It's weird that he is so insistent on knowing your story; he never asks a thing about me. I think he wants to know because you'll be the public face of this business when we go to market."

"Have you told him that I'm an axe murderer? I wanted to keep that quiet."

"I told him how solid, smart and ethical you are."

"Harry, how come you've never challenged me about selling our beef without testing it?"

"I trust you, Aurora. If you say it's ok, that's enough for me. And I know we've tested the corn seed over and over. The DNA doesn't lie. Every way we look at it, it has the qualities we want – or I should say it lacks the qualities that make beef high in cholesterol and unhealthy enzymes. Right?"

She frowned. "You don't think we've been drinking our own Kool-Aid? I mean, the effect on the cattle from our corn is all theoretical. We could be creating something toxic. Professor Fraser would never have done what we're doing. In fact, he specifically declined to do what we are doing."

"He didn't develop it – you did. And he was a cautious academic. He never did anything practical. That's why he was a teacher. He was afraid. You're not like that, Aurora."

"I don't think we should market it without testing the cows."

Harry's jaw dropped. "You are kidding, right? That would take years. I'm kind of shocked you're getting cold feet all of a sudden. Hey, suck it up, Aurora. We're all counting on you. There aren't any specific problems that you know about, are there?"

"No, it's just..."

"No, no, there are no ifs here. You did this. And you sold it to Conrad. And he's a tough, analytical businessman. He wouldn't do this unless he was confident in what we were doing and believed in us. This is happening, Aurora – don't lose your courage now."

"Ok." She forced a feeble smile.

CHAPTER 6

It took almost two years for the first herd raised on Aurora's corn to be ready for slaughter. Aurora, guided by what her Mother would have told her, advised Frank and Harry that she would not sell the meat unless it was tested by an independent company. They agreed, aware that she was going to do the testing despite their objections.

Aurora considered using one of two standard methods, SFE and Bligh, to determine the fat content and the fatty acid composition of the cows raised on her corn. She decided to do it both ways and contracted with independent labs to perform the tests.

When the results came back, they exceeded her most optimistic expectations. The cholesterol content of the beef was forty percent less than from conventionally fed cows – fully comparable to high quality grass-fed animals. In addition, a four-ounce portion of her beef had eight hundred milligrams of CLA (conjugated linoleic acid) – the highly beneficial omega-6 fatty acid that improves blood sugar regulation, provides immune and inflammatory system support, and reduces body fat and risk of heart attack as well as maintains lean body mass. Her meat also had twice the amount of beta-carotene and lutein as regular meat had. It even had the yellowish fat color found in grass-fed beef. She had produced beef as healthy as the best available grass-fed beef, and at the same low cost as conventional beef.

Aurora and Harry flew down to LA to visit a good-sized grocery chain, Bristol Farms, the first to sign on to carry their product. They took a cab from LAX to Wilshire Boulevard, a palm tree-lined canyon of high-rise condominiums, and onto the shopping store street, Westwood Boulevard and then into the parking lot of an upscale grocery store. Harry told the cab driver to wait. As they approached the meat section, they could immediately see it in the case: a fire engine red heart shaped logo with the brand name "Healthy Heart" affixed to plastic wrapping on sirloins, T-bones, New York strips, and hamburgers. The branding wasn't clever but it made the point – after all, what other meat product could legitimately call itself Healthy Heart? Aurora stood transfixed in front of the meat case, shivering from the cold and the excitement of seeing the end-product of her work. She told herself that whatever happened after this was nothing compared to what she had achieved today: getting their product on supermarket shelves, and a front page article in the business section of *USA Today* about the company and the meat and her, with a color photo of her image in pale, translucent color – ethereal, blond, beautiful – with the headline, "Young Woman Genius Behind Scientific Healthy Meat Breakthrough."

Since they'd landed in LA, Harry had been receiving texts and emails from media outlets asking for interviews with Aurora. *60 Minutes* wanted to do a segment on her; *People* magazine asked to send a reporter to San Francisco to interview her; the *Wall Street Journal* was writing an article. Tweets from @aurorashealthymeats, their own Twitter account, were trending.

"You are going to be our star, Aurora," Harry said. "You'll have to decide whether you want to step in to the spotlight or lay back."

"Whatever's best for the company."

"You. Without you, we're under the radar screen. It could take us years to convince the public of the benefits of our product. But with you front and center, that will supercharge our growth."

"I'll do whatever it takes, Harry."

"It means giving up your privacy, Aurora. You're going to become a public person."

She laughed. "I've been pretty much a nonentity all my life. The change might do me good."

"This is your decision. No one would fault you if you had our PR firm handle all of this."

"You would fault me, Harry. So would Frank. So would I."

"I think we need a PR coach to work with you before you start giving interviews."

"I'm fine. I can do it. Don't worry, I won't let you down."

Aurora said yes to every request for an interview regardless of the size or status of the media outlet. *60 Minutes* did a fawning fifteen minutes interview with her, letting her extoll the benefits of her meat and her unselfish dedication to improving everyone's health. In her new uniform, a white, V-neck cashmere sweater with matching tailored silk trousers, she was not following any fashion look; she was creating one, a modern-day Katherine Hepburn style. Her cool, understated appearance matched her on-screen demeanor — controlled, detailed, and credible. She was not like anyone else in the public eye. She fielded every question with poise and assurance and she managed to come across as both a brilliant young scientist and a desirable woman.

While Aurora was unfazed by the interviews, she was taken aback by the way colleagues and strangers treated her. Before her rise to prominence, her coworkers knew who she was; but now they acted as if she were someone entirely different. When she walked into a room, their attention centered on her, their conversations with her were overly animated, and they were reluctant to contradict her even when they disagreed with her. She could see that her new acquaintances had no real interest in who she really was; they wanted only to make an impression on her. As a result, Aurora felt further distanced from others. Throughout her transformation from nonentity to international celebrity, only her friendships with Harry and Jane remained unaltered; they were the two people she could trust and confide in.

The initial reaction of customers to Healthy Heart meat products surprised even the most optimistic of her corporate team. Propelled by the media stories about Aurora, the Bristol Farms chain sold out immediately. As soon as they were able to replenish their stock, they sold out again. The new company could not keep up with customer demand. Consumers all over the country, including young people who followed Aurora Blanc on social media, asked their local grocery stores why they didn't carry Healthy Heart products. When it was made known that the product was available only in Southern California, a third-party vendor established an app called "WeDeliverHealthyHeartToYou," which guaranteed overnight delivery anywhere in the country at a substantial premium above the normal retail price. (The vendor got the beef by buying it off the shelves at the Bristol Farms stores and doubled the sales.) It was soon shut down for violating health laws, but the demand for the product continued as the public wrote their elected officials insisting that this healthy meat be made available everywhere. *The New York Times* wrote, extravagantly, that there had been nothing like the anticipation of nationwide distribution of Healthy Heart meats since the Beatles came to America.

Harry, Frank, and Aurora convened in Frank's office for their first meeting together since the moment when Frank committed to fund their expansion.

"Aurora wants to go from zero to hero again," said Harry.

"What exactly does that mean?" Frank asked.

"You know what it means, Frank. We have this tiny, marginal operation in Southern California with a small window of opportunity to be in every major grocery chain in the United States. We have all this visibility – essentially free advertising and unprecedented customer demand for a grocery product – our product. We need to take advantage of this now."

Frank said, "To do this, we would need our own land to grow massive amounts of corn. We would have to raise our own cattle, which would involve buying grazing fields and feedlots. We would need our own slaughter operations and distribution channels. I don't even know what else we would need because we have no experience or background to run a large business like that."

"We can do it," Aurora said, looking pointedly at Harry.

"Well, we can do a combination of subcontracting and buying our own operations," said Harry.

"Even if we could do it, it would cost hundreds of millions to make it happen," Frank said.

"It'll cost more than that," said Aurora. "This is a multi-billion-dollar business. Tysons alone sells over thirty billion dollars of beef, chicken and pork a year – that's just one company."

"That's a public company."

"So what?" said Aurora. "We are offering something that no one else has. We have good patents on the corn seed, but eventually others are going to replicate what we're doing. We need to lock down the advantage that we have right now."

"I agree with Aurora," said Harry.

Frank stared at the table.

"Frank!" Aurora said.

He looked up.

Aurora stood, walked around the table, sat in the chair next to Frank and brought her face inches from his. "We can do this. This is what you were born to do. This is what we were born to do."

Within a month, Frank reported to Aurora and Harry that investors were lining up; the money was there and they could get as much as they needed. The biggest issue was how to structure the investments. Aurora told Harry that she was comfortable with him sorting through the options with Frank while she worked on finding contractors, property, and operations to purchase.

Harry's assessment of the potential investors was quick and visceral. The deepest pocket was Helena Foods, a multinational company, which sold a range of food products, including meats. Even though Helena said that they would not interfere with the production of Healthy Heart beef, Harry and Aurora were afraid that even a passive involvement with their operations would sully the purity of their product in the public eye. Harry also worried that the private equity firms that wanted to invest would be too intrusive in the management of the company. Aurora was moving rapidly to find resources to get their product into the national market and Harry did not want new investors to hamstring her. Harry was most interested in a Shanghai businessman, Xu Feng, who said he could invest a billion dollars or more, depending on the rate of the company's growth. Frank and Harry flew to Shanghai to meet with him. They were impressed with his enthusiasm for the company and disinclination to have anything to do with the management. After thoroughly checking him out, they were satisfied that he had the means to support everything they wanted to do and leave them alone to do it.

The *Wall Street Journal* got wind that Healthy Heart had funding to go national. This notice helped Harry and Aurora's credibility as they approached corn farmers and beef operators to buy or enter into subcontracting deals. Motivated by a combination of desire to be involved in a good cause and greed from the premium prices that Healthy Heart was offering, Harry and Aurora quickly acquired land, feed lots, slaughter operations, and employees. Almost overnight, Healthy Heart went from a tiny operation to a major player in the beef industry, not nearly as large as the giants but with sufficient production ability to supply grocery stores nationwide. Harry and Aurora quickly hired executives and managers to oversee the day-to-day operations, as well as experienced sales staff to deal with the grocery chains. Commensurate with their expanded responsibilities, Harry and Aurora each took salaries of 1.2 million a year, modest by Silicon Valley standards but a fortune for them — not that they had any time to spend it as they both continued to work round the clock. Aurora stayed on in her old apartment. On the infrequent occasions when she was not traveling to oversee the Company's far flung national operations, she slept there.

Healthy Heart Beef's Rapid Growth May Be Tied To Its Unusual Funding (*Wall Street Journal* May 7):

"Healthy Heart, a privately-owned beef company, is like other successful Silicon Valley startups in one respect — it has taken in hundreds of millions in venture capital funding. But in contrast to companies like Facebook, which received its money from many sources, including other companies (Microsoft), venture capital firms, private investors, and, ultimately, from a public offering, the source of most of Healthy Heart's funding is one investor, a little-known Shanghai businessman, Xu Feng. Another difference is the extraordinary speed, only one year, with which Healthy Heart received the bulk of its funds, reportedly one billion. It took Facebook about eight years to raise that amount before it went public.

"Healthy Heart has quickly put the money to quick use in

a frenzy of acquisitions, including large corn and beef operations, and the company is booming. Its steaks and burgers are
available throughout the United States, selling out at grocery
stores. Even with the relatively low profit margins in the beef
business, the company is generating strong positive cash flow.
It also has an efficient business model – growing its own genetically modified corn, using its own cattle operations and dis-
tributing its product through its own network. With demand
for its products exceeding supply, Healthy Heart will soon
be assessing a number of options, including acquisition by a
larger company or going public. Company CEO and founder,
Aurora Blanc, insists the company will remain privately held.
Given the Company's thirty billion dollar valuation of which
she owns twenty-five percent, she will have quite a bit of say
in the future of the enterprise."

CHAPTER 7

"He essentially owns us," Frank said.

"He's an investor with equity, not the owner," Aurora responded.

"In this case, his equity and the terms of the deal put him in the driver's seat."

"What the fuck does that mean? I thought the whole point of letting him invest was to keep out corporate and venture capital investors who would try to control us."

"It was. If we had taken their money, they would be controlling us. But with him, we hoped he would be true to his word that he would be a passive investor."

Aurora looked at Harry sitting across the table. "Harry?" she said sharply.

Harry looked sheepish. "Frank's right."

"Why would he do this?" Aurora asked.

"Come on. You know."

"You told me that every time you met with him, all he could talk about is the great good we are doing. He's never asked about return on investment or any details about the business."

"Well, we've done a good job of providing all of our financial data to him," Harry said. "He didn't have to ask any questions."

"It seems like we did this to ourselves," Aurora muttered.

"Aurora, for being such a smart person, you're pretty naïve. You can't just go out and get one billion dollars from someone without recognizing the possibility that he may want to exercise control over his investment. He gave us the money, let us spend it without any oversight, and we've been successful beyond our wildest dreams."

"You're wrong about the last part. The success was exactly what I planned. It was no dream."

To assess their situation, Harry consulted with a different law firm than the one that had negotiated the investment contract with Xu Feng. According to the new lawyers, the contract had a clause that could be interpreted as giving Xu Feng the right to take over management of Healthy Heart if certain revenue numbers were not met. At the time they negotiated the contract, Harry, Frank and their lawyers believed that clause simply identified "growth targets" and that there would be no adverse ramifications if the targets were not achieved. But the new lawyers pointed out that the language was ambiguous – that Xu Feng had a strong legal position to say that a "contract covenant had been tripped" giving him the right to exercise complete control of the company. Xu Feng did not even give them the courtesy of notifying them that he wanted to take over the company. Instead he covertly contacted the giant beef company Helena Foods and entered into negotiations to sell Healthy Heart to them. Harry found out about it when an accountant from Helena called to ask to review their books in order to do due diligence on the pending acquisition.

There was no clear path forward to reverse the situation. The new lawyers wanted to file a court action for declaratory judgment, asking the Judge to stop Xu Feng and Helena from proceeding with the sale, but the problem with this approach was that they would be putting everything in the hands of a Judge — where the odds, according to their lawyers were fifty-fifty, at best. Even if they won, Xu Feng would certainly appeal, putting everything in limbo for years, likely crippling the growth of the company.

Frank was sanguine about the whole situation, telling Aurora and Harry that if they had to sell, they would be multi-billionaires, not just paper-rich, as they were now. He said they should simply acquiesce and let Helena buy them instead of getting into years of litigation that would place a cloud over the entire enterprise. While Harry privately expressed his outrage to Aurora at Frank's willingness to cave in, he felt responsible for the fact that he had not understood the landmine within the contract and was now unable to come up with any idea as to how to fix it.

"You want to consult with me!" Jane laughed. "Aurora, you've got one of the best law firms in the country working on this problem and two smart partners. I don't have any good ideas. Except maybe you should just take the money and run. There are worse things than being financially secure for your entire life."

"This business is my entire life, Jane."

'You're young. There is so much you could do with the money. Hey, let's take a trip around the world for a year. We've never even been out of the country."

Aurora stared at the floor.

"Come on. Snap out of it."

She managed a weak smile.

"That's better."

Aurora wiped her wet eyes.

"God, I don't think I've ever seen you cry."

"I'm not," Aurora murmured.

"It's ok. I'm here for you, sweetie. What can I do for you? I have a great idea – let's go out for some great Chinese and those martinis you like with the chocolate cake flavored vodka. We'll drink them all night till we can't see straight."

Aurora didn't respond.

"What do you want to do, sweetie?" said Jane encouragingly.

"I do want to eat some Chinese food, but not in Palo Alto."

"I know a great place in San Francisco. I'll drive."

Aurora stood up. "Go home and pack for a couple nights away. I'll pick you up in a limo as soon as I get reservations. You have a passport? I'll text you with the pick-up time."

"That's my girl. I've got a passport. Where we going?"

"Shanghai."

It took a couple of days for them to get their visas and reservations in place, and then they were in a two-bedroom suite at the Peninsula Shanghai hotel. The rooms were black-and-white, comfortable and contemporary, with a light Asian flavor. There were bamboo screen bathroom doors and green and grass paper on the walls.

"Gorgeous rooms," said Jane.

"Given the number of hotel rooms you've seen, that's high praise.

"Your mean sense of humor is back!"

"Actually, I got this nice suite for you. They gave me a

good rate — ten thousand dollars a night. But, you know, I couldn't care less about where I stay."

"You're meeting with Xu Feng tomorrow, right. What's the plan?"

Aurora smiled brightly. "I have no fucking idea."

Jane put her arm around Aurora's shoulder and squeezed. "That's my girl. Just don't beg him."

"No, that definitely is not an option."

"What then?"

"I've never even met him. All I know is, he speaks perfect English and he's a billionaire."

"Well, that's something, I guess."

"It's all we have to work with. This gentleman is very, very private. Virtually no press on him, probably because he has spent most of his life in China. I don't even know how old he is, probably around sixty, but that's just a guess."

Frank called Harry to ask what Aurora was doing in Shanghai with their investor. "No idea," said Harry. "She didn't even tell me she was going."

"I thought you two were close."

Harry considered this. While Aurora had always been an enigma, she usually told him everything she was thinking about the business. But since the takeover crisis, she had shut him out. Harry thought that was unfair. It was not his fault that this had happened; he was just being practical in suggesting that they agree to the sale in the first place. But obviously she didn't see it that way.

"Well, what do you think we should do?" Frank asked Harry.

"She's not looking for my opinion. Maybe you should send her an email telling her that she has no authority to act on her own with Xu Feng."

Frank pondered this. In an ordinary business deal, he would not hesitate to tell a partner to stand down. But he was hesitant with Aurora. Their trysts a few years before worried him. She'd never said a thing to him about them; she acted like they had never happened.

No one in Silicon Valley had scared Frank until Aurora. From the first time they met at his house, he sensed a determined quality about her. Now, several years later, he believed she was ruthless. While he had little reason to believe she would try to destroy his marriage or screw him in some other way, the wisest course of action was to leave her alone to deal with Xu Feng. In any event, he told himself, she had no leverage to stop the sale and she was too smart to do anything to harm their business. Her trip to Shanghai was a Hail Mary; she would come home empty-handed.

The night before the meeting with Xu Feng, Aurora had difficulty falling asleep. In the morning, when she arrived at his office and was ushered in, she felt like a child entering a regal room, confronting a large, scornful, dark-haired Asian man seated behind a shiny mahogany desk. He barely acknowledged her presence, waited for her to say her piece. She blurted it out, as if she were a student standing in front of a stern teacher. When she finished, he nodded his head, signifying that the meeting was over. As she walked out of the building into the stifling atmosphere, she felt dread. She gasped for air, as if she were under heavy blankets. She straightened up, pulling off the covers, and then realized that she was not in the street, that there had been no meeting and that she was in her hotel room bed.

In the morning, she telephoned Xu Feng's assistant, saying that she had become ill, apparently from something she ate, and requested that he come to her suite for the meeting. Her contrite request was effective. He showed up at the hotel at the appointed time.

Jane ushered him into the living room, where Aurora was settled behind a small flat mahogany desk. When he entered, she continued to tap on her laptop keyboard. Clad in a sleek, black silk turtleneck and slacks, she stood to greet him. She was several inches taller than he was. He looked older than his photos, a web of wrinkles across his face.

Before he could speak, she said, "So very kind of you to come to me. I'm afraid I'm used to healthy California cuisine. This Asian food makes me sick."

"I'm so sorry. I must tell you we have some of the finest cuisine in the world here in Shanghai."

"Unfortunately, no one here invited me out to dine last night so I was left to my own devices. I probably made a bad choice. I won't make that mistake again. However, I am beginning to feel better."

"When are you leaving?"

"Oh we'll be here for a few more days." She looked at him pointedly.

"Perhaps I could take you to dine at one of our exceptional restaurants. I own several."

"Thank you, but I'm afraid our schedule is full."

"Oh well, next time then." He appeared taken aback by her refusal.

"That depends."

"Depends?"

"On whether we remain partners or become competitors."

"Competitors?"

"In the beef business, my business."

"I'm afraid legal constraints will prevent you from continuing in the beef business, because of our non-compete agreements and patents."

Jane walked in from the bedroom. "Can I get anything for you? Coffee, croissant, tea?"

Aurora settled back in her chair. "Now that you mention it, I am feeling better and a little hungry. Please see if they have Eggs Benedict. And dark coffee – Ethiopian, preferably."

Aurora and Jane looked at Xu Feng. "No, no, thank you."

"The food is quite good here. This is not where I got sick. I think the hotel is owned by Americans. Please have something. I'm sure you'll enjoy it," Aurora said, smiling brightly.

"No, thank you."

"You're missing out. Now where were we?" She paused waiting for him to respond.

"Well I was..."

"Oh yes, the non-compete clause. Well, that's nonsense. I'm the owner of the company. I never signed an agreement like that. Our employees sign non-competes. Did we make you sign one? Oh, it doesn't matter because they're worthless anyway. And you said patents? Well, we don't have patents on the genetic engineering of the corn seed because it's all in my head. And I've got a new corn seed anyway. It's different – more effective. It's designed to vitiate the carcinogens – cancer causing elements in processed beef. That means we can sell bacon, hot dogs, sausage. I'm not using it for Healthy Heart. We are already too immersed in using the original seed to switch to my new one."

Xu Feng looked at his hands.

"I know you're trying to figure out where this is going," Aurora said. "You think you hold all the cards. You don't. I hold the cards. You think this is like some kind of real estate or manufacturing deal that you can manipulate. But this is completely different because it's science and you don't know anything about science. The success of this venture is all about me – what I've invented and who I am. Take me away from this company and you've got nothing. I don't need you. I need big resources in order to dominate; the best way to get those resources is for me to partner with one of the big beef conglomerates like you're trying to sell to. They would be much better partners for me than you, because they have all the resources and money to let me scale up fast."

"Ms. Blanc, you would have to start all over. That's not feasible."

"I've already done that. I negotiated an agreement in principle with Tyson, one of the conglomerates, as you know. They're willing to give me everything I need to get the beef product on the shelves nation-wide in less than twenty months. I'll do the ad campaign and all the promotion. It will be bigger, much bigger than Healthy Heart. No one will buy Healthy

Heart after I say it is inferior to my new beef. I'll bury Healthy Heart."

"You are trying to bluff me, Ms. Blanc. I'm very sorry you are losing your company, but that's business."

"I keep telling you: I am not a business person, I'm a scientist. I deal with verifiable facts. I don't know anything about bluffing. I'm sure you could teach me about it if I was interested, which I am not. Here are the verifiable facts of this situation. You have two choices. You can try to sell the company. I use the word "try" because once your prospective buyer learns that I will be in direct competition with them, they will rethink things. Even if the sale goes through, you will be in competition with me and our resources. That is, Tyson's multi-billion-dollar business will squash you like the cockroach you are. Or you can gracefully pull out of the sale. If you do that, our lawyers will need to make sure the deal is irrevocably dead. Then we can kiss and make up. So, we can be partners like before or I can fuck you over. Those, Mr. Xu Feng, are the facts."

He stared at her.

"I know your English is very good but I want to make sure you understand the term 'Fuck you over'. Do you understand it?"

Xu Feng smiled and rose from his chair.

"Jane can show you out." Aurora glanced down at her lap top, and then, as an afterthought, murmured, "Please let me know in twenty-four hours. Otherwise, I'm moving forward with Tyson. And thank you for coming over here. I am feeling much better. I think I can enjoy my breakfast now."

★

Fifteen time zones away, Harry ignored a call from an agent of the Federal Drug Administration to inquire into the scientific procedure behind Healthy Heart's corn seed genetic modification. Harry was aware that the FDA had traditionally refused to regulate genetically engineered foods, having taken the position they were as safe as natural foods. As a result, the government had permitted GMO products to be sold without testing or even labels to inform consumers that they were genetically engineered. Harry was also aware that public pressure was mounting on the government to exercise some level of oversight in this area, and guessed that this call from the FDA agent probably resulted from that pressure. Ordinarily, Harry would have been worried about this, but with the pending sale, it would be the new owner's problem, not his.

That evening, as he sat his office, his mental state swung between mild happiness and mild depression. The big payday that was coming to him (around ten billion dollars) was beyond his wildest, craziest expectations. This, he told himself, was what he had dreamed of achieving: making a little startup into a successful company and then selling it or going public with it. Still, he felt guilty about Aurora, even though he'd had nothing to do with Xu Feng's surreptitious take-over and sale of the company. Her coldness towards him ever since it happened caused a relentless angst. He wanted to fix it with her but did not know how. He also felt angry with her for believing that he had the power to stop Xu Feng from going through with the sale. Perhaps her Hail Mary trip to Singapore would show her that they were helpless to reverse the situation and she would forgive him for giving in so easily. But he could not suppress the cold economic calculus in his head – the company in its current unsold status made him a paper billionaire, meaning that the money was not really his; whereas when the company was sold, he would become an actual billionaire. While Aurora did not seem to care about that, he did. So in that sense, they were not in the same place anymore – no longer close partners sharing a common view. Of course, he never would have gone behind her back to sell it but since it happened he was secretly glad. He also recognized that he would not feel so conflicted if she was just a regular business partner, but she meant much more than that to him.

As if his thoughts had conjured it, a text from Aurora popped up on his phone. Addressed to Frank and him, it stated: "After meeting with Xu Feng today, he has agreed to abort the sale of the Company. Please notify our lawyers to work with him to document termination of the transaction. Include ironclad legal language that prevents him from making any future unilateral efforts to sell. I DO NOT WANT THIS TO HAPPEN AGAIN. I've agreed to do promotion and advertising for our products going forward and it's okay to put that in the legal papers in any way his lawyers wish. It's time for us to get back to work. "

Shocked, Harry took a breath and exhaled. The world had spun on its axis again.

In the aftermath of the Xu Feng sale crisis, Aurora became the dominant figure in the trio of Harry, Frank and herself. Xu Feng, apparently confident in her leadership skills after meeting with her, receded into the background. The two principal challenges facing the company were: how to ramp up production fast enough to meet the explosive demand for their beef products and what to do about the FDA's repeated requests to review the scientific protocol behind their corn seed and beef production. The FDA wanted a step-by-step explanation as to how Aurora had modified the corn seed and how that corn feed affected the cows that consumed it. While Harry worked at deftly putting off the FDA agent, Frank used his connections to retain a Washington lobbyist to advise how to block the government intervention.

Several weeks after Aurora's return from Shanghai, the lobbyist, Frank, Harry, and Aurora got together on a telephone conference.

"The good thing is that the FDA has implicitly said that GMOs are harmless to human health, and have pretty much supported agricultural and scientific genetic engineering research," the lobbyist, Greg Murdock said. "The government has rightly recognized the economic benefit of genetic engineering through cheaper food and more efficient agricultural production. Of course, there is the important political component — the enormous profits of companies like Monsanto and DuPont and their big donations to political candidates of both parties. So, it's been smooth sailing for agricultural and food GMOs."

"I know, I know — public pressure is changing all that," Aurora said impatiently.

"Well, yes, there's the First Lady's campaign for healthy foods. She even gave a speech to the big grocery association telling them they should start producing better foods. But her husband hasn't followed up with any legislation or regulations. You know, the government is like a big ship – it takes a while to change course."

"Then why are they bothering us?"

"CRISPR-Cas9 genome engineering. The FDA scientists understand that this is a far more powerful gene-editing tool than the old ones; it's like advancing from gunpowder to the hydrogen bomb. Anyone can genetically engineer using this tool in their bedroom, and some FDA scientists believe it needs to exercise forceful oversight. That's the internal debate going on now at FDA. And your company has been so high-profile with your product, it puts you in the crosshairs."

"Then let them bother some amateur who is playing with this in his basement," Aurora said. "Our team is made up of Stanford-educated scientists. We are better equipped to do this than most of those second-raters at Monsanto. And I'll bet the government is leaving Monsanto completely alone." She turned to Harry. "Just tell that federal agent to go away. We're not going to show him our confidential formulas, particularly since he has no authority to come in here."

Murdock shifted in his chair. "If I might make a suggestion. The better way to handle this is to get a top lawyer who specializes in FDA law and have him or her diplomatically deal with the agent. That way you can buy time while we figure out an approach to get some help from our elected officials."

"That's good advice," said Frank.

"Alright," said Aurora, grimacing, looking at the ceiling.

After Murdock signed off, Frank caught Aurora as she was heading down the hallway to the restroom, the first time he had been alone with her since the hotel room. "Can we talk?"

She stopped and turned in his direction. "Yes."

"I'm on your side, Aurora."

She stared impassively at him.

"I did not sabotage you with Xu Feng. I think you know that."

She said nothing.

"We need to work together if we're going to make this work."

"If we're going to continue to work together, you need to trust me."

"What does that mean? I've always trusted you."

"Then let me figure out what to do about this government interference. It threatens our entire business. I know they're out to get us — to put us out of business."

"There is absolutely no indication of that at all. And they do have the right to come in here."

"That's where you and I disagree, Frank. I trusted you before and we came this close to the end of everything with Xu Feng. I am not going to let that happen again."

"You came that close to becoming a real billionaire. I would hardly call that betraying you."

"I am a billionaire and I own this company and I intend to keep it that way."

"You're in charge. Just keep me in the loop."

"I will, I am."

"I would like to meet once a week for breakfast — just you and me."

"What about Harry?"

"How do you feel about Harry?"

"I don't trust him. He just wants the cash. You're already rich."

He smiled and shook his head. He groped for the right words but didn't find them.

"Ok. Breakfast once a week."

Aurora followed Murdock's recommendation and hired a law firm to deal with the FDA agent. The federal agent told the lawyers that his superiors had instructed him to investigate precisely what the company had done to the corn seed and how that corn seed was affecting the beef. Murdock then tried to persuade several sympathetic congressmen to put pressure on the FDA to back off. That didn't work. Aurora told the lawyers that she wanted to sue the FDA for harassment, but while the lawyers said they could frame a lawsuit to accuse the FDA of exceeding their legislative authority in trying to meddle in the company's confidential scientific work, the suit would likely fail because the FDA had considerable discretion to oversee the food industry. The lobbyist was concerned that such a lawsuit would make it seem as if the company had something to hide – a bad public relations move. Aurora backed off, but she remained worried that the FDA would hurt her company. And she was angry at her high-priced experts.

Although she knew little about the legal aspects of all of this, her analytical mind figured it out quickly – that the FDA, an agency of the Executive branch of the federal government, reported to the President, who could do whatever he wanted as long as he stayed within its legislative authority and limits. There was, of course, no reason to believe the President had

had any involvement in the FDA's attempts to interfere with her business; however, if the President found out about the blatant intrusion into her private business affairs, he could tell the FDA to back off. The course of action was clear, but she was not going to discuss it with Frank or Harry or the useless lobbyist and lawyers; they would only tell her to be patient and see how things played out. She would try to fix this herself.

Jane had a surprise for Aurora when they met up at their usual drinking spot, Antonio's. Jane brought along a short, slightly pudgy, dark-haired man, who was wearing shorts and a San Francisco Giants T-shirt. As Aurora was assessing his hairy neck and arms, Jane said, "This is Horace, my fiancé. Horace, meet my closest friend in the whole world, Aurora." Jane paused, taking in the dismay on Aurora's face. "I wanted to surprise you, but apparently I shocked you."

"I told you that you should have given her advance notice of this," Horace said.

Aurora managed a wan smile. "Sorry, but I had no idea you were even seeing anyone." Frowning, tilting her head towards Horace, she said, "He's right, you should've told me."

Jane said, "I should have told you. I know. But you've been so busy; we don't talk as much as we used to and I thought I'd surprise you. Not a good surprise, right?" Jane smiled. "Come on, let's not ruin this for me. Be happy for me, okay?"

Aurora pulled herself together. She hugged Jane, then Horace, whispering in his ear, "You better take good care of her. She always took good care of me."

He pulled away and looked into her eyes. "I have her back. I love her, admire her, and I know who she is. And if you let me be your friend, I'll have your back, too."

"Pardon me, Ms. Blanc," said a young man, tapping Aurora's shoulder from behind. "Thank you for the amazing work you have done. You're an inspiration to me, to all of my friends."

Aurora was used to this. "Thank you. That means a lot to me. We're going to keep on working for everyone's health."

"May I take a selfie with you?"

As Aurora was posing, several more people waited to talk to her.

Jane took Aurora's arm. "I've got to visit the bathroom. Come with me, Aurora." She gently pulled Aurora away from the group and led her across the barroom into the dingy bathroom. They went into a stall. "Aurora, I am so sorry for not telling you. Be happy for me, okay?"

"I can't believe I'm losing you."

"You're not losing me. I'm not going anywhere. I needed this. He's a great guy. He wants to take care of me. You should find somebody too."

"Ha. I'm not even dating."

"You're one of the most desirable women on the planet. You need to find somebody. Start going out."

"I can't. I just don't feel like I could have a relationship with anyone."

"That's ridiculous. Of course you can."

"I'm so focused on, obsessed with, surviving in this business. I feel angry from the moment I get up till I go to bed. I don't trust anyone except you. I don't feel any emotion toward anyone but you. I have no physical desire at all. When I was escorting, I was so in control of the situation with those men, I think I permanently turned myself off emotionally and sexually. I know I could date famous alpha men but I don't want them. At the end of the day, I don't want to see anyone."

"Try. For me, just try going out. I give you good advice, don't I? Listen to Jane: somewhere out there is someone you can trust and rely on." She took Aurora's chin in her hand. "OK?"

"I'll think about it."

"You're going to be fine."

"Tell me about Horace."

He's a business guy, works for a big company in public relations. He's smart. I trust him. He knows everything about me and it's fine with him."

Back in the bar over sandwiches, Aurora tried to connect with Horace. "Jane says you're a public relations expert."

"I don't know about the expert part but I've been doing it for my whole career. I admire what you've done with social media advertising. That video that went viral with you talking about how you lost your dad to bad nutrition and how you founded the company so other children would not lose their parents to a harmful diet — it was brilliant. Jane says it was your idea."

"Thanks. Watching too much TV as a kid evolved into social media expertise, I guess. But I'm having a harder time figuring out kind of another kind of PR issue."

"I would be happy to brainstorm with you about it if you

want."

Aurora did not say anything.

"You can trust him," said Jane.

"It's not technically PR although it ultimately could be a PR problem," Aurora said. "The FDA wants oversight on what we're doing scientifically. I don't want them involved in our business or science or anything else. Apparently they have the right to inspect us, but it's discretionary on their part. I'd like to get the President to tell them to back off, but I can't seem to get any access to him."

"The President of the United States?" He looked skeptical.

"Yes."

"He's running for reelection with terrible poll numbers. You would have a very difficult time getting to talk to him or his people on this."

"I'm thinking I would wait until after November when he could focus on my issue."

"If you want access, forget about the sitting president — approach the Republican most likely to beat him."

"Rockwood? He has a record as governor of trying to regulate the food industry. He's much worse than the President."

"What is the downside in talking to him? You could do him a lot of good. Big campaign contributions, of course, but beyond that, you're a hero to a lot of people. You could help him get votes."

"He's the enemy. He's on the record about getting stricter food industry regulation which he did in New York when he was governor."

"He wants to get elected. I certainly wouldn't tell you what to do but if it was me, I would talk to him. What do you have to lose?"

"So, I just call him up by phone?"

"No, no. We can get him to call you."

"You can arrange that?"

"Yes."

"I'll have our procurement guy call you to discuss your fee."

"No fee."

"Absolutely no fee," Jane emphatically repeated.

The next day Aurora received an email from a Thomas Rockwood aide asking if she could take a call from the candidate at 3 PM. At precisely three, her cell phone rang. "It's wonderful to get an opportunity to talk to you," he said. "I am a big admirer of yours and would love to have you as a supporter." His voice was warm, as if he was talking to an old friend.

"Sir, I appreciate the opportunity to talk to you. I do wonder about whether we could work together in light of your positions on stricter regulations on the agricultural industry which are contrary to my company's interests."

He didn't pause. "Absolutely, Aurora. May I call you that? We'd really like to have your full support – your endorsement and some appearances with me and of course we would appreciate financial support."

Aurora, unsure if he had understood her, said, "Well, I am a little concerned because your public position on GMO food oversight by the FDA is at odds with, you know, what's best for my business."

"I know all about what you are doing with your wonderful

food products. I support what you are doing and the government should not be a hindrance to your work. I would be honored to visit your operations during my campaign."

Unable to believe what she was hearing, she went on, "Sir, I don't want the FDA getting involved in our scientific work."

"Understood, understood. I'm with you. We're doing a swing through California later this week. Let's schedule a get together."

"I look forward to meeting you."

"In the meantime, can I have one of our donation people call you or your staff? "

"Yes. Have them call me directly."

Within an hour, a Rockwood staffer called. He told Aurora that the candidate would be grateful for any monetary support but hoped for a seven-figure contribution over the course of the campaign. If Aurora was concerned about the publicity by giving that much, she could make a modest donation under her own name, endorse him, do public appearances with him, and provide the bulk of the money through a 501(c)(4), which, he explained, is an IRS-non-profit social welfare organization where donors remain anonymous. Using these donations, candidates can advertise or promote issues such as why their opponent is on the wrong side of a particular issue. By setting up a trust, Aurora would be able to transfer all the money she wanted to one of the candidate's preferred 501 organizations – all perfectly legal. The staffer recommended several Washington election lawyers who could easily set this up for her.

And so, Aurora, heretofore an apolitical person, jumped into the Rockwell campaign. She donated two million dollars of her own money, and at the same time she got Frank and Harry to triple her salary, so she had enough income to cover it. Over the three-month period leading up to the November election, she received periodic calls from the campaign asking for cash transfers of various amounts. This was all done covertly and quickly, as if it might be illegal, but the lawyers assured her it was not. She also fulfilled her promise to campaign with Rockwell by publicly endorsing him and appearing with him on his swings through Northern California. As she traveled with him, she assimilated his Republican, pro-business ideology. In October, she asked her new friend Rockwell to appear at an event at her Palo Alto headquarters. Speaking to her employees, who were present at Aurora's "request," Rockwell spoke warmly of his close relationship with this brilliant young innovator who was single-handedly transforming the way Americans eat and advancing their health and longevity. Aurora's politically liberal employees suffered through Rockwell's presentation but were impressed, despite themselves, by his warm words about their boss.

When the November election came, Aurora's man narrowly won. Several days later, one of his campaign aides told Aurora to ignore the increasingly insistent requests from the FDA. In January, after the inauguration of the new President, the FDA calls stopped. At Rockwell's first press conference, he mentioned that he opposed efforts to label GMO products, which he said would chill scientific work to develop healthier food.

Aurora avoided Harry, except for the necessary business meetings. After a briefing by him on projected fiscal expenditures, he congratulated her successful support of Rockwood.

"I thought this would be the end of it," she said, "but it seems it won't go away."

"You mean the Congressman," Harry said, referring to an Illinois Democrat who was vocally pushing for legislation to monitor genetically engineered foods.

"I would like to start work on defeating him – maybe use a 501(c) to run ads against him."

"Aurora, you can't take on the political establishment yourself. We can't afford it and it's going to get us in trouble."

"We can't afford not to oppose our enemies. And we're not doing anything illegal."

"It's sleazy. And, look, I'm your friend, so I can say it: we bought a Presidential candidate with money in exchange for direct favors. That's wrong."

"You're naive, Harry. You wanted to get into business and now you're afraid to defend it against people who want to take it away from us."

"Say what you want, it's too much to get involved in minor Congressional races."

"Everyone does it."

"I don't care. We are doing well – successful beyond our wildest dreams – we don't need to cheat."

"Tell you what, Harry. You worry about our numbers and operations and I'll take care of those things you find distasteful, ok? We need to fight our political enemies and help our political friends."

"Just be careful."

"That is exactly what I'm doing."

CHAPTER 8

"This is Dana Devere, the editor of *Vogue* Magazine," the voice on the telephone said.

"I know who you are, Ms. Devere."

"Dana, please call me Dana. We are putting together this year's Met Gala and our theme is organic — natural clothes, food, and so on. We'd like to invite you to be one of our co-chairs. In past years, Caroline Kennedy, Beyoncé, and Jeff Bezos have served. It's a wonderful fundraising event for the Metropolitan Museum and we think you'd be a great chair."

Aurora knew about the Met Gala, probably the most glamorous and prestigious social event in America. The press covered the red-carpet parade on the steps of the museum like it was the Oscars. If her mother were alive, she would not believe that she had been asked to do this.

"You know my product is not organic, I assume," Aurora said. "It's the opposite; it's genetically engineered. I'm really not the right person to chair an organic fundraiser. But thank you for thinking of me."

"Oh, that's just a technicality. Your beef is basically like grass-fed, right? So it's natural. You used science to make something organic-like. We'll make that clear in our press releases. We really would like to have you. It's a good cause. Can we count on you?"

Aurora thought her mother would be angry if she said no.

"Yes, I'd be honored. What do I have to do?"

"First thing is to look beautiful, which for you is easy. If you'd like, my team at *Vogue* can advise you on your dress and hair and makeup."

"I'd like that."

"I'm having a little party the night before at my house. Please come. I want to spend some time getting to know you and introduce you to my friends. I think you will find them interesting – Tim Cook, Taylor Swift, people like that. It will be fun. I promise you."

It was a very summery evening for early May in New York as Aurora tentatively got out of the cab on Sullivan Street in East Greenwich Village and self-consciously walked toward a grey townhouse with a red door. She wondered why she was subjecting herself to this unnecessary stress. Perhaps it was because Jane said she would kill her if she backed out, or maybe because she was simply curious about all the icons who were supposed to be at this private party. In any event, here she was, all alone, like an eighth-grade loser going to a dance.

A servant opened the door, handed her a glass of wine and led her through the lavishly decorated house out the back door into a narrow deep garden, landscaped with mature oaks, lush summer flowers and beautiful people sipping wine. Aurora stood awkwardly on the edge of the gathering, preparing herself as if she were going to dive into an ice cold lake.

"Aurora, you are as lovely in person as in your pictures." She felt a firm grasp on her elbow, then turned to see Dana Devere at her side. Devere gave her a brief hug, stepped back and assessed Aurora from head to toe. "A beauty but an unorthodox one – glistening pale Scandinavian face set off by eyes that are like dark pools," she said, as if speaking to herself. "I'm sorry. That was inappropriate. I can't stop working, I'm afraid. I was just doing a professional appraisal of you."

"Well, thank you, I think." Aurora laughed nervously.

"You need to be in the magazine – *Vogue* – on the cover with a full feature about you. You can trust me to do it right; it will promote your business, too. Please consider it."

Before Aurora could respond, Devere guided her into the throng, introducing her to one person after another, some famous, some unknown to her. "This is our brilliant co-chair, Aurora Blanc – Aurora, this is Frank, Bill, Tim, Beyoncé, Kim, Mitt," and on and on, so quickly that Aurora could not get a word out before she was moved on to the next personage. A minute later, she was back on the periphery, alone, breathing hard, as if she had completed a marathon.

"Tonight is your introduction to this world, isn't it?" A black man with a British accent, murmured into her ear.

Aurora knew he looked familiar, bigger than life, movie star handsome, but couldn't place him. "Is this your world?" she asked.

"To be honest, it is. It's like an elite school where there is the coolest kid clique. This is the coolest kid group. I'm in it now, but I could be kicked out of it any time, without notice." He laughed.

"And do you like being part of it, does it make you feel good?" Aurora asked.

"I do. It feels good to be accepted. I was a poor kid in Manchester, England. I consider myself really lucky to have gotten classical training as an actor, to get paid to act and be part of all this. I worked hard on being an actor, but I don't know how this happened — they wanted me to be part of it for some reason. What about you, do you want to be part of this?"

"I hadn't thought about it. I'm busy with my company. I really don't have much time to socialize."

"Oh this isn't social, it's business."

"It doesn't look like business to me."

"These people can open any door for you. You want to have lunch with the President of Russia — someone here can do that for you. Or have a date with a particular pop star — no problem, done."

"I can have lunch with the President of the United States whenever I want or get someone else a meeting with him — I can do that already."

"Of course, you can. That's why you're here. You're one of them, one of us."

Aurora smiled and shook her head. "I guess I am now. I thought this was just about glamour, superficiality."

"This is about power, access, and influence. They didn't do you a favor by asking you to co-chair this. You're one of the people they want access to. And they think you're fashionable too, which you are. If you were just a scientist, no matter how brilliant, you wouldn't be here. But if you were just a scientist, you wouldn't have achieved what you have."

Aurora began to relax. She was actually having a good time.

"Do you know my name?" he asked.

"John Kerry?"

He laughed. "Malcolm Cullers, nice to meet you, Aurora. You are a gorgeous woman."

"Thank you. No actor has ever said that to me before."

"You are. And sexy, too."

"Well, I already know I'm sexy."

"So at least you learned one thing from me."

"Oh, I learned more than one thing from you tonight."

"They are calling us in for dinner. May I sit with you?"

"They gave me a table card when I walked in."

"Don't worry about that. Let's go in."

Over dinner, Malcolm politely but persistently asked her questions about how she developed her corn seed and turned it into a business. While Aurora was normally circumspect about what she revealed, a practice honed from dealing with media interviews, Malcolm was so warm – that was the word that best described him – that she told him much more than she had ever publicly divulged. Of course, she left out the parts about bringing her beef to market without testing for safety and stealing the seed formula from Professor Fraser.

Entertainment Weekly/ May 6:

"Among the Met Gala party highlights were the pop group The 1975's infectious music which had everyone on the dance floor, in some interesting pairings including the previously non- social Silicon Valley entrepreneur Aurora Blanc (Gala Co-Chair) with British film and stage star Malcolm Cullers (two time prior Gala Co-Chair). They were inseparable all evening and were later seen smooching at an after party."

People magazine/ May 26. Photo with caption:

"Aurora Blanc and Malcolm Cullers coming out of NYC theatre after taking in the musical *Hamilton*. The two have been seen out and about in town all week."

London *Evening Standard*/ June 12. Photo with caption:

"Malcolm Cullers, back in London for rehearsals for his latest role in a West End production of *Othello*, coming out of his Mayfair townhouse with house guest Aurora Blanc. The American billionaire CEO of Healthy Heart Beef has been visiting Mr. Cullers for several weeks."

Wall Street Journal/ July 17:

"Healthy Heart Beef opened a corporate office in London which it will use as a base to examine the feasibility of production and distribution of its meat products in the UK. CEO Aurora Blanc will split her time between London and Palo Alto."

The New York Times/ September 28:

"Aurora Blanc, CEO of Healthy Heart Beef, was married to British actor Malcolm Cullers on September 26 in a small, private ceremony in London. Mr. Cullers' parents were present, along with Jane Smith, a friend of the bride. The couple will reside in London and California."

"This is my favorite park," Malcolm said, as he and Aurora walked arm in arm through Postman's Park, an old landscaped romantic place in central London. "You can stroll or sit and read for hours here and no one will bother you."

"The problem is getting by the paparazzi outside our house."

"That's the price of being who we are."

"I didn't sign up for that part of it."

"Ok. Then let's move to a remote island in the South Pacific."

"You are the only one I could do that with." She kissed him. "Wouldn't you be worried about your career if we did that?"

"No. With actors like me, the attention can end in a minute regardless of what you do. One day, everyone is interested in every little thing about you and the next, they couldn't care less."

"You handle the attention so well, Malcolm – it's one of the many, many reasons I admire you." She kissed him again.

"We've got a mutual admiration society of our own, don't we, dear?"

"Don't let this go to your head but I've never been so happy in my life. Truthfully, I have never been happy before."

"I've just bewitched you with my charm and prowess."

"Yes. That, too." She laughed and then gently elbowed him. "Do you think we can just stay here and live like this?"

"Seriously?"

"Yes."

"I supposed I could be selective with projects and work only in England. I would probably have to pass on American TV or films but I'd be fine with it if you wanted me to. But won't you need to go back for your business?"

"I told you, I'm staying on top of it by working here virtually. I'm not missing a beat. The day-to-day operations part is being managed by my partner."

"I'd like to meet him Harry. Seems like the two of you are joined at the hip."

"We were once, but not so much anymore."

"From what you've told me, it doesn't seem like that attempt to buy your company was his fault. It seems he is the reason you have the company in the first place. One thing I've learned in my career is: know who your friends are and keep them. Once you get some fame, everyone wants to be your friend. The old friends are the ones who were there before all of that."

"When your play ends next month, you'll come with me to Palo Alto and meet him. I should go back and show my face anyway."

"You can show my face to all your friends too."

"Malcolm, I don't have any friends except you and Jane."

"And you told me no boyfriends either. I mean, Aurora, you were not a virgin."

"You know, casual stuff in college. It didn't mean any-thing."

"So why me? I asked you that before we got married, but you never really answered."

"I think, well, my friend Jane got engaged. It shocked me because I always thought she was so independent and self-re-liant. And at Dana's party, the night I met you, I felt so off balance when I walked in and you came up and..."

"And what?"

"You fucking swept me off my feet, ok."

"That's what I wanted to hear."

She leaned in against him.

CHAPTER 9

Aurora's marriage and relocation to London astonished Harry and Frank, both of whom were used to her unconventional behavior, but not to this. And while she maintained an ongoing online micromanagement of the company from London, her physical absence changed the balance of things at headquarters in Palo Alto. Frank, reluctant to bother her, no longer communicated with her. He grew closer to Harry, meeting with him for breakfast several times a week.

"I think she's losing interest in the whole enterprise," Frank said, dipping his spoon into a dish of oatmeal and blackberries.

"I don't agree. This company is her whole life."

"With her gone, you have to run around the country looking at feedlots and corn stalks. She's dumping everything on you."

"It's ok. She shouldn't have to do that anyway."

"Maybe, but it shows her lack of interest. We should sell this business while it's got a high value. If she continues to hang out with her jet-set friends, the business will go downhill." He shoved away his oatmeal.

"Frank, there is no indication at all that she needs to be physically present in order for the business to thrive."

"Steve Jobs at Apple, Bezos at Amazon, Zuckerberg at Facebook – they all showed up every day. Aurora hasn't shown up in months."

"Well, those guys invented virtual business and communications but maybe she's the first one to actually run a company virtually. She's online with us all the time and she's doing so-cial media and advertising from London. No one even knows she's not here."

"We know. Look, last time she blamed us for trying to sell the business when we had nothing to do with it. Let's actually do it now. Between the two of us and our Shanghai partner, we have enough control to sell it. A big food conglomerate should be running this anyway."

"No."

"You're not thinking like a businessman. We should cash out. This business will never be any more valuable than it is right now. You understand that, don't you?"

"Doesn't matter. I'm not going to sabotage her."

"You're thinking with your heart, not your head. Do we really trust her? Does she really give a shit about us? I don't think she's ever asked a personal question about me or my fam-ily. It's always about her. You've known her since college, Har-ry. What was she like then?"

"She was poor. She a hard time fitting in at Stanford. She wasn't part of that socioeconomic class."

"You're not really answering my question, Harry."

"I was drawn to her. I was her boyfriend for a while. But she was different. Maybe that was the attraction. She was kind of in her own world. I mean she was smart and focused on everything around her but she was mainly focused on herself."

"That must've been frustrating for you as her boyfriend."

"It was a one-way relationship. She never reciprocated. Looking back, I don't think she was ever interested in me. She never asked me anything about myself. She never really opened up about herself. She was desirable to me, I guess, because she was so unattainable. A virgin princess."

"A virgin princess?"

"I think she was a virgin until she married Malcolm."

"And what about when you went into business together? Did you become close friends?"

"We only talked about the business. I stopped asking about her personal life and didn't tell her about mine because she clearly wasn't interested."

"And now? Are you close with her now?"

"Frank, honestly it's not a normal friendship. It's still one-way – she talks about herself. I don't think she has any real interest in my life. But I feel close to her. We'd had this extraordinary journey together. And I trust her."

"But it's all about her, isn't it? You feel loyalty to her but I think she would sell us down the river if it was in her best interest to do it."

"I'm not going to sell out. I'm sorry, Frank – the answer is no."

Frank pulled the now cold oatmeal back in front of him.

Harry increased the frequency of his calls to Aurora in London, asking what he could do that she would do if she were in the States. She told him that she would visit some of the feedlots to monitor how the cattle managers were taking care of the cows. Harry said he'd like to do that; it would be a good opportunity to see the big operations. He flew out to Texas to inspect their biggest provider.

As he rode in a truck with the manager, his first thought

was of a concentration camp. A long expanse of rectangle wire held what seemed to be tens of thousands of cows crowded together, all facing the same direction, their heads sticking through the fence, as if hoping for liberation by the Allied armies. Harry asked his guide to confirm that this was how the cattle were confined during the months they were fed Healthy Heart corn prior to slaughter. "Don't they get sick, standing together like that in their feces?"

The manager, a youthful-looking middle-aged graduate of a university agriculture program, said, "Oh, we give them tons of antibiotics."

"Tons?"

"Yes, tons. We don't want them to get sick and die, and the drugs make them grow faster, too."

"Grow faster?"

"Yeah, we give 'em Ionophores as growth promotants and that particular antibiotic also prevents diseases."

"Do our people know about this? Does Ms. Blanc know this?"

"Everything we do is under her direction."

"Antibiotics just to make them grow? We should stop that."

"Well, that would cost you big time. The faster the cattle get ready for market, the better your profits. That's why your management uses them."

"We're promoting this beef as healthy, yet it's full of antibiotics. My God."

"It's not my place to argue with you, but you advertise that your beef is heart-healthy. Well, it is. We have stringent standards in place to make sure your corn seed is used in the right proportion in the feed mix, and the final beef product is as lean as naturally grass-fed cattle. So, sir, if you will come along with me, I'll show you the corn seed, how we mix it and test and monitor everything here. Yes, sir, this is a precise scientific operation."

Harry took a last look at the cattle. "Do they get any exercise?"

"There's room in those pens for them to walk around."

Harry raised his eyebrows. "I don't see much room."

"No point in letting them roam around a lot. We just want them to eat so they get big enough for slaughter quickly. Letting them run around doesn't help us get them ready any faster. It has the opposite effect."

"They look miserable."

"You're putting human feelings on them. That's a mistake if you are in this business. They're just big dumb beasts."

Professor Fraser's funeral brought Aurora back to Palo Alto. Malcolm, still doing *Othello*, did not come along. The mourners included many of Professor Fraser's colleagues and former students, some of whom were now working for Aurora's company. Aurora saw Harry on the other side of the church, and on the way out caught up with him, whispering that she would meet him at the gathering at Professor Fraser's house after the burial.

At the Professor's house, the mourners' talk was all about the Professor's selflessness, his dedication to his students, and his worship of pure science.

"It seems like what he stood for is the opposite of what

we're doing," Harry murmured to Aurora, as they drank coffee.

"Nice, Harry, I haven't seen you for months, and the first thing you do is try to make me feel like shit."

"Do you think he'd be proud of us?"

"Why shouldn't he be proud? How many people are we saving from heart disease and obesity related diseases?"

"I used to believe that one hundred percent. But now I'm not so sure. We're giving them meat filled with antibiotics and God knows what else."

"I shouldn't have let you visit those feedlots."

"Why didn't you tell me about all that poison in the meat?"

"It's not poison and there's no science that any of it harms people."

"So, you're telling me you have no concerns about what we're selling."

"I didn't say that, Harry. I told you a long time ago there was something I was worried about and you said don't worry about it. So, Harry, please get off your high horse. I'm happy to see you. I appreciate how you're holding down the fort here. And I forgive you for what happened, OK? Let's put things back to the way they used to be with us."

"I'd like to have things better than the way they used to be between us. Let's be real partners Aurora. That means I'll have your back and you'll have mine."

To his surprise, she hugged him.

"Wow, that's a new Aurora. This husband of yours must have softened you up."

"He's helped me see things a little differently. But you

better hope I've not gotten soft or else we're in trouble." She smiled. "Let's go talk to Mrs Fraser. I think we should donate some money to Stanford for a student scholarship in her husband's name."

Malcolm surprised Aurora by flying in from London for the weekend, having arranged for his stand-in to take over his role, despite the producers' complaints that attendance would severely drop off without him. That weekend, Aurora did something for him that she had never done, that he didn't know she could do – she made dinner. Not just any ordinary dinner. She steamed tiny broccoli florets, provided by a local organic farm; roasted Japanese sweet potatoes, imported from the island of Okinawa, which she bathed in scallions, miso paste, and unsalted low-fat butter; and opened a 2012 Italian Barolo from the small Luciano Sandrone vineyards. Finally, she unwrapped two Healthy Heart sirloin steaks, used her fingers to rub in pure olive oil, sprinkled them with hickory-flavored small-batch sea salt and cooked them in a George Foreman grill for 2 1/2 minutes.

She served the food at their rarely used dining room table, which she'd decorated with candles and Asiatic red lilies afloat in a crystal bowl of water. Malcolm, accustomed to the world's finest cuisine, happily tasted what he expected in the potatoes, broccoli, and wine. But the steak surprised him.

"It reminds me of what my mum served when I was a kid," he said. "Steak was always a special treat. This has the same taste and texture. My God, it takes me back to that time."

"But do you like it?"

"It's sort of odd... there's almost no fat. But it's tasty. It tastes like old-fashioned meat. I'd forgotten what that was like. And the flavoring you put on it, it's discernible. Yeah, I really like it."

"It reminds you of your mom's steak because in the UK, when you were a kid, all steak was grass-fed. Now everyone is accustomed to fatty marbleized meat. But this, Malcolm, is the way it's supposed to be. And it won't give you gas. No greasy fat messing up your digestion."

He continued eating, enjoying himself. "Honestly, it really does make me feel nostalgic to eat this meat."

"So, what do you think of an advertising campaign aimed at baby boomers with a tag line something like 'Healthy Heart has the steaks and burgers like your Mom gave you when you were young? She cared about you so much she gave you meat that was both delicious and healthy. Healthy Heart Beef will take you back' or something like?"

"You made this meal just to use me as a guinea pig for an ad campaign!"

"I thought maybe we'd license the Beatles song 'Get Back' for the TV commercial? That would work?"

He grimaced.

"You don't like the idea?"

"Tell me, Aurora, are you putting the food and wine for this dinner on your business expense account?"

She looked pained. "Oh, come on, Malcolm."

He pushed back his chair, and left the room.

★

Aurora telephoned Frank to tell him she was back in Palo Alto for a while.

"I'm happy for you about your marriage and even happier that you are back in the saddle here," he said.

"I've never been out of the saddle, Frank."

"I mean, here with us advancing the business."

"I have been working on something to advance the business — some new science that I developed in London — I rented a lab there and hired some students to assist me."

"I thought you were honeymooning."

"I was but I also did some work to 'advance the business' as you put it. I said I would keep you in the loop with what I was doing. Do you want to hear about it?"

"Yes, yes, of course."

"Well, do you know what photosynthesis is?"

"Yes," he said. "I've heard of it." He chuckled.

"Plants use sun energy to convert water and carbon dioxide into glucose to grow the plants."

"And oxygen for us to breathe."

"I don't care about the oxygen part. I only care about the efficiency of producing our corn. The corn is not efficient because its photosynthesis process uses only three carbon atoms. So do almost all plants, which is very inefficient compared to using four carbon atoms, which is fifty percent more efficient."

"And?"

"So, if our corn used four carbons atoms, the yield would be fifty percent higher. The same crop on the same acreage would produce one and half times more corn. That would mean we could charge the same price for our beef but our overhead would be drastically reduced. We would have the most profitable beef of anyone and could produce more of it, because we'd have much more corn to raise them on."

"You're proposing to reengineer photosynthesis?"

"Certain tropical crops, through mutations or evolution, if you want to call it that, do photosynthesis with four carbon atoms. Millet, sugar cane, maize — those crops are easily grown, because they photosynthesize efficiently. There are biologists in the Philippines who are trying to replicate this four-carbon photosynthesis in rice. I did it in my lab to our corn seed."

Frank shook his head.

"With genome editing. I added DNA from maize in situ to our corn seed. I used the CRISPR-Cas9 tool to move the DNA from the maize. Now the corn seed has enzymes from maize that drive the corn to produce glucose. So, our corn is replicating four-carbon photosynthesis with all its benefits, particularly a super-high crop yield."

"This is a lot to take in."

"There's nothing for you personally to do. We'll start adding the new seed to our fields now. We'll have to harvest twice this season because the corn will be ready much faster. In a year, we'll be fully converted to the new seed. You can buy some new toys with your profits, Frank — a fleet of yachts, maybe."

Aurora spent the next eighteen months in the States, supervising the breeding and integration of the newly modified corn seed into production. She visited her large farmers to oversee replacement of her original seeds with the new seeds, monitored the feedlots to assure that the cattle were consuming the new corn, and otherwise slipped right back into her obsessive work routine. Malcolm, to be closer to her, accepted a supporting role in a run-of-the-mill TV detective series in Los Angeles, commuting up to Palo Alto on the weekends. The series was a career comedown for him. But despite his sacrifice, the honeymoon was over.

PART III
RABBI SMITH

CHAPTER 1

Timmy Smith was afraid to tell his parents about his illness. What had started as only mild nausea turned, in a few days, into dizziness, restlessness, and the sweats. He avoided his mom and dad by "playing" in his room.

It had started with a forbidden hamburger that his friend John's mom, forgetting that Timmy was an Orthodox Jew, had served for lunch. If he told his parents he was sick, he would also have to tell them he had eaten the burger. John's mom, a vegetarian, usually served food that Timmy could barely stomach, so he was excited when she offered the boys burgers, which she claimed were "really good for you guys." That was enough to convince Timmy to ignore his parents' religious convictions and devour the delicious meat. Five days later, lying in bed covered in sweat, he was beginning to think his parents were right about God forbidding the consumption of non-kosher food. He booted up a game on his phone hoping it would distract him. But the screen images wobbled and blurred, as if underwater. He stumbled to the bathroom. Standing before the toilet, he tried to pee, but nothing came. The floor tiles began to shift, as if they were pieces in a video game, and then everything went dark.

His mother found him on the bathroom floor, breathing shallowly, unresponsive to her words. The emergency room doctors could not diagnose what was causing what appeared to be some kind of shock syndrome. They tried everything in their arsenal to revive him, but his blood pressure continued to decrease until, a few hours after he was admitted to the hospital, his heart stopped.

The family sat Shiva with friends and members of the synagogue. Timmy had been the Smiths' only child. The reactions of the two parents could not have been more different. Timmy's mom, Rebecca, was shell-shocked, almost mute as she sat with the visitors. The Rabbi, on the other hand, talked incessantly, asking how a healthy young boy could suddenly die without injury, illness or even a scratch. Some of their friends noted that he never mentioned God.

The parents of Timmy's friend John stopped over several times. They said that John could not accept that Timmy was gone.

"I can't believe it myself," John's mom told Rabbi Smith. "When he was playing at our house the other day, he was as normal as always, a perfect little boy. I never, ever, could have believed that he would pass away from an illness a few days later. Please know that we loved your boy, too."

The only media coverage of Timmy's death came from the *East Bay Express*, an alternative newspaper for the Oakland and Berkeley area, in an article entitled *Why Did Timmy Die?*:

"The sudden death of an 11-year-old boy has prompted his father, a prominent Oakland Rabbi, to publicly call for a police or public health agency investigation into the cause of death. 'There is absolutely no medical reason why my son suddenly went into shock and died without any previous symptoms or known cause,' Rabbi Smith said. 'We pay our taxes with the expectation that the government will step in and investigate when there is a suspicious death, but no one seems to care what happened to our son.'

"The East Bay Express has reviewed hospital medical records for the boy, provided by his father. Documents show that he died shortly after being admitted to the hospital and that the medical tests and autopsy showed no cause of death other than shock from an unknown cause. Shock is a life-threatening condition that occurs when the body is not getting sufficient blood flow; consequently, the organs cannot function and without immediate treatment, deterioration rapidly occurs. Approximately twenty percent of people who suffer shock will die. Hospital records for Rabbi Smith's son Timmy identify none of the usual causes, such as heart attack, significant bleeding, infection or severe allergic reaction. According to Rabbi Smith, the doctors treating Timmy could not provide an underlying cause of his death.

"Neither the Alameda County Public Health Department nor the Oakland Police Department returned our calls for comment."

Harry, a regular reader of the *East Bay Express* for its arts coverage, skimmed the Timmy Smith story. He, too, thought it was odd that an excellent hospital that treated the son of a prominent local religious figure could not find a cause of death.

These days, Harry had much more time to read the paper. When Aurora had returned from London, she'd taken back the day-to-day management of company operations. She'd quashed Frank's concerns that she was losing interest in the company. Her prediction that her newly modified corn seed would significantly improve profitability proved to be correct.

The increase in Healthy Heart's net profits gave it the best margins of any beef company in the U.S. Since the grocery stores shared in the profits, they clamored for more product. Aurora complied by expanding the feedlots as well as the number of cattle. In the year and a half since her return from London, the privately held company had come to rival the big beef conglomerates in size. Harry, Frank, and Aurora were billionaires, not just on paper.

The Smiths tried to get on with their lives after Timmy's death. Rebecca threw herself into synagogue-related events. She smothered her grief with activity. Her husband devoted himself to ascertaining why Timmy had died. Rebecca asked him not to discuss his investigations with her. They stirred up too much pain.

He read medical literature and talked to prominent physicians. The physicians told him that it was best if he just accepted what had happened. "You are a man of God," one doctor advised. "Perhaps you have to put it down as the will of God." Rabbi Smith was a devout Jew who believed in God, but he did not accept that counsel.

The Rabbi made a calendar and penciled in the approximate time Timmy collapsed in his bathroom — a late Wednesday afternoon in November. Timmy had come home right after school every day that week and gone directly to his room to do his homework and play. After dinner on the night of death, he'd gone back to his room. That was not his routine, but it was not unprecedented. At dinner during the preceding week, he was quiet and ate sparingly, but that was not unusual, either. Rabbi Smith scheduled appointments with each of Timmy's teachers. They all said essentially the same thing: he was a wonderful boy and there was nothing different about his behavior or activities during the days before his death. The school nurse reported that he did not visit her that week and she wasn't even sure she would recognize him because she could not recall him coming to her office and there were no records of him ever doing so.

Rebecca reminded her husband that Timmy had also attended a weekly gym class. Rabbi Smith scheduled a meeting with the teacher.

"I teach gym at four different schools and unfortunately I can't remember most of the kids' names," the instructor said. "That's not my strong suit, I'm afraid."

Rabbi Smith showed him a photo of Timmy.

"Oh, yes, yes, of course, I know him. A serious, obedient kid. He tried really hard, never screwed around like most of the kids. I wish they were all like him."

"Was there anything unusual on that Monday?"

"You know, I think – but I'm not sure."

"What do you think happened?"

"We did laps around the outside track that week. A lot of kids can't keep up because they're overweight. But Timmy was in good shape. I think I remember him stopping to catch his breath along with some of the heavy kids. I'm pretty sure because I thought it was strange since he was usually energetic."

"Why didn't you ask him what was wrong?" Rabbi Smith said, with an edge in his voice.

"I am so so sorry for your loss," said the instructor.

Rebecca Smith threw herself into every possible activity at the synagogue, including the Hadassah book club, for which she provided refreshments even when she hadn't read the book. And though her manners were always perfect, the synagogue ladies couldn't help but notice the strain and artificiality in her demeanor. Some whispered that her time would be better spent ministering to her husband, who seemed less interested in his rabbinical duties than in "interviewing" the physician members of the congregation. Many in the congregation thought the Rabbi and his wife were a mess, but at least Rebecca was channeling her grief into congregational work. A faction of the ladies decided to appoint one of their own, Sandy Stone, to talk to Rebeca to see if they could help. Sandy waited in the parking lot for Rebecca after the book group luncheon.

"Thanks so much for helping out today, Rebecca. You know we all appreciate and love you."

Rebecca opened her car door and got in. Sandy situated herself by the door so that Rebecca could not close it. She said, "Please don't think me forward. I'm talking to you out of love and concern. Can I ask whether you and the Rabbi have received any grief consulting?"

Rebecca, taken aback, dropped her defenses. "Why, no, we haven't. My husband is trained in grief counseling. He understands what we are going through. We don't need a stranger, another professional, to tell us what we already know."

"Rebecca, everyone respects your husband. The congregation will give him as much time as he needs to be himself again. But you should know that most people here think he is not acting like himself."

Rebecca glared at Sandy.

"It's like he's here, but not here," Sandy continued. "And everyone knows he's been conducting a detective-type investigation about Timmy. He's talked to all the teachers at Timmy's school and Lord knows who else. These teachers are not medical professionals – they don't know anything – and he's making them uncomfortable. It's as if he thinks there's been foul play. Some of us, many of us, actually, think he needs to get professional help; maybe both of you would benefit from it."

Rebecca tried to pull the door closed, but Sandy did not budge.

"I'm telling you this because we care so much about both of you."

"Thank you," Rebecca said. "I've got a meeting. May I go now?"

"Yes, of course."

Rebecca later recited the parking lot conversation to her husband.

"Ignore them," Rabbi Smith muttered.

After exhausting every possible professional source, Rabbi Smith drew up a list of all of Timmy's friends and acquaintances. Even in his obsessed state of mind, he knew he could not directly contact the children, so he went to the parents instead. As to the order of the calls, he decided he would not do it subjectively by the closest friends but instead go through the list alphabetically. Timmy had a fairly wide range of friends and acquaintances – about thirty. Each evening, Rabbi Smith telephoned two or three of the parents. The conversations were lengthy because parents couldn't stop offering condolences and telling stories about Timmy and making small talk.

Several weeks into the process, he telephoned John's parents. They lived only a block and a half away, and it was one of the few homes that Timmy had been permitted to visit on his own without permission, so the Rabbi was not surprised when John's mom told him that Timmy had been there on the Sunday before he died.

"I'm sure I already told you that we had just seen Timmy a few days before when we were at your wake." She paused. "I can't remember the Jewish word for it."

"Shiva."

"Yes, right. Anyway, he was at our house."

"How did he seem to you?"

"Like his usual self. Happy, hungry, sweet."

"Energetic?"

"As far as I could tell, yes. I'll ask John and let you know if he wasn't."

"Would you?"

"Of course."

"And he had a snack?"

"Lunch."

"He ate it all?"

"He gobbled it down."

"I'm happy he had a good time."

"He did, Rabbi. He did."

CHAPTER 2

Malcolm had finished his work in LA and was spending all his time in Aurora's Palo Alto apartment. He busied himself by looking for a bigger place for them. Aurora, who had been too pre-occupied with work to search for real estate, consented to Malcolm's house-hunting, as long as the place was in Menlo Park and not too big. When he suggested that they needed a house large enough for a family, Aurora gave him an inscrutable smile. In the end, she consented to a gated, five-bedroom, twenty-year-old house on a midsize lot in Menlo Park, priced at nine million – modest by Silicon Valley standards. Malcolm handled the move, disposing of all of Aurora's old furniture and purchasing the artwork and new furnishings himself.

When they moved into the house, it seemed, even with all its contemporary furniture and art, a vast, shadowy space. No matter how many lights they turned on and shades they raised, it always felt dark. They felt lost in it.

Rabbi Smith hired a criminal forensic scientist. Without telling Rebecca, who, he knew, would not consent, he authorized the man to do another autopsy, which would cost twelve thousand dollars. A week later, the forensic scientist said he found no evidence of foul play and could not otherwise provide an explanation for Timmy's death.

Over the next few months, the Rabbi came to see Timmy's passing as an act of God that had some purpose that God had decided was not for the Rabbi to know. He refocused on his Congregation.

Malcolm received an offer for a role in a high-profile Hollywood film that would require three months of location shooting in Florida and New York City. When his wife arrived home, at 10:30 PM, he intercepted her before she could go to the bedroom. They sat in their cavernous living room. Aurora sipped from a bottle of Evian water.

"We don't need the money," Aurora said.

"I wouldn't be doing it for the money. You don't do what you're doing for the money."

"Then do it, Malcolm."

"Will I see you?"

"Sure, if I can get away."

"You can get away if you want to. Do you want to?"

"Yes, of course."

"Then I'll see you on location in Florida?"

"Yes, Malcolm."

"Well, that's good. It's settled."

The first part of the film was shot in the Everglades. Malcolm texted and telephoned Aurora several times a day. He did not pressure her to visit, agreeing with her comment that it was a somewhat remote area, difficult to fly into. Of course, she could have easily chartered a plane but she didn't. When the filming moved to New York City, he expected her to come, but she neither appeared nor offered an excuse for not coming. He texted her: "Disappointed that u couldn't find time for me. Heading to LA for some additional filming next week. Hope u can spare a day for us."

In LA, Malcolm checked into the Peninsula Hotel in Beverly Hills, commuting thirty minutes each day to the Sony lot in Culver City. He did not try to reach out to her. Early one morning, walking through the hotel lobby to meet his driver, a man approached Malcolm and handed him an envelope. In the backseat of his car, he opened it; it was a summons in Family Law court suing for divorce. He put the papers back in the envelope and closed his eyes.

"Be honest," he whispered to himself. "You thought she was a normal person at first, but you were wrong – she's not. You're glad it's over."

During the divorce proceedings, Aurora's attorneys advised Malcolm that he was owed about five million dollars under their prenuptial agreement. His first impulse was to reject it. Upon further reflection, he decided to take the money.

Rabbi Smith participated in an ecumenical panel on Oakland child services. During the meet-and-greet after the discussion, he noticed Johnny's mom across the room. He caught her eye and walked over.

"You look like an athlete," he said. She was skinny.

"I'm training for a marathon."

He asked about her diet.

"I used to be strictly vegetarian, but I need protein when I'm training. So it's mainly greens and artificial grass-fed beef."

He laughed. "Artificial?"

"You know, that GMO corn-fed meat – it's just like grass-fed. I don't like to use the word GMO, but that's what it is."

"I don't know anything about that. We're kosher, so we couldn't eat it anyway."

"Meat is not kosher? I'm so ignorant. When Timmy was at

our house, I didn't focus on that."

"We knew you were vegetarians, so we didn't worry about Timmy at your house. Anyway, he knew what he could eat."

She paused, considering whether to tell him or not. After all, it was so innocuous, it could not matter now. She decided she had to be truthful with a man of God. "I think I gave him a hamburger made of that meat. I'm so sorry."

"He wouldn't eat meat."

"Rabbi, he did. I remember, he gobbled it down."

"When?"

"The last time he was at our house – the weekend before – you know, that Sunday."

The Healthy Heart beef Johnny and Timmy had eaten that Sunday came from Snyders Market, a small, upscale grocery. Rabbi Smith visited the store manager, who checked and confirmed that there had been no reports of illness caused by Healthy Heart at any time. Rabbi Smith googled "Healthy Heart Beef," but found no reports of ill effects. He contacted the Centers for Disease Control and Prevention and the Federal Drug Administration, but neither agency had any record of problems with Healthy Heart products.

Johnny's mother had said something to Rabbi Smith about Healthy Heart beef being genetically modified, but there was no such indication on the packaging. He checked the Wikipedia entry on GMOs, which said that genetically modified foods "have had changes introduced into their DNA using methods of genetic engineering as opposed to traditional crossbreeding" and that while it was not a "natural" process, "there is a scientific consensus that currently available food derived from

GM crops poses no greater risk to human health then conventional food." Wikipedia warned that all GMO foods should be tested before being put on the market.

Rabbi Smith was agitated again. Timmy's consumption of this bastardized, disgusting Godless food product validated his initial feeling that something untoward, even evil, had killed his son. It was one thing to eat, perhaps inadvertently, unclean, non-kosher food, but quite another to eat food that didn't exist in nature, for, if, as Wikipedia stated, GMO signified that the food's DNA had been manipulated by scientists, then the meat his son had consumed was not food at all. Cows created by God had been violated in some insidious way by goyim scientists working for an obscene corporation simply to enrich the owners. There was no doubt in Rabbi Smith's mind that a moral wrong had been committed. Timmy's death was not the will of God, as he had come to believe, but a malevolent human act: a crime.

The house was so big and empty without Malcolm around that Aurora regretted buying it. She hadn't initially regretted her marriage to Malcolm, but once they moved into the new house, he became too needy. She couldn't understand how an internationally famous movie star could be so emotionally dependent on her. Perhaps there was something wrong with him to want her so much. After all, she was not all that pretty, particularly when her makeup was off, and not all that interesting when she got off the subject of her business. And she could not handle his ongoing expectation that she come home every night and talk to him. She'd needed to rid herself of him.

She was not remorseful for doing so because she was certain he would end up with a far more suitable mate then her. She did feel guilty about the measly five-million-dollar prenup payout, because she had disrupted his career. If he had asked for more, she would have happily given it to him. She attributed his sacrifice to fuzzy emotional thinking. A business person, unlike an artist, would not have handled it that way. Anyway, he was gone now and she missed him in a way.

The *East Bay Express*, as a chronicler of local, below-the-radar news, did a follow-up story on the Timmy Smith death, prompted by his father's persistent calls to the reporter who wrote the initial story. It caught Harry's eye as he skimmed the online version while waiting one morning at Philz Coffee for his coffee and oatmeal muffin.

The East Bay Express, October 11:

"The unexplained death of twelve-year-old Timmy Smith in April of this year [link to the original article], the son of a prominent Oakland Rabbi, may have a biblical rather than a medical cause, according to the boy's father. Rabbi Smith, after extensive investigation into the cause of death, learned that his son, an Orthodox Jew forbidden by his religion to eat non-kosher food, consumed a hamburger several days before his death. According to the Rabbi, the meat was genetically engineered. Rabbi Smith says that GMO foods result from 'a brutal insertion of genetic material (DNA) from one organism to another with the intent of redesigning the food.' This, according to the Rabbi, is in contravention of God's divine plan. 'Scientists employed by huge corporations are usurping God's authority by breaching divine life forms, and creating Frankenstein foods including the hamburger that killed my son.' Rabbi Smith asserts that the unnatural food consumed by his son caused a toxic shock reaction which resulted in his death. While the FDA has consistently stated that GMO foods are as safe for human consumption as naturally produced foods, Rabbi Smith says he plans to advocate for public awareness of this generally unknown national health threat. The *East Bay Express* was able to confirm that the boy was served a genetically engineered fat free hamburger at a friend's home four days before his death. His friend, who also ate the meat, did not become ill. Medical records provided by Rabbi Smith confirmed that the cause of death was toxic shock resulting from unknown factors."

Harry reread the article as the coffee line inched forward. He forwarded the article to himself, then thought better of it and deleted it from his email and trash. He put his phone in his pocket, stepped out of the line, and drove to the office.

The receptionist told him Aurora had not yet arrived. Harry drove to her house and found her sitting at the kitchen counter, eating breakfast. In this huge room, she looked like a little girl getting ready to leave for school.

"You should lock the front door," Harry muttered. "You left the door open. People with your visibility have security."

She looked away from the TV, mounted on the wall above her, the volume turned up high. She was watching Fox News.

"Good morning to you too, Harry. You don't have security."

"No one knows who I am; everybody knows who you are."

"Did you stop over to bring sunshine into my life this morning?"

"I wish." He opened the Timmy Smith story on his phone and handed it to her. She looked at it for ten seconds, then handed it back to him.

"Read it carefully, Aurora."

"I read it carefully. I get it."

"Do we have anything to worry about?"

"We have lots to worry about, but not this."

"Please tell me if we do. I don't know all the science behind what you've done with that corn seed, but I know that you messed with it. I mean it's not even a corn seed anymore, is it?"

"It's a seed, Harry, and it's a little late to have second thoughts. Look, we've been selling the meat all over the country and no one's gotten sick. We're fine."

No one had ever successfully challenged the federal government's findings that GMO foods were safe. Even modest efforts to require labeling of the packages identifying genetically modified foods had failed. But there was a pending lawsuit brought by some professors and a group of evangelical religious leaders, who contended that they were being denied their First Amendment right of free exercise of religious beliefs because when food was unlabeled, they would not know if they were consuming godless genetically altered food. The logic behind the case seemed sound to the Rabbi – if your religion prohibits eating GMO foods, you've lost your constitutional right to avoid them if the government does not require a label. Rabbi Smith decided that this case might be a way toward vindicating his son's death. He wanted to be part of this lawsuit.

He called the plaintiffs' lawyer, Craig Tamasi, who had an office in New York City. After he introduced himself and began to explain his purpose, Tamasi said, "Before you go on, you should know that we need an initial ten-thousand-dollar retainer from each plaintiff to finance this case. There is no monetary payoff if we win, so we need support from the litigants. The other religious folks in the case got the money from their congregations."

"I would like to be part of this," Rabbi Smith replied. "But I need to talk to my wife about the fee. We would have to pay it personally."

"Frankly, I'm surprised that a Jewish minister would want to be part of this."

"Why?"

"Because you Jews are so rational."

"You don't think your case is rational?"

"Of course I do, but, as you will learn if you get involved, it's an uphill battle. The government has just filed a motion to dismiss the case, and the Judge has sent a strong message that he is likely to grant it, even though he hasn't seen our brief yet. We will probably get dismissed, but if we do, we'll appeal."

"Maybe I can add something new. My son died after eating GMO meat."

Tamasi said, "Tell me about it."

Two days later, Tamasi phoned Rabbi Smith.

"I was intending to call you today, Mr. Tamasi."

"It's Craig."

"Ok, Craig. My wife and I discussed this, and it's beyond our means. We can't do it."

"I'd like to have you in the case, Rabbi Smith. Actually I don't want you yourself, really, but I'd like to have your son as a co-plaintiff."

"Mr. Tamasi, you seem like a person who is proceeding in good faith here and if it was up to me alone, I'd sign up. But my wife is adamant. She wants us to get on with our lives. She's a woman with good judgment, better than mine. She should be the Rabbi."

"Let me be frank with you. We need your son — it's Timmy, right? — in the suit."

"Why on earth do you need us?"

"There is a part in the Federal Food, Drug and Cosmetic Act, section 402 that provides that a food is adulterated if it contains any 'deleterious substance which may render it injurious to health.' Deleterious — that's a very important word here, Rabbi."

"I'm sorry, I'm not following you."

"The meat your son consumed — we don't know much about it, but we do know, according to the company, that it comes from some weirdly altered corn seed that has DNA insertions from other things, you know, other organisms. Your son ate it and died. You understand what I'm saying — food is adulterated if it contains any deleterious substance that may make it injurious to health. I want to amend our lawsuit to claim that the inserted DNA to the corn seed that fed the cows is a 'deleterious substance' as defined by the law. We'll tell the court that we have a right to find out exactly what it is and how it affected Timmy."

"I can't afford to do it."

"Ten dollars."

"Pardon me."

"Ten dollars – that's the retainer for Timmy's participation in the case."

"What will the other parties who paid ten thousand dollars say?"

"They will thank you for saving their lawsuit."

The Rabbi took a moment to process this turn of events. "Ok then. We're in."

"Good, good. You know what deleterious means Rabbi? I want you to understand our case."

"It means bad."

"Close, but much better for our case than just 'bad'. The dictionary definition is 'harmful often in a subtle or unexpected way such as deleterious to health.' You understand what I'm saying – food can have a substance added that affects it in an undetectable fashion – like putting foreign DNA in it – and if it hurts people, that violates the U.S. adulterated food laws. That's our lawsuit, Rabbi: that there is a legal presumption that GMO foods are harmful. If we can make that case to a court, it will change everything."

Rabbi and Mrs. Smith – Bill and Rebecca – sat across from one another in his office. She had just finished a committee meeting, about a silent auction fundraiser, and had intended only to poke her head in to say hello, but was now glaring at him.

"This was supposed to be a joint decision. We discussed it and decided we were not going to do it and now you're telling me that you told this lawyer yes. You can pick up that phone and tell them no."

"It's costing us nothing to do this."

"We have no idea what it's going to cost us, and I'm not talking about money. I am not exposing myself, our lives, to public scrutiny for something we have no control over."

"I checked out this lawyer. He's ethical – a public interest lawyer. He's smart. He can do this for us."

"What do we want him to do for us Bill? Bring Timmy back? No. We cannot spend the rest of our lives buried in your quest to blame someone. That's not what Timmy would want and it's not what I want."

"Someone's to blame. They must be held accountable."

"Tragedies happen. We believe in God; we understand that sometimes it's God's will and we have to accept it."

"This meat company – I know they're responsible."

"I read about them, Bill. Their meat is saving lives for thousands, millions, I don't know how many. No one else has claimed that the meat has made them ill. People are eating it all over the country and no one is sick."

"I don't care – I know what I know."

"I can't live like this. I'm not going to stop you from doing this, but I'm not getting involved. I don't know if I can continue to be with you. You make your decision and I'll make mine."

With Rabbi Smith acting as Timmy's legal guardian, the lawsuit pending in the U.S. District Court for the Eastern District of New York was amended, adding the boy as a named plaintiff, asserting, pursuant to section 402 of the Federal FD&C Act, that Timmy consumed adulterated food manufactured by the Healthy Heart Beef Company injurious to his health, causing a toxic shock reaction that resulted in his death.

CHAPTER 3

When Aurora, Frank, and Harry met with the lawyers hired to advise them on the lawsuit, Aurora insisted that they sue the Smiths for libel. The lawyers opined that the best course was to do nothing at all; Healthy Heart was not named as a defendant, the government was aggressively defending the suit, and it would likely be dismissed. Moreover, they pointed out, since the media was paying no attention to this lawsuit, it was better not to provoke coverage by getting involved in the case. Frank agreed with the lawyers, saying that every business was subject to crazy lawsuits and the mere fact that this kid may have eaten one of their burgers did not prove anything. "For all we know, the boy was doing illegal drugs, like half the kids in the country."

Frank was making one of his periodic visits to Healthy Heart's new headquarters in Palo Alto, walking the halls, introducing himself to everyone in sight. The building had been purchased a year ago from a defunct chip company and remodeled into a state-of-the-art working space for the employees handling marketing, sales, research, and administration. While Aurora had initially resisted spending the money for the new facility, Harry and Frank convinced her that the costs were the de minimis, given the enormous profits now being generated by the company. When Frank walked to the lab area and looked through the windows, he saw rows of stainless steel workstations attended by researchers in light yellow lab jackets. He wondered if the color, which had been selected by Aurora, was meant to honor corn. He found himself admiring one of the lab people, a tall young woman, whose erect posture made her the dominant figure in the room. He continued to stare at her until she turned her head toward the door. She smiled and nodded, and then held up her index finger to signal that she'd be with him shortly.

"Let's have lunch," Frank said when she appeared in the hallway.

"OK."

Frank drove them to a downtown restaurant, a sunshine-flooded room buzzing with intense chatter. The owner greeted Frank by name, then escorted them to Frank's favorite corner table in the back.

Aurora realized this was the only time the two of them had shared a meal alone together. She assumed this was about the lawsuit.

"Frank, there really is nothing to worry about." She smiled reassuringly.

"I told you, I'm not worried about it," he said impatiently, looking around the room. "Just normal business bullshit. You can't run a business without getting involved in litigation."

She sat back, waiting for him to set the agenda.

"I really didn't come to the office to have lunch with you. I saw you in the lab from a distance and I thought to myself, who is that beautiful woman? Then I saw it was you and decided I would like to have lunch with that beautiful woman."

Aurora tried to maintain a neutral expression, wondering where this was going. It had been so long since their intimate

BAD SEED

encounter, she had stopped thinking about it. "Well, okay then, thank you. I don't hear that very often."

"That surprises me. Aurora, I didn't say anything to you at the time but I am sorry about your divorce. I really hoped you would be happy."

"It wasn't his fault; it was all mine. I was never meant to be married."

"Maybe he was the wrong guy."

"He was a good man. It was me."

"I truly hope you find some happiness in your personal life."

"I'm happy in my business life, and *that* is my life."

"Good."

Her cell rang but she ignored it.

He put his elbows on the table and leaned closer to her. "I did have something I wanted to share with you. It's confidential. Can you promise you won't say anything to anybody?"

She laughed. "We both know secrets about each other and I certainly haven't shared them with anyone."

"My indiscretion and your former part-time job."

"Our indiscretions will go to the grave with me." She sipped her water and grinned, now having a good time.

"Your little secret will go to the grave with me, too. I'm afraid that may happen sooner rather than later."

Aurora stopped smiling. "What are you talking about?"

"I was diagnosed with leukemia about six months ago. It's not treatable with any conventional chemotherapy and I've decided not to try any of the experimental stuff they've offered. It's too much of a long shot and will make me sick. I'm

191

feeling good, a little tired sometimes but mostly fine and I'm going to enjoy what time I have left."

He could see that she was shocked.

"It's okay, Aurora. I've made peace with it. I mean, I've lived the equivalent of two or three really good lives, so I have nothing to complain about."

She could not find words.

"No one knows about this other than my immediate family and that's the way I want it. I'm telling you because of the business. I want you to give this some thought. I think the very best thing would be to sell it to one of our big competitors. When I die, my share will go to the family and then I have no idea what will happen to it and I'm afraid you'll lose control of the company. Better to sell out now and get the money. You can use the money to do something else."

She murmured something.

"I can't hear you, Aurora."

"I said I would die if I lost this company. This is my whole life. This is all I have.'

"I don't know what else to do. Everything I've done, including what I'm suggesting now, has been solid business advice. I know you haven't always appreciated it, but I've always acted in your best interest."

"The best overall business advice – the best business moves – are not always the best for me."

"I think I understand that now. But just think about what I've recommended."

"I have thought about it. Let me buy you out."

"That's what you want?"

"It is."

"You'd have to raise a lot of capital."

"I can do it."

"What about Harry? If you bought me out, he would be a true minority owner; he would lose his power as a partner. You would be the sole owner of the company, in effect."

"Yes."

"He'd be unhappy about that. No one has been more loyal to you than he is. I think he would hate you for doing that behind his back."

"Are you going to say anything to him about any of this?"

"Do you want me to?"

"No."

"You realize what you're doing, Aurora. I'm leaving and you're pushing Harry out. You will be the last person standing in this company – all alone."

"Yes. That's what I want."

"Alright, Aurora."

"Is there anything I can do for you Frank?"

He laughed. "That's a tempting offer."

"Take care, Frank."

"You will need to take care yourself, Aurora – more than you know."

It played out as Frank had predicted. Aurora raised the money from large commercial lenders, who were delighted to underwrite a thriving business, particularly at the higher than market interest rate agreed to by Aurora. Under the terms of the deal, she acquired all of Frank's share of the company. With

Harry and their Shanghai partner now holding minority interests, all decision-making authority rested with her.

After Harry learned that she had bought out Frank, he retained counsel to assess his options. Several weeks later, his lawyers asked Aurora if she wished to buy him out. Within days, she obtained the financing and purchased Harry's portion of the company. After the sale closed, Harry sent a friend to headquarters to clean out his office.

When it was over, she spent a morning roaming the hallways of her building. As she passed employees, they nodded, smiled, and greeted her. It seemed, on the surface, as if nothing had changed, but she understood that everything had changed.

CHAPTER 4

Rabbi Smith, who had separated from his wife, attended a hearing in U.S. District Court in lower Manhattan, where the government would argue that his case should be dismissed without a trial or even pretrial discovery. The government claimed in its brief that the case was so baseless it should not be permitted to proceed through the normal litigation process.

The courtroom was a 1920s building, with prominent granite steps surrounded by four-storey-high Corinthian columns leading to the front entrance doors. The courtroom was in a quintessentially formal hall of justice – dark wood paneling, a high ceiling, and a broad marbled space separating the Judge from the lawyers. In contrast to the setting, Rabbi Smith was struck by the informality of courtroom protocol. The place was nearly empty, except for the two lawyers seated at separate tables and the four plaintiffs huddled together in the front row of the gallery. Rabbi Smith heard the government lawyer, a middle-aged, somewhat disheveled woman, tell Craig Tomasi she had flown from Washington on a 6 AM flight and was still trying to wake up. She seemed bored as they waited for the Judge to appear.

Fifteen minutes later, a short, stockily built man in a business suit emerged from a side door and walked up to the bench. The two lawyers rose.

"Please sit down," he said, waving at them. "Pardon me for not wearing my robe, but I'm late and I've got to leave shortly for a meeting in midtown. Let's get on with it. I have read your papers. Tell me what else you think I need to know." He nodded to the government lawyer, who jumped up to introduce herself. She outlined the procedural background of the case. The Judge interrupted, saying, "Do you have anything to add that's not in your papers?"

"Well, no, Your Honor, but I would like to summarize our position."

"No need. Please sit down. Mr. Tamasi, what about you. Anything you'd like to tell me that's not in your brief?"

"Yes, Your Honor. I think it's important to underscore..."

The Judge cut him off. "Isn't this about these religious men interfering with a regulatory agency trying to do its job? I mean, we all rely on the expertise of the FDA to keep us safe from untested, potentially dangerous drugs. Don't they have enough to deal with without your clients trying to impose their religious beliefs?"

"With all due respect, I don't think that properly characterizes our claim. Nor does it recognize our amended complaint focusing on adulterated food, this beef that may have killed a child."

"Mr. Tamasi, it's the 'may have killed' part of your claim that troubles me. What evidence do you have that this meat did kill a child?"

"The child consumed the meat and died several days later."

The Judge cut him off. "There's nothing in your complaint alleging that the meat made him sick. Do you have any affidavits or anything concrete that would show the court that the meat killed him? Isn't this simply speculation?"

"Your Honor, if we were permitted to conduct discovery,

we would flesh out the facts."

The Judge shook his head. "That's the problem, isn't it, Mr. Tamasi? You have no facts to flesh out. You can't proceed with an unsubstantiated religious theory, and then burden the FDA, whose resources are already strained, with months of document production and depositions."

"With all due respect, the adulterated food part of the case has nothing to do with religion."

"I thought it was brought by a Rabbi. You're saying it wasn't brought by a Rabbi?"

"The child who died was the Rabbi's son."

"Yes, that's exactly what I thought. I've heard enough. We get a lot of frivolous cases, but I am particularly disturbed when a government agency like the FDA gets pulled away from the important work it's doing to defend something like this. After reviewing the briefs and hearing your arguments, I can see no basis for your claim that that the agency has violated its statutory mandates. Accordingly, the case is dismissed. I will file a more detailed memorandum later. Thank you."

One thought that kept recurring over and over as the Rabbi sat on the front row bench listening to the Judge's words – "I've thrown my marriage away for what – for this."

After the hearing, Craig told the little group of plaintiffs that they would appeal as it was clear that the Judge had not even read their arguments and had jumped to a hasty conclusion that their suit was a baseless religious protest claim. When he left to return to his office, the four plaintiffs (one scientist and three men of God), dismayed by the morning's events, conferred outside. The scientist noted that the Judge was a supposedly highly respected jurist, and that perhaps their lawyer had not competently assessed the merits of their case and maybe the Judge was right: the whole thing had been an ill-conceived, wasteful undertaking.

The Rabbi returned to his life, or what was left of it. His small house that had been so happily occupied just a year ago was now dark and forbidding when he came home at night. During the day, he performed his congregational duties by rote, convinced that his flock would fire him, if they were not constrained by the tragedy of his circumstances. Despite his despair, his religiously trained mind kept working. He was wired to reason, analyze, and solve complex problems. Talmud study was a strict academic discipline, in many ways similar to a legal education. While Rabbi Smith tried to bury his obsession with his son's death, he could not stop himself from formulating a plan to avenge it. The solution, he reasoned, should not be a complicated one; if anything, the lawsuit had been too complicated and confusing for the Judge to fully grasp. Things needed to be simplified just as they were when he wrote his sermons. He looked up the federal statutes governing the FDA and the state laws designed to redress personal injury. He considered the Judge's hostile response to the lawsuit. He sat down and wrote an email to Tamasi and his fellow litigants.

"Let us look frankly at the situation. A highly respected U.S. District Court Judge dismissed our case, characterizing it as the ravings of religious zealots. We are now appealing to one of the most rigorous appellate courts in the country. In my view, the only chance we have is to remove all of the religion-based First Amendment arguments from our complaint. I realize that many of you are in this case only to prosecute the free-exercise-of-religion claims, but the inescapable truth is that if we pursue those claims, we will simply validate in the Court of Appeals what the district Judge believed. The only issue on appeal should be the FDA's long-standing reluctance to require testing or even oversee the creation and sale to the public of genetically engineered foods. Our legal argument should be that federal law could not be clearer about the FDA's responsibility to outlaw adulterated foods — that is the heart of the law. Yet how can that Agency possibly follow its legal mandate if it refuses to even perform tests to determine if genetically engineered foods are adulterated? While this issue has existed for years, our case provides a stark example of the government's failure to act. Here we have a meat company that says, according to its own marketing statements that its meat is created through genetic engineering of the cattle's corn feed. Here we have hundreds of thousands, perhaps millions, of people who eat this meat every day with no knowledge of what is in it or how it was made. Here we have a child who consumed the meat and died a few days later. As to the child, my son, we should not argue to the court that his death proves anything; rather it simply illustrates the possible harm that can result from the government's failure to act. We should acknowledge that we don't know whether the child died from the meat, but we should be able to learn the truth and that's the government's job under the federal statute — to determine whether this meat is adulterated.

"We also need to take the kind of action that will make the

Court of Appeals pay attention to us. We have prominent scientists as plaintiffs in our lawsuit and there are many other scientists who agree that the FDA should be closely monitoring genetically engineered foods. Let us mobilize these resources. We can get public attention in several ways including picketing the FDA headquarters in Washington and reaching out to the press to get coverage of this appeal. If we make some noise, we can get heard. Court of appeals Judges read the newspapers like everyone else. They are subject to influence like everyone else."

The Rabbis' email achieved the desired result. Tamasi began drafting an appeal adopting Rabbi Smith's recommendation. The plaintiff scientist called his colleagues to ask for help in mobilizing public attention on the issue. They all began reaching out to contacts in the press. Tamasi gave the draft of his brief to Rabbi Smith to review and the Rabbi revised it to make it less legalistic, more compelling. When the appeal was filed several months later, twenty-five prominent scientists picketed the FDA building, demanding testing of GMO foods. The media began to pay attention.

Aurora didn't need Harry to find the media coverage of the appeal and the picketing – it was in *The New York Times* and *The Washington Post*. Without Harry or Frank to talk to, the only person she trusted was Jane, but their conversation on the subject was more a support session than practical advice. Jane pointed out the positive aspect of the articles: Healthy Heart Beef wasn't even mentioned. They both agreed that the oblique reference to adulterated beef in the articles was unlikely to cause the company any harm. As it turned out, sales continued to grow at the same pace as before and there was no follow-up by the media regarding Healthy Heart.

Craig Tamasi and his plaintiffs were encouraged that their case received major news coverage and they hoped that those articles might have an influence on the U.S. Court of Appeals. Tamasi subsequently received notice, from the court, that oral arguments on the appeal had been scheduled three months hence in the Foley Square Federal courthouse, the same place where he and his clients had been humiliated by the district court Judge.

CHAPTER 5

Now that she had sole control of the company, Aurora micromanaged everything. Although her legal people assured her that she had nothing to worry about with the lawsuit in New York, she could not sit by and leave matters to chance. She telephoned the aide to President Rockwell, whom she had worked with on the campaign and asked if she could set up a call with the President. She was told the President was in Asia for an economic summit but he would do his best. Four hours later, the White House called, announcing that the President was on the line. Aurora gave him a short summary of the lawsuit. He said he would look into it. The following day the President's aide called and said the President was working on it.

Rabbi Smith was back at the lower Manhattan courthouse for the oral argument before the appeals court. It was a snowy winter day and the Rabbi, who had traveled to New York with an old raincoat and no galoshes, was cold, his feet wet. He sat next to the handful of other plaintiffs, all scientists. The religion-minded plaintiffs were absent, having lost faith in the case. The Rabbi felt optimistic. Unlike the lower court hearing, these proceedings were formal, with three robed Judges sitting high on the bench in a lordly manner, overlooking a hushed court room.

The government table had three lawyers from the Department of Justice. The government lawyer who had argued before the lower court was not there; in her place, as the lead lawyer, was the Principal Deputy Associate Attorney General. The scientist sitting next to Rabbi Smith, who apparently understood who was who on the government side, whispered in the Rabbis' ear that he was one of the highest law officials in the U.S. and that it was highly unusual to see someone of that stature arguing a case. "I wonder why he's arguing this case," said the scientist.

"I guess we got their attention," the Rabbi whispered.

Tamasi went first. He emphasized the statutorily required need for the government to exercise diligent oversight, including testing, where the DNA of foods had been manipulated or altered. He explained how insertion of DNA from the gene from one organism to another was a profound change in a species and how such alteration raised a reasonable presumption that the food from that organism had been adulterated as defined by the statute. Tamasi's presentation did not include religious arguments or references to dead children. It was measured, calm and eminently reasonable. The Judges listened respectfully and did not interrupt. Rabbi Smith was encouraged. But the plaintiff scientist leaned over to the Rabbi, murmuring, "Their silence is not necessarily a good thing."

When Tamasi sat down, the Principal Deputy Associate Attorney General stood and cleared his throat. He spoke in a monotone.

"Scientific advances to reduce world hunger, cure cancer and other genetically based diseases – these are the miraculous gifts that genetic engineering will be providing through our extraordinary American scientists and researchers – if, and only if, they are permitted to do their work without excessive and burdensome government restraints."

All three of the Judges leaned forward to better hear the Deputy Associate Attorney General. One Judge asked him to speak up.

"You'll have to excuse me. I haven't argued a case in court in twenty years and I'm a bit nervous."

One of the Judges smiled.

"I just can't understand why this high-level person would be doing this," the scientist muttered.

The government lawyer continued, "In the late 1970s, many believed that the greatest upside of genetic engineering would result from applying it to agriculture. The hope was it would lead to better nutrition, higher crop yields, and less need for fertilizers and pesticides. For that to happen, big government had to get out of the way. And it did – it stepped back and let scientists do their work. As a result, today American agriculture is the most efficient and cost-effective in the world, and the safest. Despite the concerns raised by the anti-GMO lobby, there is no evidence the GMO foods, which are consumed by millions of people every day, are unsafe. Moreover, the mainstream scientific community concurs that consumption of genetically engineered food does not cause health issues – no increase in cancer, autism, allergies or stomach problems. There is no indication whatsoever of harmful toxins in the GMO food nor adverse effect on health, whether the modified food resulted from conventional breeding or genetic engineering. In an era where the Federal government has been blamed for just about everything, no one has ever shown any evidence of negligence by the FDA or any other federal agency overseeing our food supply."

He paused and then resumed in an even lower voice. "The advances that we've seen over the last thirty-five years are insignificant compared to what we will see in the next thirty-five years, assuming we don't interfere with progress. As I understand it, the essence of the plaintiffs' position is that foods containing DNA altered by adding genes from a different organism are inherently adulterated under federal law. But there is no science to back up these claims; the plaintiffs are like global warming deniers. I won't recite in detail the studies contained in our brief, such as the one from the *Journal of Animal Science* covering thirty years of research data on livestock that consumed both non-GE and GE feed, and which found no difference in the animals' health or human health."

He looked down at his notes as if to locate something he had forgotten. "The FDA – the defendant here today – is not taking the position that it believes that genetically engineered food should be held to a lower standard of scrutiny. The Agency has stated in the past and repeats to the court today: 'Foods that come from genetically engineered plants must meet the same strict Government requirements in all respects, especially safety, as do foods that come from traditionally bred plants. The FDA is not aware of any information showing that foods such as beef raised in whole or part by genetically engineered feed present any greater safety concerns than any other foods.' This Agency has successfully protected the American food supply for decades. It recognizes that it is not its role to impede progress. Our food supply will continue to become more plentiful, be less expensive and healthier if we do not let big government block scientific progress. That's what the plaintiffs in this case wish to do and we respectfully ask the court not to let that happen."

He paused again and glanced down at his watch. "I have a few minutes left in my allotted time. Do you have any questions?"

The Judge in the middle said, "Thank you very much." With that, all three Judges stood and exited.

As their small group left the court room, Rabbi Smith whispered to Tamasi, "What do you think?"

"No questions from any of the Judges – that's unusual. I have no idea."

The Rabbi went back to Oakland. He tried to give his attention to his synagogue duties but he did so as if on autopilot.

Two months after the oral arguments, Tamasi called, "I just got the decision and the news is bad. I wanted to call you first. I'm sorry, Rabbi."

Rabbi Smith felt numb, as if he had just chugged a glass of scotch. "What did they say?"

"I'll email it to you, but essentially the Judges said the law about adulterated food predated genetic engineering and the legislators could not have contemplated insertion of DNA in different seeds as being 'adulterated'; in other words, GMOs are not covered by the statute because the statute existed before GMOs. That does not make sense to me but there is legal logic behind it. They also said that the courts must defer to the FDA's evaluation of scientific data in determining safety, and that there does not have to be unanimity within the FDA for it to make a valid decision. The court reviewed the scientific information and said there was plenty of science to support the FDA's decision not to interfere with this type of genetically engineered food."

"Can we appeal to the Supreme Court?"

"We are done, Rabbi. This is a bulletproof decision. We have nowhere to go with this. Go back to your life."

"What life, Craig? This is my life."

Rabbi Smith consulted with six personal injury lawyers in the Oakland area about filing a wrongful death civil action. Everyone said the same thing: "No proximate cause." When Rabbi Smith pressed them to explain what that meant and why it was a problem, they struggled to explain it. Rabbi Smith wrote down what one of the lawyers said: "Proximate cause is an act from which an injury results as a natural, direct, uninterrupted consequence and without which the injury would not have occurred." The Rabbi thought this sounded like legal gobble-dygook but he understood the essence of it and the problem it created in his case – there was no provable direct link between Timmy eating the meat and his death. Another lawyer put it this way, "Look, you can't sue an air conditioner manufacturer just because Timmy inhaled air from it the day before he died. You got to show his death would not have happened unless he ate the meat."

The Rabbi told the lawyers that if they filed a lawsuit, he was sure that the information they would get in discovery from the meat company would show that the beef was poisonous. But all the lawyers told him that Judges will not permit someone to file a lawsuit based on speculation and that was all he had here. One of the lawyers told him, "Rabbi, the law is not like religion, where you can proceed on faith alone; you must have facts."

The Rabbi disagreed – faith alone was enough. His faith in God was tied to his belief that Timmy did not die in some random, meaningless way. There was a reason for his death, an evil reason – and it was Rabbi Smith's mission in life to eradicate the cause of that evil. He considered himself a thoughtful, gentle and decent person. If he was so obsessively determined about righting this wrong, it wasn't because he was being irrational, as the lawyers implied. He accepted the lawyers' assessment of the law, but he did not accept their refusal to take his case.

He spent more time at home and did less and less for his congregation. Once a good sleeper, he was now afflicted with insomnia. During the excruciatingly monotonous hours lying in the dark trying to sleep, the events starting with Timmy's death replayed in his head like a mental tic. His physician prescribed a sleeping medication which brought unconsciousness for two or three hours followed by a confused wakefulness where he would momentarily forget what he had lost; then he would regain a clear mind and the accompanying anguish. He contemplated his options – suicide, acceptance of the unacceptable status quo, or a yet-to-be determined something else. He wanted to end his pain and loneliness, and he felt that no one would care if he was gone. But he lacked the courage to end his life.

The remaining option – the "something else" – was the best of the bad lot of choices. He had to come up with something else.

He researched Healthy Heart Beef Company. The news articles contained no information about the science Aurora Blanc supposedly used to develop the corn seed fed to the cattle to produce the low-fat meat. Nor was there much information about how the company was operated or who was in charge. Rabbi Smith did not feel hatred for the owner, because he did not believe that she had invented anything or actually ran the company. Her face was all public relations to sell the product. Rabbi Smith understood what the corporation was doing – if consumers knew Healthy Heart was just another giant profit-hungry company, they would distrust it and not buy the meat. It was all a marketing ploy – a beautiful, genius woman scientist invents a product to bring revolutionary health benefits to the masses while finding the time to marry a movie star and appear in *People* magazine – a dream advertising campaign devised by Madison Avenue. Rabbi Smith understood what was going on; he just needed to figure out how to stop it. But he had run out of effective strategies to do it. Perhaps a Hail Mary was the only thing left. After all, he was a man of God and he appreciated the power of that Catholic metaphor.

The media and the legal arena had both failed the Rabbi. At this point, more news coverage of Timmy's death would do no good. But the legal avenue, even though unsuccessful so far, felt right to him. It was a Hail Mary, perhaps, but a personally satisfying forward pass nonetheless. And so, he decided he'd bring the damn lawsuit himself. He was smarter than those narrow-minded attorneys anyway.

He researched the format for a wrongful death personal injury complaint and found a standard form that required him to fill in the blanks. In one section, he was asked to explain the specifics of the cause of action. Since he was representing himself as Timmy's trustee, he said that he was bringing the complaint "pro se". The form was short and easy, and he did not need a Harvard law degree to do it. As part of the requested relief, he asked for a permanent injunction to cease production and distribution of all Healthy Heart beef products and a hundred million dollars in damages. He drove to the Alameda County court house, paid the fee, and filed the complaint with the clerk of the Superior Court.

"What's a pro se complaint?" Aurora asked the three lawyers she hired to deal with the Timmy Smith lawsuit.

"It's Latin for 'on one's own behalf'. What it really means is that this guy couldn't get a lawyer to represent him, so he brought the case himself," William Newly, the senior lawyer of the trio, responded. "This fellow was one of the religious people involved in the New York case against the FDA. He's like one of those jailhouse lawyers who keeps filing case after case."

"You're not concerned?"

"I always worry," said Newly. "That's what you pay us for – so you don't have to worry. We are going to file a motion to dismiss arguing that this case is so frivolous on its face that it should be thrown out of court immediately."

"We want to stop them from conducting any discovery," the youngest lawyer interjected.

Newly glared at him.

Aurora smiled at the young lawyer. "Thank you for being

forthright. I understand perfectly well. If he can do discovery, he can see our proprietary scientific work for our corn seed and everything else."

The young lawyer, encouraged by her praise, asked, "Should we be concerned about that?"

Her smile faded. "You should worry about winning this motion to dismiss and getting rid of this lawsuit."

The young lawyer, unfazed by the change in Auroras' demeanor, continued, "What do you worry about?"

"I worry about people who don't give up, like this Rabbi Smith guy."

Aurora's lawyers filed a motion to dismiss, arguing that the complaint on its face showed no connection (proximate cause) between the child's death and Healthy Heart Beef.

Rabbi Smith, with his usual Talmudic intensity, went to the Berkeley Law School library to research and prepare a response brief. His research showed that the Healthy Heart lawyers were correct, inasmuch as his brief did not show legal proximate cause. He was in a Catch-22 situation. He needed discovery to get facts to show there was something inherently dangerous in Healthy Heart beef that caused Timmy's death, but he was not permitted to do discovery because he didn't have the necessary facts to plead proximate cause.

While Rabbi Smith was a man schooled in logic and rationality, he also knew how to preach faith and hope, so he prepared an eloquent, heartfelt and persuasive legal brief asking the court for the opportunity to conduct discovery to support his claim. It accurately described the proximate cause standards and also argued that it would be impossible for anyone to satisfy them in a case like this, where the composition of the allegedly lethal product was a corporate secret. It asserted that it was contrary to public interest to allow a big corporation to shield its so-called proprietary information when a child's life may have been lost as a result of that product. His legal brief was a Hail Mary but an exceedingly skillful one.

CHAPTER 6

Aurora received a group email from Frank Conrad's wife, telling friends and family that he had died after his battle with cancer. Aurora told herself it should not be a shock because she knew he was dying, but knowing that and learning that it had actually happened were different things.

Since the end of her marriage and her business and personal relationships with Frank and Harry, the only passion Aurora had felt was for her company, and her only relationships were with employees, customers, consultants, and lawyers. While she was amiable enough with her business associates, she cared only how these people could help her. The person with whom she had deepest and longest lasting friendship of her life, Jane, was now focusing her attention on her husband. Aurora recognized she was partly at fault for their drifting away from each other, because she rarely called Jane. But she also wondered whether Jane resented, in some way, her success, or if Jane believed that Aurora should have rewarded her financially for helping her over the years. And there was the nagging resentment that Jane had taken advantage of her by turning her into a prostitute and profiting from it while Aurora put herself at risk. Her best friend had been her pimp.

Despite the ambivalence of her feelings toward Frank, she felt compelled to do something meaningful in the wake of his death. She called Frank's wife, whom she barely knew, to express condolences and to offer to speak at the funeral services. The hesitancy on the other end of the line, Aurora concluded, probably related to Frank saying more negative things than good things about her. But Mrs. Conrad said, "Yes, of course, Frank would be so pleased to know that you would do that."

Waiting outside before the service, attended by hundreds of people, Aurora saw Harry. She smiled and waved. While there was no doubt he saw her, he turned his back and talked to another guest.

During the service, when she went up to the podium to speak, she could see anticipation in the faces of the mourners. She had done so many corporate and PR presentations that she was entirely comfortable in front of an audience but her problem today was she had nothing of substance to say. She spoke for two minutes about what a wonderful person Frank was, how he had faith in her as a young scientist and aspiring business person when no one else did. He would be missed, she said, by everyone who knew him.

When she sat down, she was disappointed in herself, not only for her pathetic little talk but for her tepid emotional reaction to his death. To survive in business, she had developed a ruthless demeanor – without it, she would have been destroyed long ago. Maybe she had gone too far and internalized that toughness, and that was why she felt so unaffected by Frank's death.

In her office, seated across from the newly hired new senior vice president of human resources, whom she had poached from one of her competitors, Aurora got right to the point. "I want you to fire fifteen percent of the workforce – across the board: blue-collars to executives."

The VP, a veteran of corporate politics and a shrewd executive, said nothing, waiting for her to continue.

"I know I told you I had a great workforce when I hired you," Aurora said.

"I believe you also told me that the company was appropriately staffed and that my job would be to bring in talent as the company continued to grow," he said. "I don't think you said anything about cutting back staff, unless I missed it."

"That's right."

He waited for her to clarify.

"I want the company to have the best talent in corporate America. I want to get rid of the lowest performing people even if they're good employees."

"Even if they're loyal, productive employees?"

"Everybody here is loyal and productive. I want the best of the best."

"May I be frank, Ms. Blanc?"

"I hired you to be honest."

"First off, we will not to be able to get the best people in corporate America to work for a meat company. Second, I don't see the benefit of going through a wrenching, disruptive layoff when you already have a solid workforce. Third, you are respected and well-liked by the employees. If you institute a massive, bloody firing, they will blame you."

"I don't care. Everybody here is complacent. It's too easy for them. Our enemies – competitors, the government, others – want to destroy us. In our organization, we need to dump the mediocre and hire strong people. Pay them what we have to and convince them this is not a meat company – it's a Silicon Valley company. I need strong people to help me. I can't do this all myself. Right now it's all on me."

He nodded.

"And I want it done fast."

He nodded again.

"Another thing. I want a board of directors."

"Ms. Blanc, you own the whole company. You don't need a board."

She glared at him. "I want one. They should be high-profile, influential people who can help me deal with the government and the courts, and also help me get good media coverage. Do some research and put together a list of candidates. I don't care what we have to pay them. If we throw enough money out there, we can get former senators, cabinet members, big-name finance guys. I want a board made up of people who are so impressive that it tells everyone that we are an extraordinary company."

"I'll start on it."

"Next Wednesday," she said.

"Pardon me?"

"I'd like the list of potential board members by next Wednesday. Once we have a list of whom we want, I'll call them myself. I can convince them to join. And I'll make sure they are loyal to me." Expressionless, she extended her hand. "Glad to have you with us."

CHAPTER 7

Rabbi Smith read the two-line ruling from the Judge over and over again, looking for alternative meanings.

"Defendant Healthy Heart's Motion to Dismiss is denied. Discovery is permitted only with respect to the scientific process relating to the composition of Defendants' proprietary corn seed. An appropriate confidentiality provision will apply to all discovery."

The Rabbi wished he had a lawyer with him to interpret it, but it appeared to be a victory – his lawsuit would continue and he could get documents and information from Healthy Heart about the development and genetic composition of the corn seed. He remembered the legally savvy fellow plaintiff scientist, Bill Bradford, from the New York FDA case, and how he correctly understood what was going on during the Court of Appeals arguments. Rabbi Smith telephoned him.

"I'm a lawyer too," Bradford told Rabbi Smith. "I practiced for a couple of years with a Wall Street law firm in the litigation department. Hated it; ended up going back to school and getting a PhD in bioengineering. Anyway, it looks like this Judge scrawled out a two-line decision. It's clear that he's giving you full authority to find out everything about how they developed the corn seed and what's in it. In other words, you got what you asked for. Hope it doesn't turn out for you like the Chinese proverb, you know, 'Be careful what you wish for.' Can I assist you with this?"

The Rabbi was taken aback that someone actually wanted

to help him. "Yes, yes of course."

"I wouldn't volunteer unless I thought I could add some value to what you're doing. My two years in legal practice were all spent on discovery – drafting document requests and interrogatories, reviewing responses and documents, and attending depositions that involved taking opposition witnesses' testimony under oath. You'll get to do that in your case, Rabbi. That's a big deal. This Judge has allowed you to get into their underwear. He probably figures that as a non-lawyer, you'll get nowhere with it. The other side probably isn't worried either. I've never actually taken a deposition myself; I was too low on the totem pole to be allowed to do it. But I've read and attended lots of them. And, of course, I've got something else that will be useful to you."

"What is that, Bill?"

"I'm a bioengineer. I've done work in genetic engineering. I actually know something about this."

"Thank you. I'm grateful."

"This is what you want, right – to pursue this?"

"Yes, absolutely, this is all I want."

"We'll need some money. I will ask the other co-plaintiffs who funded the FDA case if they can contribute."

"Only if they agree not to interfere with what we're doing here."

"Yes. We will tell them what our goals are and give them periodic status reports."

"And what do you see as our goals, Bill?"

"Why, to destroy that company, of course."

Bradford raised thirty thousand dollars from his former

co-plaintiffs. They hired an inexpensive Oakland lawyer, Jeb Ebinger, to handle court filings and provide advice on local law practice. They also lined up, at Bradford's suggestion, an outside consultant who would use software programs to analyze the tens of thousands of pages of documents they expected to receive in discovery from Healthy Heart.

Bradford, with the help of Ebinger, prepared document requests and interrogatories aimed at obtaining all of the proprietary scientific formulas and processes used to develop and propagate the corn seed. The discovery requests were served on the Company with a thirty-day response time. The Healthy Heart lawyers asked for a thirty-day extension, which Ebinger said was reasonable under the circumstances.

Rabbi Smith waited. He had a purpose now. He approached his congregation work with renewed interest, and his flock noticed for the first time in a long while that he showed genuine compassion toward them.

When the sixty-day response period expired, Ebinger received a call from one of Healthy Heart's lawyers, a partner with a large San Francisco firm. He told Ebinger that they were still working on the discovery responses and needed yet another thirty days. When Ebinger refused to consent, the Healthy Heart lawyer said they were taking the time anyway.

When the discovery responses finally arrived, Rabbi Smith opened the envelope and eagerly read the papers. He did not need a lawyer to interpret them. The responses were unequivocal – there were no documents describing or reflecting the development of the corn seed nor were there any documents that showed the composition of the seed. After all the meticulous drafting of their document requests and the long wait, they had received nothing.

Ebinger filed a motion to compel production of the documents, and the Judge, for the first time in the case, scheduled a hearing. Rabbi Smith appeared with Ebinger in a courtroom in Oakland, within a nineteen-thirties Art Deco building that he had driven by many times but never been inside. The light gray, cube-like building, elegant and majestic, had been a WPA project. The courtroom had been modernized with marble and wood walls. Judge Justin Hodges was in his early forties, and Ebinger knew he had been saddled with too many cases. Ebinger told Rabbi Smith that the Judge was competent and fair, as well as interested in keeping his docket under control.

The court was crowded, dozens of lawyers and clients waiting for the Judge. When he appeared, exactly on time, the court call began. The Judge quickly disposed of them.

"This is known as a cattle call," Ebinger told the Rabbi. After a forty-five minutes wait, their case was called. Two lawyers, tall, athletic-looking, Waspy, went to the podium, along with Rabbi Smith and Ebinger, and introduced themselves as counsel for Healthy Heart.

Ebinger argued to the Judge how the absence of any documents from Healthy Heart was not credible. The corn seed, a complex, genetically engineered creation, simply had to have underlying documentation of its development and composition.

The Judge nodded, turning to the Healthy Heart lawyers with raised eyebrows. "What do you say to that, gentleman?"

The older lawyer responded, "The founder of the company developed the seed over a period of time when she was at Stanford. She did it by trial and error and did not keep records. Apparently, she scrawled notes as she worked in the lab and they were thrown away when she was a student or soon thereafter, well before there was a company. There is no current need for any record of the corn seed formulation because the company has the corn seed itself which now naturally reproduces itself. And because the formula is proprietary, the company has chosen not to write it down."

"Well, ok then, it appears there are no documents," said the Judge. "At least that's what the company says. And if there are no records, then there is nothing to produce. Next case, please."

Ebinger tried to speak but the Judge cut him off. "Didn't you hear me, Counselor? I said next case."

Another group of litigants approached the bench. Rabbi Smith, who had turned away, now turned back and approached the Judge.

"What is it, sir?" the Judge said.

"We should get..."

The senior Healthy Heart lawyer interrupted Rabbi Smith. "This gentleman is not even a lawyer. He should not be speaking."

"I am permitted to speak," Rabbi Smith said. "I'm appearing pro se on behalf of my deceased son. I'm permitted to act in the capacity of a lawyer."

"That is correct," said the Judge. "However, you're not permitted to disrupt my court. We're finished here."

"The corn seed. They should provide us the actual corn

seed as part of discovery, if they have no documents explaining what's in it."

"Now, wait a minute," said the Healthy Heart lawyer, hurrying up to the podium. "They never asked for the actual corn seed in discovery. And in any event, it's not a document."

The Judge glared at the Healthy Heart lawyer. "First, you tell us you have no documents relating to this proprietary corn seed. I personally find that hard to believe, but since you are an officer of the court, I must accept it. Now you are saying the plaintiffs can't even have the corn seed itself. Provide it to them within thirty days. And, please, don't be clever by just providing one seed – give them sufficient seeds to work with. OK, then, are we through, Mr. Smith?"

"It's Rabbi Smith, Your Honor. We also need to take the oral deposition of the company founder who they say developed the corn seed formula."

"This is harassment," protested the Healthy Heart lawyer. "They're talking about dragging the CEO of the company into a ludicrous lawsuit. If she had to testify every time some person decided to launch a baseless case against the company, she couldn't do her job."

"Two hours," said the Judge, glaring at Rabbi Smith. "I'll give you two hours to depose her and she gets to pick a location that is convenient for her. Are we done?"

Much to Rabbi Smith's surprise, the Healthy Heart lawyers quickly made Aurora Blanc available for deposition, for a date only three weeks after the Judge's ruling. Bill Bradford could not get away from his university duties to come to the West Coast and Rabbi Smith did not trust his local lawyer to conduct the deposition, so the Rabbi decided to do it himself. Bradford helped him prepare a list of questions. While Rabbi Smith was determined to make the most of the opportunity, he did not feel confident of his abilities as an interrogator.

The drive from Oakland to Silicon Valley, where the deposition was scheduled, in the Healthy Heart attorneys' offices, was like a trip to another country. Rabbi Smith's GPS route took him through green mountainous terrain, past lakes, into the boutique town of Palo Alto where everything was perfect and pristine. No wonder, he mused, so many of the wealthiest people in the world chose to live here. The law offices, located on a side street, were expensively appointed in wood and contemporary furniture.

Ebinger was waiting for him. They were escorted into the conference room, where the Rabbi got his first look at Aurora Blanc. She stood by a long conference table, poised, tall, slim, blonde – statue-like in her perfection. She towered over Healthy Heart's senior counsel. She took the Rabbi's breath away. Two other lawyers sat at the table along with a court reporter, stenographic equipment in front of her. No one in the room, except the court reporter who smiled and whispered a request for their business cards, acknowledged their presence. The reporter, Rabbi Smith, and Ebinger seated themselves on one side of the table and the others sat across, acting as if they did not exist.

Eventually, the senior lawyer motioned for Aurora Blanc to move to the head of the table and, still not looking or in any way acknowledging Rabbi Smith, said to the court reporter,

"This deposition will end in exactly two hours, not a second more, unless they stop before that. You are to terminate your work after one hundred and twenty minutes, not a second longer. Are we clear on that?" Without waiting for her response, he turned to Ebinger, "Let's get this over with. You can start."

"I'm taking the deposition," said Rabbi Smith.

For the first time, the Healthy Heart lawyers looked at him, and the youngest one smirked.

"Please get started," said the senior lawyer.

Without looking up from his notes, Rabbi Smith read the canned introduction and instructions to the witness, then looked at the prepared questions provided by Bradford. He took a deep breath. "Your lawyers have provided us the corn seed that your company uses to feed Healthy Heart cattle. I have one here which I will mark as Plaintiff's Exhibit A. Am I correct that it is a genetically modified corn seed that you developed?"

She gazed at him, silent and expressionless. Thirty seconds passed, and then she spoke in a cold and confident tone. "I developed a corn seed that we use for our cattle. I don't know if the seed that you have in your hand is mine. I wouldn't have any way to know that, Mr. Smith."

"Well, let's talk about the one you developed. Do any documents exist that contain the procedure or methodology used to genetically engineer the seed?"

"No."

"Don't your lab assistants or employees need instructions to make these seeds?"

"No."

"Do you have any documents that show all or even part of the composition of your genetically modified seeds?"

She looked at her watch. "Do we have to sit here for a full two hours?"

"Can you please answer my question?"

"I did. Again, the answer is no."

"How can your employees make seeds if they don't have the formula?"

"They can't."

"Well, then who makes the seeds?"

"Me. I was told my lawyers already gave you all this information. This is a waste of my time and yours." She raised her wrist and tapped the face of her watch.

Rabbi Smith was sweating and he started to rush his words. "Am I correct in understanding that you developed this corn seed when you were at Stanford?"

"Yes and no."

"What does that mean, Ms. Blanc?"

She smiled slightly, the first change in her blank demeanor since the deposition had begun. "You want me to define the words yes or no?"

"No. I want you to explain your last answer."

"I already answered your question to the best of my ability. Do you have any more questions or can I go?"

"Did you or did you not develop a corn seed when you were a student at Stanford?"

The senior lawyer spoke for the first time. "Asked and answered."

"What do you mean?" said Rabbi Smith.

"I mean you already asked that question and she already gave you an answer. You can't ask the same question again if she's already answered it. If you are out of new questions, then we are done. I'm not going to permit you to harass Ms. Blanc."

Rabbi Smith took a deep breath, trying to dispel his panic. "Am I correct that you started your work on your genetically modified corn seed when you were at Stanford?"

"Yes."

"Did you alone work on it?"

"Yes."

"Did you make any notes as you worked on it?"

"Yes."

"Where are the notes?"

"I lost them."

"Do you have any idea where they are?"

"No."

"You continued to work on the seed after you left Stanford?"

"Yes."

"Did you make notes of your work then?"

"I don't remember."

"Where are those notes?"

"I said I don't remember if I made notes, so how would I know where they are if they exist?"

The senior lawyer interjected, "As reflected in our discovery responses, we conducted an appropriate search. No such notes exist."

"Did anyone ever work with you or help you develop the corn seed?"

"No, I did it myself."

"And to your knowledge, there were never any papers anywhere that contain information about the composition of the seed or how it was developed?"

"That's correct, except possibly for handwritten notes that I discarded around the time I wrote them because I didn't need them. I have a photographic memory."

"What if you died and the company needed your process used to create the seed?"

"Objection," barked the senior lawyer. "That's a hypothetical question and calls for speculation."

"No, it's not," said the Rabbi. "Everyone dies.'

The senior lawyer looked at Rabbi Smith with his mouth open. "You may answer if you are able to speculate on his hypothetical question, Ms. Blanc, but you don't have to guess."

"They could reverse engineer the genetic composition of the seed," she said.

The senior lawyer looked uncomfortable.

Rabbi Smith fumbled through his notes.

"You're done now, aren't you?" said the senior lawyer.

"Yes," mumbled Rabbi Smith.

Aurora Blanc walked out of the room without a backward glance.

Later, when Rabbi Smith checked his cell, he found three calls from Bill Bradford. He tapped in Bill's number.

"I've been on pins and needles all morning," said Bradford. "What happened?"

"Nothing, it was a complete bust. Same story that we got from their lawyers."

'Shit. Excuse me, Rabbi. It's hard to believe. Did you ask her the questions I gave you?"

"I asked all the questions you gave me."

"And the question about how the company would know the composition of the seed if she died?"

"Yes, I asked her. We got nothing."

"What did she say?"

"They could reverse engineer it."

"Really! That's good. In fact, that's great."

"Why?"

"It means the seed can be deconstructed. I can do it – I'll have one of my students help me."

"OK."

"Keep the faith, Rabbi. We've only begun to fight. By the way, what is she like?"

"An ice maiden."

The waiting after the deposition was the worst part for Rabbi Smith. His synagogue duties were not enough to occupy his mind. Every day, he checked and rechecked his email, text and voice mail for something, anything, from Bill on his progress with the reverse engineering. After three weeks, he called Bill.

"I know you want to know what's going on," said Bill. "It's complicated."

"Oh."

"Not bad complicated, just not what we expected. When Blanc testified that we could figure this seed out by reverse engineering, that was bullshit. We thought we'd see a normal corn seed with an inserted gene from flax. That is there, but there's much more. This seed has been altered beyond recognition. It's hardly a corn seed anymore. Apparently, they had to make all kinds of DNA insertions in the seed to get the result they wanted – you know, to make corn feed to produce fat-free cattle meat. And they changed the seed for other purposes that I'm not yet sure of – maybe for growth reasons so the corn doesn't need as much water to grow. I'm not sure but what is clear is that all these numerous DNA inserts disrupt the genome and cause unintended mutational defects and antigens."

"What in the world does that mean?"

"It means, in layman's terms, that this is a totally fucked-up seed that could cause dangerous unforeseen consequences. We haven't taken our analysis as far as we can yet, but, Rabbi, I promise I'll get back to you as soon as I get something more concrete. Keep the faith."

CHAPTER 8

Harry was snowboarding down the Big Burn run at Snow-mass in Colorado. He loved snowboarding in conditions like today's – the glittering azure sky and pristine white snow; the sun warm on his face, the powder so light that he could almost float down the slope using just enough exertion that he was physically engaged but not exhausted. At the bottom of the mountain, the pretty girl who was spending the weekend with him, had skied ahead to secure a window table in the private, members-only dining club, where the wealthy and well-known (and the not-so-well-known) could check the others out while drinking three-hundred-dollar bottles of white burgundy with their eighty-five-dollar lunches.

He moved in a dance-like rhythm, staying in the wide-open middle area, avoiding the tall pines on the periphery, which he knew could be lethal if one had a collision, as had happened to other rich, overconfident, fair-weather skiers. He had worked too many hours on his business over the past decade to have time to be more than an average snowboarder, but he was good enough to enjoy it. Physically he could not have felt any better than he did at this moment. Materially, he was a so-called master of the universe, rich beyond his wildest dreams, respected and admired by friends and strangers, and free to do whatever he wanted. But in his head, he was not where he wanted to be.

Since Aurora had forced him to sell his share of the company, he had divided his time between having fun and reviewing potential startup investments. A good life? No. By any reasonable standard, he had a great life. All was well, except for the anger in his gut. He understood that he had stupidly regarded her as his best friend – that he had loved her as a friend. They had taken a magical journey together, transforming themselves from non-entities to icons sitting at the top of the world. And he had invited her on that magic carpet ride after he found her, depressed, sitting in the middle of a filthy apartment, going absolutely nowhere. On the other hand, so what if she had fucked him over? In the words of the great sage Liberace, Harry "laughed all the way to the bank" after she bought him out. Looking at the whole thing dispassionately, he knew he was crazy to be so obsessed just because she had underhandedly and disrespectfully forced him out of his own company. After all, it was just business and the payday that he received was more than fair. But he felt as if he'd been dumped, and couldn't stop being angry about it. Perhaps he should try something extravagant to get past it – maybe marry one of the young ladies who wanted him, or start a new business venture. Or perhaps find a way to confront her, call her out for her conduct. No, the best course was to forget about Aurora, to be positive and forward-looking.

Ebinger received a call from the Healthy Heart senior litigation counsel, Franklin Lumar. Their conversation, as Ebinger told Rabbi Smith, was about a settlement offer from Healthy Heart: without admitting guilt or liability, and for the sole purposes of avoiding the expense and time of more litigation, Healthy Heart was willing to pay two hundred thousand dollars, provided there was a confidentiality agreement. Lumar emphasized that the settlement was not Healthy Heart's idea, but his own, as he often advised his clients to settle to avoid the distraction of litigation.

"It's a sign of weakness, isn't it?" Rabbi Smith asked Bill Bradford. "They're afraid. We've hit a nerve."

"It's more likely they're surprised we've been able take the case this far," said Bill. "They're not afraid of us, but any good lawyer knows, and Healthy Heart has good lawyers, litigation is always uncertain and that it's worth a few dollars – two hundred grand is nothing to them – to bury this case. What we're seeing is routine. The question is, do you want to settle? If the opening offer is two hundred thousand, you could probably get a little more with some negotiation."

"We're not in this for that, Bill."

"I know, I know, but maybe you shouldn't let this become a crusade that takes over your life. Maybe it's time to stop."

"Bill, this is my life. I understand what you're saying about why they're trying to settle, but I think they're worried about something else. That woman who runs the company – she's tough. She wouldn't have authorized a settlement unless she was hiding something. She has a secret. I know it."

Several weeks later, Bill called the Rabbi. "I've got very good news."

Rabbi Smith's pulse quickened.

"We've been studying the composition of their corn seed. They transplanted foreign DNA from flax and Lord knows what other genes into their seed. You already know that. But the big thing is, all that transformation has caused significant turmoil in the corn organism. As a result, several things happened – all potentially dangerous. The disruption turned on – like a switch – biochemical pathways that are usually dormant, which created roadways in the corn seed that didn't exist before. The inserted genes also produced an enzyme that upsets the entire plant's metabolic balance so that it overexcites certain cellular molecules. So we see toxins in higher concentrations than should be in a corn seed. You understand what I'm saying. These are foreign toxins, noxious substances, that shouldn't be there, and this corn seed is swamped with them."

"And they harm people?"

"Scientists have known for years that genetic engineering can have unintended consequences in a plant, but it's usually something you can foresee. For example, some years ago, researchers tried to increase the shelf life of tomatoes and the result was a tomato that looked like a Christmas bulb."

"I'm struggling to understand this. What effect does it have on the meat?"

"You know how protective the FDA has been about GMO foods. Even they have been worried about potential problems. Sometime ago, the FDA's Director of Veterinary Medicine wrote that they believe 'animal feeds derived from genetically modified plants present unique animal and food safety concerns,' including 'the risk that unexpected toxins in an engineered animal feed could appear in meat and milk products, making them unsafe for humans.' Listen to this, Rabbi, and bear in mind it's from an important FDA official: 'Unlike the human diet, a single plant product may constitute a significant portion of the animal diet... Therefore, a change in nutrient or toxicant composition that is considered insignificant for human consumption may be a very significant change in the animal diet.' You get it, don't you? They sounded the alarm for exactly the scenario we have here."

"That's good?"

"This is exactly what we have hoped for."

The next day, the Healthy Heart lawyers filed a motion for summary judgment, asking that the case be thrown out, because there was no evidence, despite the extensive discovery permitted by the Judge, that supported the claim. The brief contended that because there was no documentation on what was in the corn seed, as discovery had shown, there was no evidence that it was harmful. Thus, the seed had no connection with the death of Timmy Smith.

In response, Bill prepared an affidavit summarizing his scientific examination of the corn seed – saying, specifically, that there were foreign toxins in the seed that would be passed on to the cattle and then to humans who ate the beef, and that those transmitted toxins were harmful to human health. Following the Judge's order to maintain confidentiality relating to the proprietary corn seed, Bill filed the affidavit and brief under seal, so that it would not be available to the public.

Bill flew out from the East Coast to argue the motion. It was his first time in a courtroom since his days as an associate. Despite his inexperience, Bill was confident as he stood before Judge.

"We've been able to develop a lot of evidence about this corn seed and its potentially lethal effects. And we've done so without any documents from Healthy Heart. It is beyond belief, defying all commonsense that this Corporation has no documents of how the corn seed was developed and what is in it. It is also incredible that there are no records of testing on animals or people. The absence of records would be understandable if we had found the corn seed was altered in some modest way but what we found, based on our study of the actual seed, is that it is nothing like a normal corn seed. The Defendant's seed does not exist in nature, and it is filled with dangerous elements – toxins, otherwise deemed poisons. I ask you, Your Honor, do you believe a multibillion-dollar company has no record relating to any of this?"

The Judge interrupted, "I understand you find all this incredible but what exactly do you want me to do about it?"

"The founder, Aurora Blanc, stonewalled in her deposition. Let us take more depositions to get to the bottom of this."

Turning to the Healthy Heart senior lawyer, the Judge said, "That doesn't seem unreasonable to me."

"Your Honor, this is a witch hunt. Ms. Blanc developed this corn seed when she was a student and she credibly explained why the notes don't exist. There is nothing suspicious about it. More importantly, they don't have a case – everything they say is speculation. We have a valid motion for summary judgment and it should be granted."

The Judge looked pained as he turned to Bill. "Against my better judgment, I am going to permit you to take three more depositions. Choose wisely and don't come back to me asking for more. I've been more then tolerant with you and I will tell you: the Defendant makes a very persuasive case for their motion for summary judgment. Understood?"

"Perfectly," said Bill. "Thank you."

As they walked out, Bill whispered to Rabbi Smith, "We're hanging on by a thread here."

Aurora drove to her lawyers' offices for a debriefing. They sat in the conference room, but before the senior lawyer, Franklin Lumar, could speak, she said, "Do I need to bring in a new law firm?"

"Absolutely not," Lumar said.

She continued as if he had not spoken. "Because this is not going well. You told me this was a 'nothing case' but here we are, months later, with more disruption and intrusion into our business. You guys are supposed to protect me from that. You are failing. The lawyers on the other side are amateurs; one of them isn't even a lawyer and he's beating us! This is unacceptable, gentleman. Tell me how you are going to fix this, or I will find some lawyers who will."

"Ms. Blanc, we came very close today to winning. The Judge is bending over backward for them, because the plaintiff is a Rabbi with a dead child."

"Excuses! I have better things to do than to listen to this." She left.

She got into her BMW and slammed her hand again and again on the dashboard. "Shit, fuck, shit, fuck," she chanted, as she pounded.

Rabbi Smith got a call from Franklin Lumar, asking if they could sit down to discuss the case. Apparently, the lawyer had figured out that Rabbi Smith called the shots, so if he wanted to accomplish anything he had better deal directly with him. Lumar suggested meeting at a coffee shop in Rabbi Smith's neighborhood. The Rabbi invited him to meet in his study at the synagogue.

The psychological effect of facing the Rabbi as he sat behind his desk in his modest office was exactly as the Rabbi had expected. The lawyer was in a subservient position in front of a man of God. He welcomed Lumar, then waited for him to state his business.

"I wanted to resume the topic of exploring what we could do to bring this lawsuit to a close," the lawyer began.

The Rabbi gave him a paternalistic smile. "I assume this was your idea, not your client's."

Ignoring this, Lumar continued, "You will not be offended if I'm completely frank."

"I would be offended if you were anything other than completely frank. I have a pretty good detector for insincerity."

"I am not here to bullshit you, Rabbi. Our CEO does not like the intrusion into our business from this litigation or any litigation. She would like this case to be gone. I have told her the case will be dismissed in the normal and ordinary course because the Judge is going to throw it out on summary Judgement. You've been present at the court hearings and I'm sure you understand this from what the Judge has said and his overall attitude toward this case. Nonetheless, I am here to try to ascertain what you need to resolve this. I understand you've suffered great loss and I am sure that you honestly believe it is the fault of my client's product. I am not going to argue with you, but I need to reiterate that the case will be dismissed in due course and you will have achieved nothing. Now, Rabbi, that's as frank as I can possibly be. I'm not going to ask you for an answer right now unless you wish to give it. But I encourage you to give this some real consideration. If you are not looking for money for yourself, perhaps you might consider a seven-figure charitable contribution to some cause you believe in. We are open to your thoughts. But please do not view my visit as a sign of weakness on our part. That would be a serious mistake."

Despite himself, Rabbi Smith liked this man. He nodded his head, signaling that he would think about it.

"Rabbi, would you be offended if I told you a Rabbi joke? It may be instructive," the lawyer said as he stood to leave.

"Please, go ahead," said the Rabbi, settling back in his chair.

"A big flood swamped Rabbi Cohen's house, putting him in danger. As the waters covered the first floor, rescuers in a boat came by, but the Rabbi declined to get in, telling them, 'God will save me.' Several hours later as the waters rose to the second floor, a helicopter came by the bedroom window where the Rabbi stood, its pilot urging the Rabbi come aboard. Again he declined, telling the rescuers that God would protect him. By evening, the water was up to the roof where the Rabbi was perched. Another helicopter flew overhead and lowered a rope ladder but the Rabbi shouted up to the pilot, 'God will save me.' Shortly thereafter, the house became completely submerged and the Rabbi drowned. He woke in heaven sitting in front of God. Realizing he was dead, he protested, 'I have lived a pious life, but you did not save me from the flood.' God glared at him and said, 'The hell I didn't, schmuck! What about the boat and the two helicopters.'

The Rabbi laughed. "I understand your point. But he did go to heaven."

"You're wavering?" Bill asked, after the Rabbi briefed him on the phone.

"I'm thinking about what Timmy would want. A large charitable donation in his name compared to losing the case and coming up empty."

"They are not going to let you use his name. If there's a settlement agreement, there will be a broad confidentiality provision and any charitable contribution will be in their name or anonymous."

"Regardless, it would provide great benefit to some needy cause."

"Who says we are going to lose? Their lawyer must have really worked you over. This is not done. We got the tissue samples from Timmy's autopsy, as you know, and analyzed them for the reaction to toxins in the corn seed. I believe it shows that the meat killed Timmy."

Rabbi Smith knew that Bill was not prone to exaggeration, even if he had been overly optimistic before. "Explain it to me."

"You may want to write this down so you can reread it. There is a type of natural toxin called mycotoxin. Mycotoxin is a Greek word meaning poison. It's usually produced by fungus-type organisms such as mushrooms. When you think about poisonous mushrooms, you're actually concerned about mycotoxins in certain varieties of mushrooms. We were surprised to find high concentrations of a type of mycotoxin, called Citrinin, in the Healthy Heart corn and in the Healthy Heart beef that we got from a grocery store. We also found it in Timmy's tissue samples."

"That is significant."

"Yes, it is. This is what we know about Citrinin: it is a fungus, but, surprisingly, it is also found in some grains, including corn – more specifically, the type of corn used as animal feed. Researchers have determined that Citrinin can target the kidney. It's been found to have an adverse toxin effect on animals but there has been no evidence that it causes human health problems. But scientists in Germany conducted studies on the effect of high consumption of grain products containing Citrinin on humans. They observed high concentrations of it in urine, but could make no firm conclusions about health effects."

"That doesn't help us."

"What's different here is that there are extremely high concentrations of Citrinin in the Healthy Heart corn and its beef and in Timmy's tissues – substantially more than naturally occurs. When the Healthy Heart researchers made all the DNA modifications and insertions in the Healthy Heart seed, it set off a series of enzyme reactions that resulted in a huge expansion of Citrinin in their corn seed. Timmy's symptoms were all consistent with nephrotoxic injury; that is, there was injury to the kidneys. There was excess fluid in his body, high blood pressure, and, finally, kidney failure. His hospital records show all of those classic symptoms. They could've treated it by removing the toxin from his system by hemodialysis but they had no idea what was causing the shock to his system."

"Oh," Rabbi Smith said, taking the information in. He started to choke up. "Why did it kill him and not others?"

"Who says it didn't kill others. I think it did but no one has traced it back to the beef. We do know that most of the time, mycotoxins, which are usually ingested by eating mushrooms and while potentially lethal, have no discernible health effect on most people. You hear stories about people dying of mushroom poisoning all the time but that's a myth. It rarely happens even when someone eats the most dangerous kind. Little kids eat poisonous mushrooms more often than we imagine, but it doesn't affect them most of the time. In many cases, it depends on the susceptibility of that individual. Timmy rarely ate beef — so he may have assimilated the Citrinin in a more pronounced manner. Regardless of how it happened, that toxin is present at a high level in his tissues and that's what killed him."

"You think we can prove this."

"Yes. I believe with this new information, the Judge will not dismiss the case on summary judgment, which means it will go to a jury. And before a jury, we will win. I'm looking for a top-notch trial lawyer to join our team once we get past the summary judgment motion."

"Alright."

"Alright, what?"

"Let's go forward, Bill."

Choosing the three Healthy Heart deposition witnesses that the Judge permitted was not difficult. Of the two other company founders, one was dead. The surviving one, Harry Sumner, even though no longer an employee of the company, was subject to deposition through a subpoena. Bill came out to California to take Sumner's deposition, in Ebinger's offices. The parties met in a cheaply furnished conference room shared by all the office building tenants. Ebinger, who didn't have a secretary, carried in a boxed container of Starbucks coffee.

At the designated 10:00 AM start time, the witness was not present.

"Where is he?" Bill asked the company lawyers.

"No idea," said Lumar. "He's not our witness. He doesn't work for the company. You subpoenaed him."

At 10:30, a slim man in his late twenties, attired in tan trousers and a light blue cotton shirt, walked in, hands in pockets, and apologized for being late. He waited for instructions on where to sit. When none of the lawyers spoke up, the court reporter pointed to a chair next to her. It soon became obvious that he did not know anyone in the room. How could it be, Rabbi Smith wondered, that a co-founder of the company was here without being represented by the Healthy Heart lawyers or his own attorney?

Bill began the deposition of Harry Sumner by introducing himself as one of the lawyers for the Timmy Smith estate, then launched into questions about the origination of the Healthy Heart Company. Harry answered in concise sentences, explaining how, after graduation, he had talked to Aurora Blanc about her corn seed research. He explained how he had successfully sought funding to establish the company. He confirmed that Aurora Blanc was the sole inventor and that the lab assistants were subsequently hired by the company to assist her in the process of refining and testing before the beef went to the retail market. It all sounded cut-and-dried.

It appeared that Sumner had been well prepared. By the time Bill began his questions on the allegedly "nonexistent" documents relating to the corn seed, Bill was struggling.

"Did you ever see any handwritten notes by Ms. Blanc or the lab assistants regarding the science underlying the corn seed?" Bill asked.

"No."

"Did you ever see Ms. Blanc or her assistants taking notes as they worked?"

"No."

"It seems unlikely to me."

"That's not a question that I can answer."

"Please answer."

"My answer is: that is your opinion."

"What is your opinion, sir?"

"I don't have an opinion."

"So, am I correct that you're testifying that Ms. Blanc and her lab assistants made no record of their work on the development and refinement of the corn seed?"

"First, they're not her lab assistants; they work for the company. Second, you are correct with the exception of what they put on their iPads."

"iPads?"

"iPads are computer-like tablet devices."

"I know that. Did the lab assistants and Ms. Blanc use iPads in their lab work on the corn seed?"

"Yes."

"For what purpose?"

"For recording data and information on the corn seed work."

"What kind of data?"

"Any data related to their work."

"How do you know this?"

"When we initially hired our first assistants, we were working out of a little lab. Aurora was using an iPad for her work and wanted the assistants to have them, too, so they could share information. I bought them with our first infusion of investment money and I got one myself, so that I could be part of the communication chain. I was originally a Stanford biotech major. I was able to follow what they were doing."

Bill leaned forward, trying to hide his excitement.

"Were you emailing this information back-and-forth?"

"No, that would not have been secure. We had our own secure website which we used through a private server in the lab."

"Do you still have your iPad?"

"I keep all my old iPads to use as music players, so, yes, I still have it."

"Is the lab data still on your iPad?"

"I don't know, but probably. I downloaded everything at the time because I worried that our backup might not be reliable. I should have erased everything from my iPad, but, frankly, I didn't think of it."

"Where are the iPads belonging to the other lab assistants?"

"We destroyed them for security reasons."

"And where is that private server?"

"Also long gone. It crashed and became useless. We destroyed it."

"What about the data on it? Was it retrieved?"

"We didn't try. Aurora and I decided there was nothing we needed to keep."

"What about the website you used?"

"That was taken down for security reasons and the data deleted."

"Sir, I am instructing you to retain the iPad that we've been discussing and provide it to us immediately."

"Sure, no problem. I can have someone deliver it to you today. What address?"

As they drove back to the synagogue in Oakland, Bill said to the Rabbi, "I just cannot believe she lied so blatantly about the existence of records. She's probably lying about everything."

Bill fumbled for his ringing cell phone. "Why... alright... 2 PM."

Bill put away the phone. "Healthy Heart filed an emergency motion to prevent us from getting that iPad. They say it contains proprietary information and that Harry has no legal right to give it to us because it belongs to the company."

At the court hearing that afternoon before the Judge, the company's senior lawyer argued that Harry had no ownership rights over the scientific data on the iPad. It belonged to the company.

Bill said, "Your Honor, first they claim, under oath, that

there are no records of the science relating to the corn seed. Then we find out there are records and they have the temerity to argue that we cannot have them."

Lumar jumped up. "That's not true! We did not have any records. This ex-employee had the records, not the company. Moreover, he stole them and is now giving them over to these people." He turned, glaring at Bill and the Rabbi as if they were vermin. "The point is, these are confidential records regarding the scientific formula of our product and to give them to these people just because they filed this nonsense lawsuit is wrong. We don't trust these people with these sensitive documents, even if there is a confidentiality order."

The Judge looked pained. "I am afraid this case is spinning out of control. But I am going to permit both parties to review whatever is on that iPad. I'm imposing a strict confidentiality order. If there is any public dissemination of this information by the plaintiff, I will impose the strictest sanctions imaginable."

Lumar began to protest, but the Judge cut him off. "Enough. That's my ruling."

Several days later, the Judge summoned the parties back to court. He appeared in good spirits.

"Counsel, I'm recusing myself from this case. I just found out from my wife that we eat this Healthy Heart beef three or four times a week. I did not know that. She is a big believer in this product and doesn't want me to do anything that could interfere with it. Out of an abundance of caution, the case will be assigned to another Judge." For the first time since the case began, he grinned. "Have a good afternoon, everyone."

The information on the iPad contained step-by-step instructions to the lab assistants on the genetic modifications to the seed, with an explicit roadmap on how to create the new seed. It also showed that Aurora Blanc's work of genetically engineering or merging the flax DNA with traditional cattle corn DNA was already complete before she began sharing information with her assistants. In other words, it appeared she did the science herself.

The Healthy Heart lawyers waited a month to refile their motion for summary judgment. It contended that despite the liberal discovery provided to the plaintiff, there was not a smidgin of evidence showing any link between the death of Timmy Smith and the Defendant's beef products. The renewed motion came up before Judge Biglow. Ebinger told Bill and Rabbi Smith that the Judge was straight-down-the-middle, a fair and competent jurist.

Bill's response read more like a scientific research paper than a legal brief. It relied on a fifty-page affidavit prepared by a prominent MIT bioengineer stating that careful analysis showed there were unusually high levels of Citrinin in Timmy Smith's tissue samples and in Healthy Heart corn and beef. This evidence was more than sufficient evidence, Bill argued, to establish a material issue of fact for a jury trial. He added a new motion against Healthy Heart, asserting that the company and its CEO should be sanctioned for misrepresenting that there were no records of the scientific development of the GMO seed.

In reply, Healthy Heart submitted citations from prominent scientific journals, which pointed out that the Citrinin is commonly present in many grains including corn, and that studies had shown that Citrinin concentrations in the human kidney had no ill-health effects whatsoever. The Healthy Heart Brief concluded: "The so-called evidence that the deceased child's friend's mother saw him consume some unspecified portion of the Defendant's beef product several days before his death is too flimsy and speculative to allow a lawsuit to proceed."

Bill assured the Rabbi that once they had an opportunity to appear before the new Judge at the hearing, his scientific expertise would enable him to best the opposition lawyer in argument and convince the Judge of the soundness of the evidence.

Several weeks later, Ebinger called the Judge Biglow's clerk to ask when the hearing would be held so the out-of-town counsel could plan his trip. The clerk said that he was writing a draft of the opinion for the Judge. Judge Biglow had seen no need for a hearing; the ruling online would be posted online.

CHAPTER 9

Aurora was finishing a customer dinner in San Jose at La Foret, a classic and expensive French restaurant, chosen to impress the two staid businessmen brothers who ran a family-owned grocery store chain in Missouri. They had been flown in as a reward for their business and as an incentive to increase it. Aurora's new goal was to persuade grocery store retailers not to treat Healthy Heart Beef as a specialty item but to feature it as a core beef product, alongside or even as a replacement for the traditional fat-laden meats. If this strategy was successful, it would give Healthy Heart a shot at becoming the biggest meat producer in the U.S. Aurora believed that if she could convince these Midwestern businessmen to adopt her beef as their principal meat product, she could use this success as a marketing tool with the giant national grocery chains. She was working them over as they gobbled down the restaurant's signature Grand Marnier soufflé and sipped from a second bottle of 1999 Chateau Mouton Rothchild Pauillac (seven hundred dollars a bottle and well worth it to impress these guys), when she spied Jane and her husband Horace, across the room at a corner table. She hadn't communicated with Jane in months, and would not have acknowledged her except that Jane had seen her, waved and hurried across the room.

"Excuse me, gentlemen," Jane boomed, as she embraced Aurora, squeezed her head to her chest, and held her in the embrace, oblivious to Aurora's embarrassed smile. The men appeared startled by this extravagant display of affection. "My long-lost sister," Jane explained to them, clearly unconcerned about whatever she was interrupting.

The oldest of the two men said, "We should let the two of you catch up. In St. Louis, I'm usually in bed by now." The two men stood and thanked Aurora for the "spectacular evening," assuring her that they could find their way back to the hotel. As they walked away, Jane instructed Aurora to stay right where she was, signaled to her husband, who waved and left.

"Now that I've got you cornered, I'm not letting you get away until I decide you can go," Jane said.

Aurora sat back, taking Jane in. Her face had filled in and was flushed, probably from the opulent food and wine.

"I know, I know, I gained some weight but so what. I feel good, I'm happy. He's a good guy," Jane said, meaning her departed husband. "But I miss you. You never return my texts. I know you love me so I'm not offended. I just need to be part of your life again. Men may come and go but girlfriends are forever." She put her hand on Aurora's cheek.

Aurora motioned for the waiter. She ordered herbal tea and a glass for Jane to finish the Bordeaux.

"Tell me what is going on. I know you're hiding."

"I'm not hiding, Jane; I'm working. That's my life. Everything falls on me in this company. No one working for me has any self-initiative or foresight." She reddened as her voice rose. "They just show up every day and do what's in front of them. No one thinks outside the box or solves our big problems. I have to work day and night."

"Bullshit, Aurora. Everybody knows you're getting the

best people for your company. They all want to work for you. What you're really telling me is: you have no friends, you're not dating, you're a workaholic. And you look gaunt."

"Nice seeing you too, Jane."

"What about that fancy social set in New York where you met your ex-husband? Do you see any of them?"

"They keep inviting me to things, but I really don't have a lot in common with Taylor Swift. And my ex-husband is part of that circle."

"So, you have no social life at all?"

"My business colleagues and customers. You saw two to-night."

"That doesn't count. So, no dating, no romance, no sex?"

"Men are intimidated by me, Jane. They treat me like I'm a celebrity or try to get some business advantage from me."

"I thought you had a great guy with Malcolm."

She shook her head. "He was too nice for me. And he didn't understand the pressures that I am under."

"Alright, I'm sorry. I'm butting in and imposing my own values. The business is going well?"

"It's growing, but we're a big target. People want to bring me down."

"What people?"

"The government, litigants, competitors — my enemies."

"For God sakes, Aurora, you are one of the most respected women in the country."

"You have no idea. They're all circling me like vultures. I need to have my guard up all the time. They think I'm some undeserving girl, not part of their club, who doesn't know what she is doing. I'm vulnerable Jane, so vulnerable."

"Club? What club?"

"The boys' club – the investment banks, the Silicon Valley crew, the politicians, the whole fucking establishment. I'm an outsider. They want me gone."

Jane stared at her.

"Jane, you have no idea what it's like for me. Every day is a fight for survival."

"I understand," Jane said dubiously.

"You're my only true friend, Jane. You understand me. You're the only one who doesn't want anything from me."

"I do want something from you. I want us to go away for a girl's vacation. Let's go to Cobo for a week and do nothing. Beach, spa, and shopping."

Aurora had no interest in a beach vacation, but could not say no to Jane. "As soon as I have some time. I'm getting an award from the TED talk thing and I have to give an acceptance speech."

After they parted, Aurora pondered why Jane had such a powerful hold on her, particularly since she was a woman of no real accomplishments or standing. Since they first met, Aurora had emulated her, essentially tried to be her, even though Jane was hardly a shining example. But regardless of Jane's defects, Aurora had stronger feelings about her than about anyone else in her life. She loved her friend.

PART IV
AURORA

CHAPTER 1

The day after I received my TED Prize, my lawyer called me with news of the court ruling in the dead kid litigation.

"Overall, very good news."

I interrupted him. "Just tell me – I'll decide if it's good news."

"You won the lawsuit. The Judge said the alleged linkage between the child's death and your product is too tenuous to permit the lawsuit to go forward. He agreed with all our arguments – that the presence of that toxin, Citrinin, is not enough to support a lawsuit since there's no scientific evidence that it's harmful, as it is present in most grains with no ill effect; that the child's possible consumption of the beef does not tie his death to it as it could have been a multitude of things that he was exposed to that may have affected him or it could have been some congenital cause. So the lawsuit is over. They could appeal, of course, but it's unlikely that this case would be reversed, because the trial court has a great deal of discretion with this kind of ruling. There is, however, a negative aspect to the decision but I do not want you to worry about it."

"I'll decide what I need worry about."

"You should read the decision yourself, but essentially the court says that it is issuing sanctions against you and the company for misleading the court regarding the existence of scientific records. Those sanctions amount to a small monetary fine – $25,000. But he is also referring the matter to the State's Attorney to consider criminal perjury charges. Now, I need to tell you that it's very unusual – it's never happened in my experience – that discovery misrepresentations have been treated as a perjury offense. So the likelihood that the State's Attorney would do anything to you or the company is close to zero, in my opinion. And even if she did – which again, I stress, I don't see happening – we could work something out."

"That's outrageous. I didn't misrepresent anything. They asked me about notes and I didn't have any notes."

"Right, right. Ms. Blanc, this ruling is a cause for celebration. You won that lawsuit just as we forecast. It's over."

And so, I had one less thing to worry about. That lawsuit had worried me because it threatened the entire company. This new claim about the misrepresentations of documents was just another annoyance. I would do it all over again to protect my business.

I took Jane up on her suggestion that we get away. We flew down to the Baja Peninsula, stayed in the biggest suite in the best hotel, and did the whole spa thing, all of which Jane arranged with her usual expertise about the finer things in life. If she had my money, she would probably spend it in a year. But this was my first real vacation since I'd left Malcolm, and I had to admit that I actually relaxed and enjoyed it. I even had a fling with a gentleman staying in the hotel before he headed off on a fishing trip with his friends. It was only a two-night stand, but it made me realize I missed the intimacy of being with a man, if not enough to live with one.

Back at work, I became so immersed in the everyday challenges that I did not worry when I skipped my period. That had happened before, an unsurprising consequence of stress.

When I skipped it for the second month, I took a package test. It was positive. It was just another annoying problem to take care of, as soon as I found the time to schedule the procedure with a physician.

The brothers from the Missouri grocery chain informed us that they would showcase our product as their principal beef product if we would provide a wholesale price less than that of beef from the major companies. This was a breakthrough opportunity to leap from being a successful niche product to a dominant beef brand, showcased in grocery stores for a broad consumer base. I negotiated with the brothers while looking at whether we could shave our overhead to sell at a cut-rate price. My plan was to offer the same discount price to any retailer who would substitute our beef for the majors' with the goal of becoming the number-one beef company. And that was looking more and more feasible.

I worked with all my department heads to cut costs. I made staff cutbacks. I also made several trips to St. Louis with my corporate lawyers to negotiate an ironclad commitment from the brothers to feature our products front and center in all of their stores for three years in exchange for a discounted whole-sale price. Every time the deal began to unravel, I got it back on track by sheer force of willpower. If I had delegated any of the details of the negotiations to my subordinates, it never would have come together. Whenever the brothers began to waver, I reminded them of the sacrifices my company was making to give them a favorable price arrangement. In the end, when we shook hands, signed the papers and drank champagne, everyone understood that I, and I alone, had made it all happen.

With the Missouri grocery deal completed, I moved to leverage it by approaching the other major supermarket chains. After getting confidentiality agreements from each one providing that they would not share information with one another, I put my plane to good use, traveling from one corporate headquarters to another – negotiating, negotiating. I did not intend to reach a deal with all of them because we did not have sufficient cattle stock to supply all of them. Instead I focused on getting contracts with the highest-profile, most trustworthy chains.

Traveling from place to place wore me down. Fatigue, nausea, irritability, sleeplessness. I ignored it all, refusing to let it affect my performance. I reminded myself that I was still young, even though some days I felt old, burdened by the immense responsibilities of the company I created. I told myself that I was doing this to give illness free lives to American meat consumers, to provide jobs to my thousands of employees and to create tens of thousands of jobs for those who provided services to my company, employees and their families.

The deals came together. My customers' greed – the opportunity to buy beef products at a lower wholesale price and sell them at the same price as the majors – made the deals happen. In the end, the big grocery chains didn't care a whit about providing healthy meat to the public; what they cared about was a bigger profit margin.

During these months of negotiations, I didn't forget I was pregnant; I just ignored it. The work was so overwhelming that I could not risk the possibility I would be unable to do it for even a few days as a result of the procedure. Of course,

I had the means to get a qualified physician to do it anytime, anywhere even when the pregnancy progressed beyond the early stage. But I kept putting it off and by making some minor adjustments with my wardrobe, no one could tell, and most of the time, I didn't think about it.

Since renewing our friendship, Jane had become relentless about keeping in touch. Every day, I was inundated with her texts, emails and calls. She was annoying, but I could not help being touched by her loyalty and love. She didn't ask for anything, wouldn't even let me pay for the Cabo trip, insisting we go Dutch. She just wanted my friendship, and I had to acknowledge that I needed hers.

Late one Sunday night, she showed up at my house.

Leading me back into my kitchen, she rummaged through the built-in wine cooler until she found a white French burgundy that met her standards, opened it, poured two glasses, and sat at the island, serenely relaxed, as if it was her own house.

"You look better then you've ever looked in your life," she exclaimed. "Your face is filled out, your complexion is rosy, you're not wearing those severe clothes. You must be getting great sex."

"No sex. No time for that." I gave her a detailed account of my business dealings over the past months.

"Congratulations. You are the most extraordinary woman of the twenty-first century."

"You came over here just to ridicule me?"

"Well, I did hope I could tease you a little tonight, but I mean it, sweetie. Now, tell me more. What else is going on?"

"That's it, Jane. That is my life."

"Have you had any contact with that gentleman fisherman that you met in Cabo?"

"No, I don't even know his name. He was married, anyway, and I'm not getting into that kind of mess. Tell me what's happening with you."

Jane called the next day when I was in a staff meeting. When I didn't respond, she texted, telling me to call her about an urgent matter.

"What is it, Jane?" I asked, as I walked out of the meeting down the hallway back towards my office.

"Aurora," she said in an accusatory manner. "You didn't drink your wine last night."

"That's the urgent matter! I didn't waste it. I poured it back in the bottle. But you know, I can afford to pour it down the sink if I want."

"You're pregnant! I knew something was different about you."

"I'm not pregnant, Jane."

"I'm coming over there now. You tell them to let me in when I arrive."

Before I could protest she hung up. I contemplated barring her from the building but I couldn't do it.

When she arrived at my office, I thought she was going to embrace me. Instead she yanked my blouse up to my neck and placed her hand on my belly.

"You are! You can't get away with lies with me. I know you too well."

"It's not a lie. I don't lie, Jane. I'm taking care of it next week."

"You're certainly taking your time about it. How many months?"

"It's not too late for me to fix it. I've been too busy."

"Alright, sweetie. I'll go with you and hold your hand. Give me the details." She pulled her phone from her purse, waiting for me to give her the information for her calendar.

"I'll text it to you."

She stared at me skeptically. "You don't even have it scheduled."

"I will, I will."

"When you're eight months? You're already, what, five months gone?"

I couldn't look at her. "Six."

"Aurora!" She shook her head at me. "I think you want it."

She wore me out. I didn't respond.

She studied me. "Well, why not? Have the baby. You need something in your life."

"Absolutely not."

"I know you better than anyone, Aurora. There's no one more organized and focused than you. If you wanted to get rid of this baby, you would've done so the minute you found out you were pregnant. Listen to me – I know what you want – you want this kid."

This startled me. I had pretty much blocked out any emotional feelings since I split up with Malcolm. Despite myself, I had to consider the possibility that she was right.

"How would this look to everyone?" I asked.

"Aurora, you are one of the masters of the universe. You

can do whatever you want and the media will talk about how amazing you are. They'll say you're the epitome of the new woman who doesn't need a man to have a baby and still be the most successful chick on the planet."

And so, I did it. A quiet, pretty baby boy. I never stopped working; I was on the phone with colleagues a few hours after his birth. We set up a nursery down the hall from my office, complete with soundproof walls and a full-time nanny who looked like a corporate assistant, except I paid her a lot more than my own assistant (whom I paid a low six-figure salary).

I couldn't get enough of the baby. I took him and the Nanny with me on the corporate plane on every business trip. If anyone – customers or employees – looked down on this, I didn't give a shit.

With Baby, life continued as normal but it was a new normal – a much better normal. I knew I wasn't a regular mother; I had a tendency at times to forget about him. But when I was with him, walking down the hall to see him or holding him on the plane or going back to the hotel where he waited for me, it was sweet, so sweet.

I didn't believe in God, but if there was one, he tested me after I had the baby. His message seemed to be: your work will not be easy; there will never ever be a letup; every day will be hard; if you let your guard down, you will fail and lose it all.

I liked to make surprise visits to every part of my business – the distant cattle lots, cornfields, regional sales offices, retail outlets. But the visits I looked most forward to were to the lab. This was where my heart was. But I didn't visit often, because the lab was the one place where I had a manager whom I could trust, Carol Franklin. She'd been with me since the beginning and had the professional attributes that I wanted in my managers — focus, creativity, and loyalty.

This unannounced visit to the lab turned out to be more of a surprise for me than for my employees. Carol was not there. When I made inquiries, I was told she had just left the company, that they didn't want to disturb me during my "maternity leave" (which they didn't realize lasted only during my labor and delivery).

I called my Human Resources VP.

"It happened last week," he said. "Every time, I stopped down to tell you, your office was empty. I had to fire her."

"You should have talked to me before you did this."

"I've been interviewing possible replacements. I'll have a list for you next week."

"Why didn't you talk to me about firing her beforehand?"

"Ms. Blanc, you have repeatedly told me that you wanted me to make hiring and firing decisions, and not bother you with them. And this one was clear-cut; she had to be fired."

"I'm listening."

"Last year, she terminated one of the lab assistants. The employee was incompetent, but Carol mishandled it."

"You fired Carol because she fired an incompetent employee!"

"Please, Ms. Blanc, let me walk you through the details."

"I've heard all the details I need to know."

"Please."

I had to control myself not to yell at him. "Go ahead."

"The terminated lab assistant was African-American. He filed a race discrimination claim with the EEOC. Ordinarily, filing of such a claim means nothing – terminated employees often file baseless claims."

"That's right, a baseless claim," I said.

"As a matter of procedure, we do an internal investigation whenever an employee claims that racial epitaphs were used in the workplace. The EEOC charge said that Carol got frustrated with the employee and called him the N-word."

"That's ludicrous. It's goddamn libelous. I'm going to sue him."

"I hired outside counsel to conduct the investigation because it was so delicate and I wanted it done right. This is a lawyer I know and trust. I've used him a lot at my previous companies. He is one of the best – always has the company's back."

"I've got a busy morning. Get to the point."

"Two other lab assistants heard her say it – that is, call this employee the N-word. And the third lab assistant told the investigator that Carol confided in her that blacks were not cut out for scientific work and that this one must've gotten in Stanford on an affirmative-action program, because he was so stupid."

"You believed all this?"

"Doesn't matter what I believe. Those were the results of investigation and it was conclusive. There were three witnesses."

"You should've gotten Carol some counseling."

"I asked the attorney what we should do. He assured me that

the results of the investigation were covered by attorney-client privilege and that he would proceed to defend the case. Since we had such a weak case, he suggested that we might want to try to work out a confidential monetary settlement with the fired employee."

"Good, that's the right approach."

"We tried to settle but the ex-employee wanted one million and a public apology. In other words, the whole thing would've been in the newspapers. I asked him whether we had any other options."

"Right, other options."

"The lawyer said the company could probably insulate itself from liability by firing Carol and taking the position that she had acted outside the scope of her authority. In other words, the company has not discriminated – she had – and once we learned this, we fired her."

"This lawyer recommended that we fire Carol?"

"He didn't recommend it; he just explained our options. It was my decision."

"Your decision! You should have come to me."

"Ms. Blanc, everyone in that department knew about this. They knew that Carol was a bigot. As a company, we cannot condone race discrimination. It was an easy decision. She had to be fired."

"The only person that has to be fired is you. Get the fuck out of here. I want you out right now."

He laughed, thinking I was joking.

"I'm sorry," I said, calming myself. "I can't trust you anymore. She was my most valuable employee. You should have known that. You can say you resigned. I'll write you a good reference. You'll get another job."

After he left, I asked my assistant to track down Carol. When I got her on the phone, I apologized for the actions of our incompetent lawyers and human resource people, and told her to come back to work tomorrow. She asked if we could talk in my office tomorrow.

I promised myself that my next Human Resource VP would actually understand that his only job was to hire and keep the most talented employees, with no ethical bullshit mixed in.

Carol, usually self-possessed, was fidgeting in the chair in front of my desk. Her dyed blond hair was more artificial-looking than ever. She had always tried to be like me but today her face was strained and she appeared older than a woman in her early forties. "Aurora, I appreciate that you're asking me to come back but I can't."

I shook my head, rejecting her decision. "I want you back; I need you back; everyone respects you. Don't worry about the idiotic lawsuit – I'll pay them off."

"Aurora, it's something else. That kid who died, I..."

I cut her off. "We won that lawsuit and I just found out this morning they're not appealing. It's over and done with. Pure harassment. That's what happens with all big companies; you get sued by the loonies."

"I lie awake at night. I've started taking anxiety medication." She began crying. "I read this book – a book written by a doctor about the history of gene research. It really upset me,

Aurora. I mean, I already knew everything in there, but the way he said it – made me reconsider what we have done."

"Carol! You have examined and re-examined our work countless times and found nothing wrong. This EEOC lawsuit or whatever it is has really upset you."

"No, it's our seed." She said she was troubled by how we used the new scientific tool, CRIPSR-Cas9, to change the corn genome. "Thousands of genes carrying instructions on how to give life to corn – we completely altered it, not a little, but radically."

"We improved it, Carol," I said.

"We know what the specific genetic instructions say from the genes that we inserted in the corn, but we have no idea about the rest – the inadvertent instructions, the ones that spun off of what we genetically engineered." She wiped her eyes. "Aurora, I've been trying, ever since I heard about that child dying, but I can't determine what those instructions say; I can't see it – how they affect the functioning of our corn seed. It's impossible to tell because we inserted DNA with thousands of new instructions into the original seed. I'm sick with anxiety. I can hardly get out of bed, Aurora."

"Carol, I'm the one who developed the corn seed, not you. It's safe, I'm telling you, it's completely ok. I designed genetic instructions to produce healthy meat, that's all."

She shook her head, and pressed her fingers against her tired face. "We don't know what we did. We did so much to it." She looked away, refusing to make eye contact with me.

"There is no indication that it causes any harm. You're overreacting with no basis, Carol. You are a scientist – think like a scientist. "

"That book made me think. It talked about sickle cell anemia, which, as you know, is caused by tiny alterations in gene encoding. It took scientists years to figure out that a seemingly inconsequential change in the gene instructions, replacing one amino acid with another in the protein of people who inherited the disease – how that one minuscule change in the genome instructions caused devastating consequences. For people who have this mutation, their blood can't flow through their veins without excruciating pain."

"Carol, what are you talking about? Sickle cell is an inherited disease, no one genetically engineered it."

She began scratching her scalp. "Aurora, you know what I'm saying: one change can have inadvertent consequences."

"You take some time, Carol, as much as you need. I'll keep you on salary as long as you want. If you decide you don't want to come back, that's OK – I'll keep paying you. Do you understand what I'm saying, Carol?"

She nodded.

I never saw her again.

CHAPTER 2

My life settled into a new routine. I wasn't happy in the way normal people are, but it was the best it had ever been for me. I cut back on travel, left the office at six, and spent every night at home with Baby and Nanny. Of course, I was still focused on the company, determined not to let anything slow its growth. The business was my obsession. But I liked being with Baby. He adored me. I was the center of his universe. It was unconditional love. I saw myself as a good mom just like my own mom. Like her, I was there for my child, and that would never change. I watched him develop, both a biological process and a miracle. The satisfaction of observing him was equal, perhaps even better, than my business success. In a way, they overlapped because one gave me the money to give the other everything he needed to be happy and secure. He would not have to fight to grow up like me.

It's true that I didn't have the patience to play with him — rattle his toys or read to him. I couldn't change his diapers; I was too squeamish to look at baby shit. And I didn't feed him; it was kind of disgusting to watch him eat. I didn't walk him in his stroller, either; it was not safe for me to be going around unprotected with a baby. I couldn't hold him for long; it was distracting for me to work with my arms around him. I had Nanny calm him when he was crying, because he seemed to cry more when I tried to comfort him. What I could do that no one else could do was be his mother.

When I was young, I was the outsider, a social outcast.

In high school, I had tried to make friends, but I didn't have the ability to talk about the trivial things that girls discussed. I tried, but I couldn't do it. And, of course, I was big, overweight. I told myself that I didn't care, but I did. In college, I was accepted by the science students, the nerds. When I lost the weight and got in shape, it didn't change anything, except, of course, there were now men who paid to fuck me. I was always on the outside until I became successful and then it all changed. Everybody wanted to be with me, wanted my attention and approval. Now I was the coolest kid in the class and I didn't care. It wasn't real. But the baby and the company were real.

My lawyer called. He'd been talking to the Alameda County District Attorney's office about the perjury referral from the court. According to my lawyer, the DA people were apologetic about any inconvenience but felt that they needed to do some kind of obligatory investigation to satisfy the Judge – a short interview with me conducted by a staff investigator at their offices. My lawyer said he did not handle this kind of "white collar law" so he was bringing in a top- notch specialist to go with me to the interview. This lawyer, James Cohen, formerly the U.S. Attorney for the Northern District of California, represented corporate executives accused of "financial problems."

"You mean, he's a criminal lawyer," I said. "Is that really necessary?"

"Probably not, but I like to be careful since perjury is a felony, even if it is rarely prosecuted."

Mr. Cohen insisted on meeting me in person. In contrast to my company lawyer and his team, who were discreet and deferential to me, this man was overbearing, disrespectful, a know-it-all, and a slob. His stomach hung over his belt, his shirt pulled at the buttons.

When I began to tell him what had happened, he said he got the whole picture – that I had developed the seed alone; then lost whatever notes I may have had; that the company had no records at all about the seed's development or formula. The main problem, he said, was that my former partner Harry Sumner had contradicted me, testifying at his deposition that the Company had records on the seed formulation stored in a company server and that information had been provided to the lab assistants on iPads. He understood that the server and the iPads no longer existed at the time I gave my deposition testimony so technically I had told the truth; but my testimony did not go down well with the Judge and that's why he had referred the matter to the DA's office for investigation. Cohen agreed with my lawyer that the case would probably be dropped by the DA, because perjury was rarely prosecuted in civil cases. Still, he said, we needed to handle this matter carefully.

"Of course, I will be careful," I said, annoyed. "I'm always careful."

"Good. I'll call the DA investigator and tell them that you are not coming in to talk to them. I'll tell them you wanted to, but I wouldn't let you."

"You want me to take the Fifth?"

"I don't want to take any risks."

"Mr. Cohen, I don't think you understand," I said, getting

angry. "I make the decisions. You just make recommendations. I have absolutely nothing to hide. I forgot about the stupid iPads. I told the truth at that deposition – we had no records on the seed development at that time. I was absolutely and totally honest. And I'm going tell that to the DA."

That evening at home in the kitchen, eating a salad while Nanny sat across from me, holding my child in her lap, I told her about my conversation with Mr. Cohen. Since I now spent more personal time with Nanny than anyone else, she had become my confidante.

She asked, "Why wouldn't your lawyer want you to go in to show them you have nothing to hide?"

"Because he says since these DA interviews are under oath he doesn't want me talking about complex things that happened a long time ago and innocently saying something that could cause problems."

"Hmm. You mean, like accidentally lying under oath."

"Right. But he's wrong. If I don't go in, they'll think I'm hiding something. I need to take care of this myself. Whenever I rely on somebody else, they mess it up."

I did not like that the DA interview was at the courthouse where the dead child lawsuit had taken place. Because the lawsuit had been dismissed, I'd never had to go there. I met Cohen in the parking lot outside the Depression-era courthouse, and impatiently listened to him repeat my interview script four times before he would let me go into the building to get it over with. We waited in the security line behind the drab lawyers and then waited some more in the shabbily furnished government conference room. Finally, a middle-aged man appeared and introduced himself as an investigator and asked us to wait a few more minutes for his superior. We sat for another forty-five minutes, while Cohen made small talk about his second home in Montana and I tried to work on my phone. Eventually, a fortyish woman, the district attorney, entered and told the investigator to proceed.

The investigator placed a recording device on the table, and then told me that my testimony was under oath. In response to his questions, I said that there were no notes or any other records in the company's possession about the corn seed development or formula. As to the iPads, I told him I'd simply forgotten about them as they had been created to guide the lab assistants during the early days of the company, and later thrown away when they were no longer needed. I stressed that I had been totally truthful when I stated that there were no records of the corn seed formula.

As we were leaving, Cohen said, "The district attorney was in the room because of your celebrity. She wanted to make sure things were done right. She's running for reelection in a rough campaign and can't afford to have problems with a respected, high-profile person. If she were seen as picking on you, it would be bad press. And, let me say, you did a good job. You followed my instructions to the letter."

My social life consisted exclusively of Nanny and Baby. Baby treated her like a second mom which was okay with me because I couldn't be there all the time. Sometimes it seemed that Baby actually preferred her over me which was annoying, but

I was confident that once the child understood what was what, she would treat me as her only mother.

Nanny liked going out to dinner since she was at home all day, and I tried to keep her happy. So, on Saturday night, I let her select her favorite restaurant, a retro-hippie place near us. Actually, I liked going out with her and Baby, who was almost always a quiet little dinner companion.

I thought it was a God-engineered coincidence that Ellen Fraser was there. I hadn't seen her since Professor Fraser's funeral, but she looked the same, older but still vibrant. Normally, I wait for people come up to me but this time I walked across the restaurant to her table where she was sitting with another lady. She didn't recognize me until I identified myself; apparently, she didn't read *Vogue* or other fashion magazines, which would have kept her up-to-date on me. She was as warm as ever, acting as if she had seen me only yesterday.

"I was going to call you, but I had no idea how to get hold of you," she said. "I wanted to tell you that a government employee telephoned me last month to ask about my husband's work files. He said the University told him that the files had been turned over to me after my husband's stroke. The government fellow said they were looking into my husband's work on corn seeds."

"What did you tell them?"

"Why, the truth, of course."

"The truth?"

"Yes. That my husband developed the fat-free meat corn seed in the Stanford lab with you as his lab assistant; that I gave you the files on hard drive when he got sick. I'm assuming you used those for your business, although I didn't say that to the government man. I just told him what I knew."

I was silent.

"Of course, you and I know that he never intended to use that work for a commercial product. He thought it was too risky. I guess you didn't care about that, Aurora."

"Our corn seed is different from his work." I tried to smile pleasantly.

"I'm sure it is, dear. Well, it was very nice seeing you." She resumed eating.

CHAPTER 3

When I was at Stanford and for a few years after graduation, I maintained four email accounts, including my student email. But now, I couldn't remember the providers, much less the usernames and passwords. Sunday morning, hours after I'd run into Ellen Fraser, I woke at 4 AM and began going through boxes in my basement. When I'd moved into this house with Malcolm, I'd had no time to pack, so I'd sent an employee to my apartment to box everything up. I hadn't opened any of it since. After going through boxes of old photos and books, I found, under a pile of power cords, my old Dell laptop.

I found a matching power cord and turned the laptop on. I looked in the address book and found four addresses that I had used on my AOL, Hotmail, Stanford and Yahoo email accounts. I tried to open the Stanford student account, but it was no longer in existence and I assumed all those emails had been deleted. I successfully opened the other accounts, but only AOL still had my emails. In the AOL emails, I found a file titled "Miscellaneous;" under it was a single email, with no header, containing an attachment. I opened the attachment, and there it was: Professor Fraser's corn seed research, the file that Ellen had given me after his stroke. I hit the delete button and then emptied the trash. I exhaled. I was safe. No one would find this ancient account, and even if they did, the email with the corn seed information was gone.

I was no longer concerned about Ellen telling the investigator that her husband had developed the corn seed. After all, it was her word against mine. Moreover, what did she know? – she was just a professor's wife, who never went into the lab and had no science background. If the investigator asked me about it, I would explain that Mrs. Fraser was confused and misinformed. Yes, I'd worked with her husband, but not on corn seeds, and any data she may have given me after his stroke was unrelated to that and long gone.

The following morning, in my office, I felt anxious. Self-doubt was not part of my makeup, but my tampering with that email bothered me. I knew a lot about bioengineering, but nothing about computer data retrieval. What if they could trace what I did yesterday? Was it some kind of crime to mess with an email account like that? This whole absurd investigation was bullshit, but had I created a problem by getting rid of that work file? Did I do it only because I would be humiliated if it came out that the corn seed formula came from Professor Fraser? If that did come out, it would no big deal. So what if I developed the corn seed with a Stanford professor? That fact wouldn't hurt our product at all. I should not have deleted that email.

I decided the most discreet way to fix this would be to call one of my IT people to determine if they could restore the email. I randomly chose a name from the IT staff directory and asked my assistant to tell him to come right to my office. When the young man showed up, I opened the AOL account on my office desktop, showed him the empty "Miscellaneous" file where the email had been, and explained that I had accidentally deleted it and emptied the trash.

He asked if he could sit at my desk and work on it. I took a walk and when I came back, he asked if I had done the deletion on this desktop computer. I explained that I opened the account on old laptop at home, where I unintentionally deleted it. He said that it was a long shot but he would like to have the old laptop.

The next morning, I brought in the laptop, and the young man sat in the corner of my office with it while I watched.

"Is this it, Ms. Blanc?" I looked at the screen and there it was – Professor Fraser's work file.

"That's it. How did you retrieve it?"

"We got lucky. Once emails are permanently deleted, they're gone. But this attachment had been previously downloaded on this laptop so it was there. At some point, you must have thought it was important to download it."

"Can you put it back in the AOL file under 'Miscellaneous?"

He bent over the laptop for a minute. "Done!"

"Thank you. And don't tell anyone you've been working with me. You understand, don't you?"

"Understood.

James Cohen, my overbearing lawyer, called to report that the DA office was about to close the investigation. However, as a matter of routine and to satisfy the Judge that they had done a diligent job, the DA's office wanted to review all of my company emails. I reminded him that they already had all that.

"I told them that, but they want it provided again," he said.

"Tell them no. They're wasting our time and their time."

"That would be a mistake. It would piss them off. There's

nothing to hide. Before we turn them over, you'll double-check everything and so will my team."

I hated this guy, but I didn't disagree with his judgment. I was not going to snatch defeat from the jaws of victory.

My assistant pulled all my company emails and sent them to Cohen for review, who passed them on to the DA.

Months went by and I did not think about the investigation until Cohen called. "They want to interview you again."

"I thought this was over."

"They never told us it was over. I don't want you to talk to them."

"Why?"

"Same reason as before. It's under oath and you may inadvertently say something that gets you in trouble."

"That's what you said last time and everything worked out fine when I spoke to them."

"Still not a good idea. I can tell them that enough is enough; you're busy running a large corporation and we cooperated above and beyond the call of duty. I know best, Aurora."

"Please set up a meeting with them, Mr. Cohen. I will make myself available at their convenience."

The second interview followed the same procedure as the first. This time only the investigator was present. After advising me again that failing to tell the truth in the interview is a crime, he asked the same questions again. I confirmed that I developed the genetically modified corn seed; that I had provided all of my emails to the DA's office just as I had done in the lawsuit; and that there were no records of the corn seed formula other than the iPad data that we previously discussed. I was ready when he asked about whether I had worked on the corn seed as a student at Stanford under Professor Fraser. I told him that I did not, but I did remember talking about the possibility of healthy fat-free beef with Professor Fraser and his wife. I was also prepared for his question about whether any downloaded files were given to me by Mrs. Fraser. Yes, I now remembered that after his stroke, she had given me a disk to review and organize but that I never got to it, that I no longer had it, and must've lost it. I told him about the sudden death of my mom and how I took some time off and didn't do much of anything related to bioengineering for a while.

"Did you subsequently look for the information on the disk that Mrs. Fraser gave you?"

I hesitated. I had not discussed the AOL work file with Cohen, so I didn't have his input on the best way to answer this. I decided the smartest approach would be to fudge it.

"I'm sure I did. I don't have a specific recollection of it."

He pressed me. "Was there corn seed research there?"

"No," I calmly responded.

Cohen thought the interview went well. Of course, he knew nothing about my AOL email and I was not about to share that with him. Cohen told me that we should soon expect to hear that the matter would be closed.

Weeks went by with no news. "No news is good news," Cohen assured me. Even though his assurances meant little to me, I did believe the whole matter was behind me.

It was Cohen who brought *The New York Times* article to my attention. I never read *The Times* – much too left-wing for me. Entitled "The Problem With Perjury" it was about the increase in recent years of lying by corporate executives before courts, grand juries, and investigators. The article hypothesized that this so-called disregard for the truth was undermining the entire justice system which depends on truthful citizens. While common criminals have always lied, false statements by the pillars of society were a new phenomenon. While perjury is a felony under federal and most state laws, corporate leaders blithely break the law without any concern of being prosecuted and, according to the article, Judges and prosecutors usually turn a blind eye to it, since the cases are so hard to prove and expensive to litigate. However, that had been changing lately as reflected by several successfully prosecuted high-profile perjury cases as well as more government scrutiny of incredible statements by executives under oath. The article concluded by listing six prominent individuals currently under investigation for potential perjury, including Aurora Blanc.

Cohen said he was outraged that someone from the DA's office had leaked this. He told me that he had screamed at the DA, who assured him that the leak did not come from her or from the investigator. It's a big office, she told him, and people talk; it's unavoidable. As to the status of investigation, the DA told him that it was dormant; she did not say when it would be officially closed.

My chief financial officer asked to see me. He had heard from our sales VP about the new price program we were rolling out.

"Fifty percent off any beef purchase up to $75 for anyone using food stamps for the purchase? Am I getting the right information?" He was distraught.

"That's correct information. It works perfectly because we provide an unprecedented discount to the people who most need our product for their health but can least afford it. And the government is, in effect, making sure that only people in economic need qualify by giving food stamps only to them. It's one of my best ideas."

"Pardon my language, Ms. Blanc, but we'll lose a fucking fortune on this. You know better than I that the markup on our beef is minimal. We'll take a hit every time somebody buys our product with food stamps. I've run the numbers based on various scenarios of how much we are likely to sell. Every way we look at it, it hurts our bottom line."

"Thank you, but we're doing it."

"You owe it to your employees not to put the company in jeopardy."

"You are overstepping your bounds. This is my company. I can do whatever I want with it, including putting it out of business. But that's not going to happen."

"I'm emailing you all the projections. Will you look at them?"

"No need to. I already know what they look like. I can do my own math."

"Ms. Blanc, I cannot let you do this."

"You can go to the Board if you want but they have no power. It's a private company and I control them. You are a good CFO but if you don't like this, you can quit. I'll give you a good reference even though you have no vision whatsoever."

The man's hands were shaking when he left my office. It

was good to be rid of him. He thought he was smart, but all he could see was numbers. He missed the big picture.

I held a press conference in the lobby of our building, in front of the Healthy Heart logo, to announce the Food Stamps discount. The media loved it, especially *The New York Time*s. They did a Sunday front page article on it – how the Company and its founder were putting humanitarian considerations over profits; how we were acting to dramatically improve the health of all Americans where government had failed to do anything to limit or even label unhealthy foods; how my public spirit action was comparable to Andrew Carnegie and John D Rockefeller when they established national libraries, universities and worldwide medical and health initiatives, even though I was not nearly in the same economic category as those titans of industry. According to the article, I represented the best and brightest of young American leadership, an eleemosynary spirit and a shining example that all corporate executives should strive to emulate.

CHAPTER 4

My ability to read people is good and, as it turned out, I was right about Cohen. I was apoplectic when he told me that he had been having talks with the DA behind my back.

"Look, Aurora, she wants to help and she's been very reasonable."

"Reasonable! She wants me to plead guilty to a felony. You consider that reasonable."

"It's just a technical plea to resolve this thing and get it behind us. She's under pressure to do something. Her investigator believed you committed perjury and she says the whole office knows about it. If she lets you off with nothing, it will leak to the papers. She's facing a tough election, and needs to give you a slap on the hand."

"A criminal felony – you must be out of your mind, Mr. Cohen. Absolutely not."

"You take the plea deal, and they will recommend no jail time. You run a private company so it will not affect your job or the corporation. Once it's over, you can spin it to the press, you know, say that there was confusion about facts that occurred a long time ago. No one will blink. You are riding so high in public opinion – this will not affect you at all. And it will be over and done with."

"How long have these negotiations been going on?"

"It doesn't matter."

"It matters to me. You've been negotiating a felony plea with a prosecutor without telling me."

"For your own good."

"For my own good, I'm firing you. And do not talk to that prosecutor ever again about my case!"

After he hung up, I was so enraged that I told my assistant to find some scotch in the building and bring me a big glass of it.

I hired a new criminal lawyer, Larry Ellis, also a former U.S. Attorney. I told him to tell the DA to go fuck herself. "If they want to go after me, let them. I don't think they will."

Several weeks elapsed, and nothing happened. Then my new lawyer called me to say that the DA had contacted him, urging us to work something out, hinting that she would consider a more favorable deal than the previous one. She told them they had a strong case against me but they did not want to use their limited resources to prosecute an expensive, high-visibility case. It was better for all of us, she told him, to quietly work something out.

"It would be better for her, not me, to quietly work something out. Tell her no."

My confidence in not settling with the DA was not what it seemed. As a scientist, I looked at things dispassionately and objectively. As I assessed it, if I settled the case, it would forever put a cloud over my accomplishments and successes. I would be a convicted felon – a scarlet F stamped on my chest. Moreover, the DA had much to lose by going after me. I was an icon, admired internationally for my science and humanitarian food program for the poor. I established the Food Stamps discount because I was a good, compassionate person. Yes, it was expensive and took a dent out of our profits but they were my profits. As an investment, I knew, it was worth its weight in gold because it made me a saint – someone the DA would dare not prosecute when push came to shove. I had everything going for me: the fact that perjury cases are hardly ever brought; the expense and burden on the prosecutor's office in bringing one; the difficulty in proving such a case, since, as my lawyers told me, the DA would have to show that I intended to lie. It was not enough to simply prove that there was a false statement. From any objective view of point, I had made the right decision.

It upset me when my lawyer found out that the DA had taken the next step: a grand jury was now reviewing my case. That did not mean it would go any further, however; I still believed I'd made the right decision. So, it was a jolt the day that I learned that I had been indicted for perjury. I was afraid. I knew that this would be a fight to the death, but that was when I was at my best.

My new lawyer asked for permission to inquire whether the plea deal was still available to me, and I told him to go ahead. But the deal was off the table. The DA would accept a guilty plea, but would no longer waive a jail sentence. Instead, she would recommend that the Judge use his discretion to determine an appropriate penalty. In other words, even with a plea deal, I was at risk of going to jail.

I wish I could say that my friends hurried in to support me but I had no friends other than Jane, who, of course, offered her undying support, and Nanny, who stood by me, prepared to throw herself in front of a bus for me, if necessary. No one in the company said a single thing to me about it. I'm sure they were just too uncomfortable to mention it. But the media, the motherfucking media, had a field day with the story, running long, detailed articles in the business section of every major paper, talking about it on the network cable news. I did my best to spin it: giving a press conference declaring my innocence, blaming the publicity-seeking District Attorney for trying to get elected, despite her mediocre record, by prosecuting me. I assured our employees the case would not affect our company. I would continue to run it as usual.

In the weeks leading up to trial, we didn't see any adverse impact on business. We were not a public company so there was no stock price to worry about. Sales remained steady. The public apparently didn't care.

I continued to live my life in my normal way – working, working, working. But when the trial happened, my ability to keep a cool head under pressure and to look at events dispassionately deserted me. When we arrived at the courthouse the first morning, there were reporters and camera crews at the entrance, yelling unintelligible questions. When I was seated in the courtroom at the defendants table and my lawyers began choosing a jury, I couldn't follow what they were talking about. When I looked around the crowded courtroom, all the faces blurred together and I had difficulty separating the friendly from the unfriendly. I didn't see Jane the first two days. I texted her and told her I needed her.

She showed up the next day, hugging me in the hallway. Her presence calmed me, but I still could not properly concen-

trate on what was happening. My lawyer talked to me about
the jury selection decisions, but I couldn't pay attention. And
on day three, or maybe it was day four, when the lawyers made
their opening statements to the jury, the DA, who was trying
the case herself, told the jurors I had lied, lied and lied – but I
couldn't follow the specifics of her speech. And then my lawyer, Mr. Ellis, cool and calm, denied everything, repeating that
this case was all political grandstanding by the DA.

Jane insisted we go out for dinner that night. She picked
me up at home, apparently to make sure I wouldn't back out.
She tried to make small talk but I couldn't engage. My heart
kept pumping hard, as if it were trying to escape my chest. I
wanted to lie down her on her car seat.

"Talk to me, Aurora," she demanded.

"I feel I deserve this," I said.

"You're not saying you're guilty, Aurora? I know you're
not."

"Not legally guilty. I didn't do what they're accusing me
of. But maybe, I never should've gotten my success. Maybe, it
was all a big fluke."

"That's crazy talk."

"I just can't summon the energy to fight this. I have no
strength. In that courtroom, I have to work so hard just to stay
awake."

"Sweetie, you're depressed. It's physiological and com-
pletely understandable after everything you've been through.
Let's go to my house and I'll get you something, some Zoloft.
No, that takes weeks to kick in. Better to give OxyContin.
That'll perk you up right away, I promise you."

"I don't do drugs."

"You're a zombie and this will make you feel better. I use it when I'm blue. If it doesn't help you, stop taking it. I've always taken care of you. Just listen to Jane."

"What's going to happen to me, Jane?"

"Nothing if you pull yourself together. Remember when we went to Shanghai and you got your company back from that billionaire guy? You accomplished the impossible. You're the toughest girl of them all."

I listened, but it felt like she was talking to me from another room.

I took the pills Dr. Jane prescribed. I felt better, in a surrealistic way. In court, I was more alert, but I felt like the proceedings had nothing to do with me. She was probably right to give me the pills — at least now, I could cope.

Harry was the prosecution's first witness.

"No surprise," my lawyer whispered in my ear.

It was not a surprise, but his appearance was painful. I knew he had given a deposition in the civil suit, but he'd had no choice. Now he was testifying voluntarily, for the prosecution. He repeated what he said in the deposition: during the early days of the company, the corn seed formula and other information was put on the company server by me and made available to the lab assistants for their work. I understood that this contradicted my testimony in the civil case that there were no company records about the formula but I had been truthful at that time because I believed there were no records. Harry's testimony was too weak a thread to convict me of deliberately lying.

But the next part of his testimony shocked me. Harry told the court that when we were working together at Stanford, I had told him I was working on the corn seed under Fraser's supervision and that Fraser had shelved the project, because he was concerned that it was untested and the consequences unknown.

On the witness stand, Harry was confident, smug. He knew exactly what he was doing – hitting me in the most vulnerable place, testifying that the corn seed was not mine. I felt everything crashing down around me.

My lawyer whispered in my ear, "You look upset. Put a neutral expression on your face. This is not bad. Who developed the corn seed is irrelevant here. It's got to be a material misrepresentation for it to be perjury. This doesn't matter."

I understood what he was saying. The civil lawsuit was about whether our product killed the boy, not who developed it, and this case was about whether I deliberately lied about a material fact in that lawsuit. Clearly, I did not. But that was cold comfort to me while Harry sat on the witness stand, trashing my status as the inventor of the Healthy Heart corn seed.

That night, I started feeling better. After all, it was just Harry's word against mine, and who was he but a disgruntled, former business partner who had been out-maneuvered in a corporate buyout? Anyone could see that he was just a cocky twerp. People loved and admired me.

When Ellen Fraser took the witness stand, the prosecutor explained that she was there only because she had been subpoenaed; she had not volunteered as prosecution witness.

She was composed, almost serene, and I knew that she could hurt me. I had to force myself to concentrate as the DA questioned her, bringing out the long- ago dinner at the Fraser's house when I was a student and the lengthy conversation about designing GMO animal feed to produce healthy beef. That didn't worry me because I had said the same thing in the DA interviews. Then Ellen said that she had given Professor Fraser's disc files to me after his stroke. I had also told the investigator about this in my second interview.

The DA said to her, "Did your husband talk about his professional relationship with his student Aurora Blanc?"

"He talked about her all the time."

"What did he say?"

My lawyer objected for reasons I couldn't understand, but the Judge said he would allow it.

"He thought she was the most talented student he'd ever had. He took a special interest in her for that reason and because she had pulled herself out of poverty against tremendous odds. He gave her projects to encourage her, to help her grow. This was work that he paid for out of our savings; it was not funded by the University. We discussed it in detail because of the economic consequences to us. But he considered her to be like a daughter and he wanted to help her blossom as a researcher and scientist. He had developed some innovative ideas in his field and he decided to have her do the lab work to see if they could be done."

"What specifically did he have her do?"

"Objection," barked my lawyer. "This is all hearsay. The

witness has no direct knowledge of what work was done or not done in the Stanford lab. She cannot testify about what occurred outside of her direct observation."

The prosecutor tried to respond but the Judge cut her off.

"It is hearsay. Objection sustained."

"All right," said the prosecutor. "Mrs. Fraser, going back to the disc of files that you gave Ms. Blanc after your husband's stroke, what research projects were on the disc?"

"Only one."

"Hold it!" My lawyer was on his feet. "That's hearsay, too."

The Judge leaned toward Ellen, and softly asked, "How do you know what was on the disc?"

"My husband told me before his stroke that he kept the special research that Aurora was doing separate on his personal laptop and he told me exactly what it was."

"Did you read it yourself?"

"Why, no. No reason to, because he told me all about it."

"That is hearsay, Your Honor," repeated my lawyer.

"I know what hearsay is, counsel. Objection sustained. Next question."

The DA had no more questions. I was elated. They got absolutely nothing from Ellen. My lawyer squeezed my arm. Later, he told me they made a mistake by having the DA prosecute this case. "She doesn't know how to try a case. She never should have called that professor's wife. It made the prosecution look inept in front of the jury."

One of the witnesses on the prosecution list was William Franklin, who was identified as a former employee of my company. I didn't recognize the name, but when he walked up to the witness stand, I knew him.

The DA began her questioning. "By whom are you employed, Mr. Franklin?"

"I'm between jobs."

"What was your most recent job?"

"I worked for Healthy Heart Beef in the IT department."

"Why did you leave?"

"I was terminated as part of a reduction in the work force three months ago."

"Have you ever done any work directly for Aurora Blanc, the defendant in this case?"

My attorney leaned over and whispered to me, "Where is this going?"

I couldn't respond. I felt I was watching the event from a hundred feet in the air.

Franklin shifted in his seat as he glanced at me. "I helped her with some data retrieval several months ago, in September. She asked me if I could restore an email that had a research file that she had deleted."

"Objection, this is more hearsay," my lawyer said.

"No, Your Honor, it's not," the DA responded. "This is an admission against interest on the criminal charges in this case."

My lawyer asked the Judge for permission to approach the bench. After an intense discussion, the two lawyers returned to their seats. My lawyer stared straight ahead, giving me no clue about what had just happened.

"Can you tell us what you did next, Mr. Franklin?" the DA said.

"I looked in the trash for the deleted email, but it was empty. I asked about it and she said she had emptied it out of the trash, too. So, obviously, she had taken some trouble to get rid of it. Generally, it would be gone for good, but I checked her personal computer, an old laptop, and looked through the downloaded files, and there was a file about corn seed research."

"And what, if anything, did Ms. Blanc say when you showed her what you'd found?"

"She said 'Don't tell anyone about this.'"

"Objection Mr. Franklin can't testify about corn seed research."

Before the Judge could say anything, the witness said, "Oh, I'm very familiar with this, because I'd worked there for three years. Yes, this was a scientific research file about the development of the GMO corn seed. But what struck me as strange was that it had all kinds of references to Stanford on it."

"Objection, objection. This is hearsay."

"How do you know this?" The Judge asked.

"Before I told her I'd found it, I read it all the way through."

"It's still hearsay!" my lawyer shouted. "He can't testify about what some document says."

"You can see the document if you want," the young man said. "I made a copy of it. I've got it with me in my briefcase."

I did not take the witness stand in my own defense. My lawyer patiently explained to me what I understood perfectly well – that the submission into evidence of Professor Fraser's corn seed research coupled with my action in deleting it would subject me to withering, harmful cross examination.

He would take no responsibility for the verdict if I testified against his advice.

I sat at the table, anesthetized by OxyContin, trying to maintain a composed demeanor, as the DA delivered her closing argument.

"The Judge will tell you that I have a heavy burden of proof in a perjury case, that it's not enough to show that Ms. Blanc repeatedly lied under oath in the wrongful death case and again during the DA's office investigation, that such conduct is not a crime standing alone. The Judge will tell you that I have to show more than that: specifically, that Aurora Blanc intended to lie, that it was not an oversight or a mistake on her part and that the lie was material – that is, the lie was important to the wrongful death lawsuit. Well, Ladies and Gentlemen of the Jury, we have had no problem showing all of that in spades.

"Ms. Blanc lied to keep the father of the dead little boy from getting the formula behind the genetically modified corn seed that was at the heart of the wrongful death suit. She had a motive, a tremendous incentive, to deceive, because, without it, the little boy's father couldn't begin to prosecute his case. She wanted to shut him down before he could even begin."

My lawyer was wrong when he told me that the DA was a poor trial lawyer. She meticulously, savagely, spelled out what she called my criminal behavior. I had perjured myself, she said, about everything: testifying that there were no company records about the corn seed formula when, in fact, there was a computer server that contained all of it; that there were no corn seed records from Stanford when, in fact, I had the entire corn seed formula on a disk provided by my professor's wife; that I tried to destroy those records at the same time I was lying about their very existence; that I had taken credit for inventing the corn seed that had actually been created by my mentor.

"Ladies and gentlemen, Aurora Blanc believes she is above the law. Our legal system depends on truthful testimony to function but Ms. Blanc thinks the rules do not apply to her. This case is about more than this woman. It's about the pervasive perjury by the elite and powerful who think that the law does not apply to them the way it applies to everyone else. And it is this arrogant disregard for the law that, if left unchecked, will undermine our beautiful criminal justice system – the best in the world. For the system to work, witnesses must tell the truth and let the system bring about a fair and just result. Ms. Blanc tried to game the system, and that is a grave matter – a crime for which she must be called to account."

In his closing statement, my lawyer argued that the prosecution was trying to turn the normal human inability to remember every detail into a criminal activity. He talked about all I had accomplished and how crowded my life had been over the decade since college. How, he said, could Ms. Blanc be expected to store in her mind everything that had happened to her, particularly regarding such mundane information as record keeping? Aurora Blanc is, he pointed out, a national heroine who has devoted herself to the well-being of others and this is the thanks she has received – a baseless prosecution.

When the jury verdict was read, I believed, despite all the indications to the contrary, I would walk out the courtroom door, back to my business and my child.

I didn't remember my lawyer ever telling me that the perjury in California is punishable by imprisonment of two to four years. He said he had told me several times, so perhaps I forgot, as my memory had not functioned very well during that period.

At the sentencing hearing, I felt fine, smiling as I entered the courthouse with my team, chatting about nothing in particular with them, waiting for the Judge. I felt good because at last I could take the witness stand to explain to the Judge how this so-called perjury happened. I knew my explanation would surely end this nightmare and I would receive an appropriate penalty, a reprimand perhaps. But when we arrived in court on sentencing day, there was to be no testifying on the witness stand. The Judge asked me to make my statement from the table where I sat surrounded by my lawyers. As I stood, I went blank, forgetting everything I had so carefully prepared to say in my defense. I cried as I racked my memory.

The Judge asked if I wanted to take a break.

"Please don't send me to jail," I said, as I struggled to get myself under control. "I have a child – a baby. Please don't take his mother away from him. I'm not asking for me; it's for him. Please."

He looked at me sympathetically and waited for me to continue. But I could think of nothing else to say.

My lawyer whispered, "Don't you want to tell him the rest?"

I shook my head.

My lawyer rose and made an impassioned plea for me, but I couldn't comprehend his words.

The Judge said he was taking into account my exemplary life and extraordinary contributions, but he could not overlook the damage that would be done to our justice system if conduct like mine — blatant disregard of the law — was punished with a slap on the wrist. He sentenced me to two years in a California state prison and gave me thirty days to get my affairs in order.

CHAPTER 5

I set up things with my lawyer so Nanny could serve as Baby's surrogate mother. I turned over the day-to-day operations of the business to the appropriate executives, careful not to place too much authority in any one person. I assured all my retailers that everything would remain the same during my absence. Despite my pledge to the grocery store executives, some terminated their business relationship with us, and I knew that more would follow. Our profit margins were already so small that a continuing loss of business would bankrupt us.

I was being humiliated in the media. It was a great story for them: the golden girl, it turned out, was a liar and a fraud. She didn't even invent the healthy meat that she had been bragging about for years. I could have handled this disgrace if my business had not been losing ground since my conviction. What, I asked myself, did I have to look forward to when I got out of jail: bankruptcy and scorn?

"My life is over," I said, as Jane sat on her usual stool in my kitchen.

"Nothing is over, until it's over. Have you stopped taking those pills?"

"I'm not taking them anymore. They muddled my thinking."

"You'll be clear-headed and resolute when you go to the place you're going to."

"You mean prison. You can say it, Jane. I would like to pretend it's something else, but I can't."

"You can handle it."

"I don't want to handle it. I've been thinking about it. I've had an amazing life. I've done more at 29 than anybody else has in their whole life."

"Stop it! If you try to kill yourself, I swear, I will kill you, Aurora."

"What do I have? I want to lie down and block everything out."

"You have a child. If you're gone, he loses you. It would be the most selfish, despicable thing you could do."

I had nothing to say to that.

"Answer me! It would be a disgusting, cowardly thing to do, wouldn't it?"

"Yes," I conceded.

"You are going to get through this."

"I don't know how."

"You will."

I nodded.

The night before my incarceration, I held Baby. He was a precocious one-and-one-half-year-old; he could understand everything I said.

"You are the only thing I have left. If it wasn't for you, I couldn't go on." I started crying again. "When I'm away, please don't forget me. And don't think Nanny is your mommy. She loves you but I love you more and I will always be there for you, no matter what."

"Where Mommy go? To office?"

"Yes, Baby, to office."

"Can we have French Toast Sticks for dinner tomorrow?

You like them too."

"I'll make sure you get them but I won't be here."

"Well then, see you later Mommy. I'm sleepy."

"I know you are but let's talk some more."

"You go talk to Nanny. Good night, Mommy." He wiggled out of my lap and set out alone towards his room. He was just like me: if he wanted to do something, he just did it. As I watched him make his way up the stairs, my heart broke.

My lawyer prepared me for prison by hiring a "consultant", an ex-con, to "school' me on what to do and not to do. What she had to say was so stupid and obvious that anyone who needed this advice deserved to be in prison. It was very important, she said, to respect other inmates. Don't cut in line or look at them funny or get into fights; don't engage in homosexual conduct; stay away from gangs; don't use drugs. If these instructions were meant to ease my anxiety or lift my depression, they failed.

I flew alone in the company jet, without friends or colleagues, to the California Institution for Women, outside of Los Angeles. When I first saw it, it reminded me of a third-tier state university campus – but with a barbed wire fence. During the intake procedure, I tried to concentrate on the prison officials' instructions and questions, but I was too anxious to absorb it. Nausea overcame me and I vomited. A guard led me into a restroom to clean up, but when I came out, I did it again. I was so shaky that it took all my energy to remain standing. As I stood there, weaving, perspiring, gagging, they stopped the intake process and a guard took me to a little room, telling me to rest for a while. There was a toilet and cot, nothing else. Through the small window on the door, I saw someone watching me from the hallway.

Dry heaves, diarrhea, sweats and chills came and went in waves. A prison official came in to ask about my condition. I told her I would be alright. I slept, waking up every few hours.

The next morning, there was pain in my muscles and joints and more chills and sweats. I looked around the room and realized it was a cell. I was brought breakfast, which I couldn't eat. Later, a woman told me that we were going to the infirmary. She helped me out of the cot, but I could not stand on my own. She left and returned with a wheelchair and got me into it. I tried to sit up straight but didn't have the strength.

"Let me give you some advice," she said, as she wheeled me down a hallway. "You will be better off to just accept it, get on your feet and fit in. Being a prima donna won't work. I've seen inmates try everything in this place, including what you are doing. Take my advice."

They put me in an infirmary bed, screened off from other patients. I could hear them as I lay there, floating in and out of reality. When I came fully awake, overwhelming hopelessness seized me. I wanted to die. When I drifted off, there was a black nothing. I refused the medications they tried to give me, insisting I would be fine soon, telling them that it was just nerves. I told them I was allergic to Tylenol, Ibuprofen, and aspirin – untrue – but I was afraid to take their pills.

I lost track of time, suffering alternating bouts of fever and chills. I defecated in the bed. When they tried to examine me, I pushed them away. At some point, they got an IV into my arm, but when they left, I yanked it out and watched as I bled on the sheets. When they tried to put a catheter in me, I rolled into a ball so they couldn't do it. When I ate their food, it came back up.

Finally, I slept for a prolonged period. When I woke, I felt a weight on my chest, and had to fight it to breathe.

"Looks like cyanosis," a male voice said. "See, her skin is blue."

"We'll get a doctor. Just rest," said a woman.

"No, please, don't leave. If I fall asleep, I'll die."

"You are not going to die. Just breathe and we'll get the doctor."

The story was in the newspapers, and then on *The Today Show* – the second news story at the start the broadcast.

Hoda Kolb: "Aurora Blanc, the founder of Healthy Heart Beef, is in critical condition in a California state prison where she is serving a two-year sentence for perjury. She has an undisclosed illness that has her in a fight for her life. Ms. Blanc has been internationally recognized for her pioneering work in genetically modified food."

Samantha Guthrie: "Hoda, since the story broke yesterday, there has been mounting criticism that this respected scientist and entrepreneur is in prison. You may recall, she was convicted of failing to disclose documents in a routine civil suit against her company. Many are questioning why she was sent to prison, saying that it would be a miscarriage of justice if she dies there."

Hoda: "During her perjury trial, it came out that her scientific work was actually done in conjunction with Stanford University and that perhaps she took credit for work that she did not do alone."

Samantha: "I buy Healthy Heart beef for my family, and I'm glad to know that a top university like Stanford was involved in creating it."

The press coverage that followed was critical of the Judge's decision to send me to prison for such an inconsequential lapse. An editorial in *USA Today* summarized public sentiment: "At a time when our national security and personal safety are under constant foreign and domestic threat with dangerous people intent on doing us grievous harm, it is an outrageous waste of criminal justice resources to prosecute, imprison and possibly end the life of an extraordinary woman whose scientific and business accomplishments have benefited hundreds of millions of people."

As pressure and protests intensified, prison officials consented to legal requests to provide outside qualified medical assistance. However, even though I was in a medically-induced coma, breathing with a ventilator, prison officials refused requests to transfer me to a hospital that could provide the sort of treatment that would improve my chances for survival.

CHAPTER 6

My dreams flowed from one precious experience to another – meals: emerald green vegetables, glowing snow colored lobster, pitchers of freshly squeezed lemonade, dark Swiss chocolate; workouts: my muscles pumping, getting leaner, stronger; beautiful spreadsheets on an iPad: continually updated, showing cash flow, profits, growth; strolling down University Avenue in Palo Alto: people nudging their companions, looking admiringly at me. I dreamed about a boy timidly approaching me for a selfie; I dreamed about Malcolm in the kitchen, making coffee, beaming as I walked in, so in love with me; I dreamed about my baby, about him asking, 'Where was Mommy? Stay now? Mommy, play with me now;' I dreamed about my own bed: fresh crisp bedsheets, stretching my limbs, feeling delightfully woozy, seeing sunlit leaves through the windows, trying to get out of bed but being restrained by tubes in my arms.

"Can you hear me, Ms. Blanc?"

"Who are you?" I whispered. I could hardly hear my own voice.

"Genevieve, your day nurse."

"Why are you here?"

"I'm a nurse."

I looked around, trying to sort out what I saw around me. "I'm supposed be in jail."

"They let you out of jail."

"When do I have to go back to jail?"

"You are not going back."

CHAPTER 7

Baby, Nanny, Jane and I took the trip that I'd promised Jane, to a private house, high in the mountains of the Caribbean island of St. Bart's. We didn't talk about my ordeal; I didn't bring it up. But I knew Jane was eager to hear the details. Late one afternoon, after having lunch in Gustavia, Jane, driving our little rented Jeep up the winding, one lane-road on the mountain's edge, said, "That pardon by the Governor – didn't you think it was beautiful? Can you read to me please? I want to hear it again." I looked it up on my phone: 'Aurora Blanc's exceptional contributions to humanity merit, even demand, an exceptional act by the office of the Governor. In granting this unconditional, full pardon to her, my sentiments today are best expressed by Shakespeare: 'The quality of mercy is not strained. It droppeth as the gentle rain from heaven upon the place beneath. It is twice blest. It blesseth him that gives and him that takes.' And so I am blessed to have the authority to provide this pardon and I hope that she has a speedy and full recovery to health and continues her stellar contributions to the health of our citizens."

"Yes, it was beautiful – and nice that he got a big political bounce in the polls for doing it," I said.

"You supported him in his last campaign, didn't you?"

"I gave him a lot of money. I never dreamed that this would happen, but if that's what you're inferring, yes, he did owe me. You know, it never would've happened if I hadn't been so sick."

"For a while everyone thought you would die."

"I could have died."

"They never figured out why you were so sick."

"I knew."

"You knew why you were sick?"

"Those pills."

"Pills?" Jane hit the brakes bringing the car to a dead stop.

"You can't stop in the middle of the road."

"You told me you weren't taking pain pills anymore."

"I lied. I took them the morning I went to jail. Jane, drive! You're making me nervous, these roads are dangerous."

We continued up the mountain.

"Pain pills don't make people stop breathing like happened to you," she said.

"I was taking Xanax, too."

"You were taking both together? That could kill you."

"I took more, a lot actually, after I was in my cell."

"They let you bring in pills?"

"I snuck them in. I thought they would find them when they did the physical during the processing, but they must have been too awed by me to do a thorough cavity search."

After we got out of the Jeep, she blocked the path to the house.

"You tried to kill yourself?" she said.

"I didn't want to die. I took a risk, a calculated one. If I had died from the pills, well, that was the downside of the gamble. But I didn't think they would let me die. I was too famous; it would have made them look bad. I believed that if I survived and they didn't figure out that I'd overdosed on pills, something good would have come of it; I just wasn't sure what."

Jane followed me up the steep path to the back deck. We sat on a garden bench, looking out on vivid green terrain running down to the curved sliver of sand bordering the bay. Beyond was the indigo ocean, extending to infinity. The sun warming my skin soothed me. I leaned over to Jane who looked stunned, and I kissed her cheek.

"I think I'll buy this place. I told you, didn't I, that the business bounced back after I got out? I want to get this as a gift for us," I said. "You and Horace can use it whenever you want, like it's yours."

I leaned back, stretched my arms and inhaled the sweet air. It felt so good, sitting there on top of the world.

RABBI SMITH

Rabbi Smith was in his office at the Hebrew Union College in Cincinnati, where he had moved to get a new start. He was a professor, imparting Jewish history to students, grateful that he did not have to talk to a congregation about moral and ethical issues. He lived alone, making no effort to develop a social or romantic life. Despite telling himself that he had acted properly and honorably, he felt responsible for all that had gone wrong and all he had lost.

When his cell phone rang, showing an unknown number, he assumed it was a solicitation. He answered it, however.

"Rabbi Smith?"

"Speaking."

"I'm so sorry to bother you, but are you the Rabbi Smith who was involved in the lawsuit with a dead child?"

His finger hovered near the red "end call" button. "Yes, that's me."

"I tried to reach you at your synagogue in California, but they said you had left. I pestered them into giving me this number."

"Who are you? What do you want?"

"My wife recently passed. She had been ill, cancer. Her immune system was weak from chemo, but her prognosis was good. Her doctors wanted her to eat more protein, so I got her some lean meat, steak. She ate it, went into shock, and died two days later. The doctors couldn't understand why it happened but said that that her system probably collapsed because of the chemo. It didn't make sense to me. Then I read about your little boy and how he died."

"I'm so sorry."

"I'm sure it was the meat. It was the same brand – Healthy Heart."

"Oh."

"I need to do something. She was forty-eight-years-old. Do you have any suggestions?"

Silence.

"Rabbi?"

"Yes."

"Yes, what, Rabbi?"

"Yes, I can help you."

AFTERWORD

I began this book project as a nonfiction account of genetic engineering in the food industry. During the months that I spent researching the topic, the deeper I dived into the science, business and politics of the subject, the more I was struck with the drama and ambiguity surrounding the facts. And so, I ultimately decided that the voluminous information I had gathered would be better elucidated in a novel than in a dry scientific book.

In writing the story, I tried to be as factually accurate as possible in describing the scientific and technological aspects of the tale. The only exception was Aurora's genetically engineered corn seed and the resulting heart-healthy beef, which I invented, although there is no question we will see such scientifically created agricultural products in the near future. CRISPR-Cas9, the gene editing tool that Aurora used for her work, is real, and like the life-changing effects on our world from the technological revolution, this biological tool (and all its future refinements and improvements) will enable scientists to bring about miraculous improvements to the health and well-being of humankind. At the same time, this unprecedented power to fundamentally alter the genetic makeup of plants and animals poses immense risks and dangers. If this book enhances discussion and debate on this momentous matter, that would be a very good thing.